I0720559

<u>Thrillers By Mark P.J. Nadon</u>

<u>Psychological Tech Thrillers:</u>

The Genesis Project

The Genesis Project (Book 1) – June 2024
Monsoon Rendezvous Novella (Book 1.5) – January 2025
Cognitive Breach Novella (Book 1.75) – February 2025

The Treatment Room – Forthcoming April 14, 2026

<u>Post Apocalyptic Survival Thrillers:</u>

Armageddon's Descendants Trilogy

The Collective (Book 1) – March 2025
The Chosen (Book 2) – July 2025
The Resonant (Book 3) – November 2025

<u>Short Story Collection:</u>

Edge of Darkness – February 2025

The Genesis Project: Book 1

Copyright © [2024] by [Mark PJ Nadon]

All rights reserved.

Published by Summit Ridge Publishing
Ottawa, Canada

Visit the author's website at www.markpjnadon.ca

The story, all names, characters, and incidents portrayed in this book are fictitious. No identification with actual persons (living or deceased), places, buildings, and products is intended or should be inferred.

Cover designed by 100 Covers

First published June 2024
Revised February 2026

ISBN (Electronic Book): 978-1-7383077-2-2
ISBN (Paperback): 978-1-7383077-0-8
ISBN (Hardcover): 978-1-7383077-1-5

For my son Matthew, who kept asking me
why I hadn't published this book yet.
I ran out of excuses.

A content warning is included at the back of the book.

Chapter 1

"SERGEANT, YOUR BEST FRIEND bled to death. Your partner was beheaded in front of you. And you have no signs of post-traumatic stress?"

Sergeant Blake Powell nodded, wondering why the unit psychologist grilled him without respite. He glanced out the window, expecting the sun to have set after hours of his legs sticking to the leather sofa, but it still dominated the evening sky and bronzed the psychologist's milky-white skin.

"No nightmares?"

Blake shook his head.

"No rage?" Doctor Kendra's wrinkles frowned alongside her mouth, making her look alien.

Blake stood, fists clenched. "We're done here, ma'am. Colonel Morse ordered me to report for assessment, but I wasn't ordered to remain here all day answering the same damn questions." He didn't care if his irritation came across as a sign of PTSD. Everyone tired of interrogations. If she wanted to hear about every battle he'd fought in where one of his men died, they'd be together for days. Blake saluted and turned to leave.

"Have a seat, Sergeant."

Blake gritted his teeth and sat, keeping his muscles relaxed to appear non-threatening.

"You're under contract with DOD. Leaving this appointment early could have consequences. Your wife relies on your income to feed your daughter, doesn't she?"

Blake waited, motionless.

"No...*anger?*"

Blake shoved his hand in his pocket and found the blade that had saved his life many times with Delta Force. It reminded him she could be dead in a heartbeat if he felt like it. "Nothing out of the ordinary." He forced a smile.

Doctor Kendra's expression was as boring as her chocolate milkshake colored pants. "Why do you think that is? Why do you think you feel no attachment? Care nothing for the lives of your men?"

Blake tightened his grip on his knife. "Who are you to tell me my men don't matter to me?" He spoke through his teeth, still straining to smile. "I don't want anyone to die. I'd love to hold my wife at night and tuck my little girl in to sleep. Am I as emotional as others? No. Blame my parents; Daddy gave me the belt too many times, and Mommy didn't let me suck her tits long enough. Does it matter? Run all your tests. I care, but I don't have a problem letting go. I clear emotional impact immediately. Ignore and override."

Doctor Kendra straightened her pants and readjusted her posture. What was she struggling to fix? Maybe a stick up her ass? Her pants were ironed to precision, and she wore a blazer. She flipped open a folder.

"Tell me about Captain James Burmann."

Here we go again. "He died in combat."

"Be more specific."

"A mission in the UK—a hostage situation. They killed him. Complete mission failure."

Doctor Kendra stood and wandered to the window. "More specific, Sergeant. You were there. You failed the mission, and men died for it. Isn't that right?"

Blake watched her eyes scan the parking lot. "That's right. You asked me that already." *Is she waiting for someone? Or is she afraid to look me in the eye?*

"But they awarded you the Medal of Valor and a Purple Heart for your injuries."

"I didn't ask for them. The team received those medals."

"You don't think you deserved them?" She adjusted her blouse again.

Blake shrugged. "We failed the mission. My men died. Hostages died. Failure doesn't deserve a reward."

"It states in your file that you declined the medals. Because of your guilt?"

Blake straightened. "Because we failed the mission."

"Tell me about the mission."

Blake debated sharing. Did client confidentiality mean anything in the military? *Stick to the facts. Talking gets people killed or court-martialed. What's she after?*

"Sergeant Powell, I'm ordering you to tell me the story." She tapped the paper. "I want your version."

Chapter 2

"Our orders were to infiltrate Multi-Diamond. I'm sure you've heard of the UK pharmaceutical company? Rescue several hostages, avoid enemy contact—no footprints. Echo team got the call. There were six of us: Wade, James, Mikey, Josh, Sparks, and me. We'd performed well in a dozen missions prior to Operation Dunk Tank, so we came highly recommended.

"We were told the US government was outsourcing research because of red tape, and that research was under threat at Multi-Diamond. Terrorists took control of the building and killed hostages—cleaners, mostly. Nobody important to the government, yet. The terrorists wanted the hostages to talk. Nobody knew what for, but we all assumed to steal research. No biological or chemical threats on site, so they said. Estimates concluded there were six to ten terrorists. Some government analyst botched the estimate. Command wanted to use three Navy SEAL Team Six units since the plan included a sea incursion, but their teams were otherwise engaged. The information was time sensitive, and no other teams could hit the ground as quickly as us.

"Mission prep went well. We conducted rehearsals off the coast in a similar building and nailed operational guidelines—as perfect as a rehearsal goes. But no plan survives contact with the enemy.

"A Mark V Craft dropped us off at the coast. We geared up and used an SDV—SEAL Delivery Vehicle—to close in on shore. We arrived on the beach without incident at the rendezvous codenamed Alice. It was midnight, and the plan was to move under cover of darkness. The moonlight left us silhouetted no matter our approach angle, so we moved methodically. No surprises. It wasted time but kept us all alive.

"I was the third man in—outside guard. We moved in a single stack. Wade, James and I had HK 416s, Josh had an MK46, and Mikey favored the HK417—Mikey preferred hitting harder and doing more damage. Sparks had a SIG Sauer MCX, and an M24 strapped to his back. All weapons were fitted with sound suppressors. Is that too much detail for you? Fine.

"Our target was a three-story building with a lobby on the main floor and several offices and labs on the second and third floors. Intelligence suggested the hostages were on the third floor, which is fairly typical of a hostage situation: it's a tactical advantage and makes terrorists feel safe.

"Command suspected the enemy was Al-Qaeda, but they didn't issue any demands and weren't known for hostage taking. The only reason we had intel at all on the terrorists was because of an employee who had called 999. The call recording had background noise that sounded like Arabic slang.

"Command expected a bomb to go off at any minute, which was their MO.

"Three hundred feet from the building, James ordered sniper overwatch. Sparks humped it to an adjoining building down the road. He didn't get a spotter because it would have left our team short. Sparks was our best shot, and we were confident he could spot his own targets from that range.

"We used a drone to scout the perimeter while we waited.

"'Fox in position,' Sparks said. 'Third floor is tinted. No eyes on targets. No movement on first or second floor. Lights are off. Should I return to your position?'"

***

Blake grit his teeth. They should have waited for a second team. God-damn government didn't care about his men, just the protection of their research.

***

"'Roger, Fox. Moving on burrow,' James said. 'Remain in position.'

"Only one entrance made sense—the main entrance. You can imagine how screwed up that made the mission feel, but the drone revealed all other entrances were collapsed. They wanted to funnel us through the front. Warning two that this mission was FUBAR. An insertion by helicopter would have been smart, but it was red flagged because of suspected anti-aircraft weapons.

"Command updated us that the terrorists demanded the release of a UK prisoner. Not a typical Al-Qaeda request. They were wasting our time. It didn't matter. We were Charlie Mike—continuing mission.

"We'd buy time with a story about preparing the prisoner for re-lease. Our team would either successfully complete the mission or die. The nearest QRF—that's a quick-reaction force—waited twenty miles out. The US and UK governments didn't intend to meet their demands.

"James signaled our advance. We stacked against the glass pane. Wade checked the door: locked.

"'Silent breach,' James whispered.

"Wade nodded, pulled out a set of lockpicks, and worked the problem. An alarm went off, and the lights in the main entrance blinded us.

"'Wade, breaching charge. Execute, execute, execute!'

"Wade slammed the breaching charge on the glass and detonated it. Shards hit all of us. Armed men threw open a door near the elevators and fired.

"We returned fire and entered the building through the broken window. I stepped inside and felt a jab in my foot. I took cover at a support beam. We all knew they probably killed the hostages, but we had to keep moving.

"Several Al-Qaeda went down hard in the exchange, but they poured into the lobby. We lost the firefight and had to keep our heads down. We already knew we faced a lot more than ten terrorists.

"'Wade, grenade!' James ordered.

"Wade cooked off a grenade and lobbed it. The explosion killed several of them. Some scrambled for cover. Others stood dumbfounded. I shot them before they recouped.

"Ammunition couldn't last forever. No resupply was coming. I'd already fired three magazines and had only seven remaining in my vest.

"'Extended line. We have to push forward and funnel them,' James said.

"We fired from our pillars, forcing our way forward. As we hoped, the poorly trained terrorists bumbled into each other.

"'Wade, flank left. Mikey, right. Rest, up the middle,' James ordered.

"Wade and Mikey inched ahead, forcing the terrorists to continue converging. I pulled a grenade from my vest, yanked the pin, cooked it for a three count, and lobbed it. It fell into the group and rolled toward the back. *Boom.*

"When the smoke dissipated, most of the terrorists were dead or wounded on the ground. We cleared the room to the back stairwell.

"'Stack up,' James said.

"We moved to the third floor. I heard gunshots above us. We took our time. Slow is smooth, smooth is fast.

"'Fox, do you see anything?' James asked over the radio.

"'Negative, no eyes on the burrow. I can't get a visual through the glass. Permission to bug out and head in.'

"'Stand by, Fox.'

"Hundreds of scattered cubicles provided the enemy with cover. 'This place is a damn maze,' I said.

"'Blake and Mikey, left flank. Wade and Josh, right flank. I'll go center,' James said.

"The top of their heads sailed across the cubicles as we cleared the room. Bullets whizzed past us. We shot down several terrorists in camo. An office with a stained-glass window on a mezzanine over-looked the room—probably a manager's suite.

"Then gunfire erupted from every angle. Camouflaged terrorists leaped from behind desks and filing cabinets. A near-empty room turned into a shooting gallery.

"'Ambush!' I'd been trained to say it, but we all knew. I raced forward, firing rounds into the enemy, ignoring everything behind me. We had to break through and gain cover.

"'I'm hit!' James said over the radio. I couldn't chance a look. I had to push forward.

"A bullet punched me in the back of the vest. Two more followed. The impact threw me forward and knocked the wind out of me. I couldn't recover before someone pinned me to the ground.

"'Do not move, or lose your head,' a voice boomed from above me. I didn't resist.

"The overbearing gunfire ceased. The air tasted acrid.

"Al-Qaeda tied my hands with zip ties. They pulled off my equipment, cursing at me in Arabic. I couldn't understand the details.

"'You here kill us?' One of the Al-Qaeda pressed an AK-47 into my eye. I wasn't sure if he expected a response.

"He cracked the butt of the rifle into the side of my head.

"'You speak English, stupid American? You here kill us?'

"I spit blood. 'I saw a light out. We were coming to replace the bulb.'

"He struck me three more times with the butt of the rifle—the third to the top of the shoulder. Each hit sent sparks to my fingers. I tried not to cry out, but the third time I couldn't help it. The guard holding me kicked my foot, further lodging the shard of glass into it.

"'You want funny? I show funny.'

"The Al-Qaeda leader unsheathed a knife from his side. I closed my eyes and thought a goodbye to Sophia and Clara, praying Sophia knew I had done my best. I hoped a place like Valhalla existed, although I didn't have a weapon in my hands. On a fear scale of one to ten, I measured a solid eight. Ten is when the situation is hopeless, reserved for soldiers who can't will themselves to move.

"Nothing happened. I opened my eyes.

"The leader stood beside James and flicked his wrist. The men jerked James to his knees and dragged him over. James looked at me, smiled, and nodded. He didn't need to speak the words. I nodded back."

***

Blake bit the inside of his cheek and squeezed his toes, trying to cut the connection to the tears burning in his eyes. If his dad could see him, he'd slap him with an open palm, call him a little bitch for sobbing like a girl, and tell him to man up.

James had meant the world to Blake. He'd selected Blake to the team when every other team leader had passed on Blake because they thought he was too cold. Wouldn't fit in. James had been Blake's best man at his wedding and Sophia's godfather. If Blake didn't come home, he trusted James to look after his family.

James never should have been the terrorist's target. Blake should have been the first to die.

"Everything okay, Sergeant?" Doctor Kendra said.

Blake covered his mouth and faked a few coughs. His dad never faked a cough to cover up tears. He went to the grave coughing blood. Blake returned his thoughts to the mission.

***

"The leader looked at me. I thrashed around but couldn't escape the two men who held me.

"'Now you watch me funny.'

"I might have chuckled at his English if I hadn't known what he was about to do. He took James by the edge of his helmet and pressed the knife to James' throat. Blood spattered my face, my eyes. I blinked away enough blood to see him hack James' neck until his body fell sideways. James' head dangled by his helmet. I thrashed again, but there was no use. 'You fuck!'

"The terrorist laughed hysterically.

"'I'm going to kill you!' I said.

"Muted expressions showed the terrorists' fear. They shifted from leg to leg. If they both leaned toward me, I could throw them off balance. I would have time to secure a weapon before they killed me—take a few more with me before I died.

"The leader punched me. Blood dripped down my head. I didn't mind the taste of blood—it reminded me of Selection.

"The leader crouched down in my face. 'You commander?' I tasted his sour breath.

"'I was tasked with climbing the ladder to replace the lightbulb. We weren't sure how many of us it would take.'

"His face reddened, and he pressed a pistol into my eye. The quicker our death, the better. His finger squeezed the trigger, but a bang from outside distracted him before the hammer slammed forward. Tinted glass on the right exploded.

"In SERE training, survive and escape, I thrived at escaping custody. I picked locks and stole maps with a thief's precision. I looked at James's corpse and tightened up—that bastard had to die. The Al-Qaeda around me must have realized it too because they reaffirmed their grips. A third man behind me yanked my helmet back, exposing my neck.

"'No.' The leader huffed.

"The third man wrenched my head sideways; every ligament in my neck groaned. They'd murdered most of the hostages. Two remained kneeling, their heads sagging forward. I knew a broken captive when I saw it. They knew they would die soon, and they'd seen enough to want to.

"Mikey, Josh, and Wade knelt on the other side of the room in the same position I was. Blood dribbled off Mikey's head. A gunshot? I couldn't tell. He wouldn't be walking out of here. He needed a medic.

"The leader stormed over to them and stood behind them, pointing at the paned glass. He barked in Arabic at a chaos of activity on the other side.

"'Corporal Johnston, United States Army. Serial number two, two, three, five, seven, niner, six, three, eight, eight.' *Damnit, don't die boys.*

"'Raven, this is Fox. The rabbits have control,' Sparks said over the radio. 'Mouse, this is Fox. I have eyes on. Going hot in five...four...three...two...'

"I relaxed my muscles to lull the terrorists into a false sense of security before I sprang.

Chapter 3

"WE GOT OUT. JAMES didn't. That's it," Blake said.

Doctor Kendra frowned. "You don't find it liberating to talk about?" She scribbled in her notes. *She's probably drawing stick-death pictures of our mission.*

"War is better left where it came from."

"Do you have nightmares, Sergeant?"

"I dream." Blake hated not knowing the purpose of this interrogation disguised as a counseling session.

"Can you describe your dreams?"

"Same as other soldiers. Brothers dying. Sometimes I save them. They die anyway—hidden snipers. Sometimes they're ghosts and blame me. Sometimes I'm locked in a dark room, and I hear them scream."

Doctor Kendra cleared her throat. "When you have these dreams, do you wake up angry? Hurt? Do you cry?"

She won't tell me why I'm here because she wants to uncover something. Do they want to declare me unfit for duty? I'm not old enough for retirement, and I'm a damn good soldier. The team is still healing. Nobody is operating. I should have more time. "No, I don't cry. I wake up, take a deep breath, and think about them. I think about their loss—the reason they died. Their sacrifice to make the world better.

Could the missions have gone differently? I should be happy I'm alive, but I don't always think so."

"Do you feel responsible for Captain Burmann's death?"

"No," he blurted. "If I had kept quiet, he'd still be dead. I wasn't the one who killed him. I didn't ask anyone to cut his fucking head off." Blake felt the knife jiggle in his pocket. He sensed Doctor Kendra's eyes on him.

"You're responding with a lot of anger for a man that claims indifference."

"I have a wife and daughter. I don't have rage. I don't drink too much or use drugs. I don't fight. I'm not haunted by the memory of the men I served with, but I still remember. I'll always remember. And it pisses me off when I'm asked if I think someone's death is my fault. I've never intentionally killed one of my own men. There's your answer: I've never felt responsible."

Doctor Kendra wrote in her pad. "Do you know how PTSD affects soldiers?"

"Sure, I have plenty of friends who've returned from combat."

She nodded, adjusting her blouse and her posture. "In soldiers, symptoms may include violence, avoidance, mood swings, reactivity and substance abuse. It has impacted skilled soldiers, and some of them don't serve for long. We've seen an increase in suicide in recent years. An alarming increase."

Blake waited for her to say more. When his patience wore out, he said, "So?"

"You're being considered for a position in a top-secret project."

Blake frowned. "No thanks. I'm going to heal up and get back to Echo team. It's where I belong. I'm only thirty-nine and feel twenty. I'm not a paper pusher."

"You won't be pushing papers. I can't share details. The next step is a monitored dream test. You'll have nightmares—bad ones—and we'll record your response. If you're the right candidate, you'll handle it. You won't recall the dream when you wake up. Are you ready to continue?"

"Aren't you supposed to be a good listener? I told you I'm going back to Echo team the second we're cleared hot."

Doctor Kendra smiled. "Take the damn test and decide later what you want to do."

"I've enjoyed this conversation. It was as cold as my marriage."

Doctor Kendra straightened her pants. He didn't like the motion. It felt like she was preparing to give him an order.

"If we offer you the position, the risk of personal injury is near zero compared to combat. The risk to your mental state...well I...the project hasn't been running long enough for us to know. But you would spend more time with your family. I know how close you are to Sophia. She's your world. I could tell when you talked about her." She leaned forward. "You could be with her every night. Blake, do stage two. Echo team is months away from active duty. Consider what other options are available."

Sophia. His mouth dried. He'd missed a good part of her life. *Always another critical mission.* "Home every night? And not behind a desk?"

Doctor Kendra leaned back. "*Some* desk time. You'll be in combat, just facing a different enemy."

I can handle a nightmare if I can be in combat and be home every night. Sounds like training cadets, but she said "top-secret project." Sophia plays the piano twice a week. I'd actually hear her play. No idea how that's possible, but it's worth finding out. "Okay, let's go to the next stage. But to be clear, good chance I'm going back to Echo team."

Chapter 4

Blake followed Doctor Kendra down the hallway. People in business suits eyed him. *Doctors? Soldiers?* Beneath the light, Doctor Kendra looked paler. Most of the other people did too.

Despite the lighting, he felt like he was being led into a dark place. They slowed at large double doors with no windows. They reminded him of a hospital.

He nearly walked into Doctor Kendra when she stopped and turned unexpectedly.

"This is your last chance to say no."

Blake nodded. "Good to go." Not knowing what awaited him on the other side of the door wasn't new.

"Just making sure."

Blake felt for the knife in his pocket, and realized he already held it in his hand.

They continued through the doors. When the doors closed behind them, the hallway darkened. Blake considered pulling his phone out to use the flashlight. A whiff of rubbing alcohol seared his nostrils. The military conducted many after-action psych workups, but he hadn't realized the building was so big.

They stopped halfway down the hall and faced another closed door. A security scanner beeped every few seconds. Doctor Kendra smiled as if a good attitude was required for entry and swiped her card.

A single bed waited in the center of the room with cables hooked up to the sides in a dozen places. It looked like a tanning bed on top and something from the Matrix on the bottom. He retreated two steps when he smelled an electrical fire. "I saw a movie once with a machine like this. A scrawny soldier went in, and Captain America came out. Is that what's happening? I'm in all the way."

Doctor Kendra blinked. Not a single wrinkle on her face curled. "Change into those clothes." She pointed at a locker with a long white gown inside.

"Nice. You provided a dress. You aren't taking my picture after I put that on, are you? I don't want to see myself on social."

"We're all professionals. It's time to get changed Sergeant. I have other appointments." Doctor Kendra turned around.

This wasn't Echo team, and they weren't going to laugh about this over a beer later.

He put the gown on.

"Lay down," Doctor Kendra ordered.

Blake paused. A bad feeling shot through him. He took a deep breath to relax. Team missions made sense to him. Grab your gun, make someone do something, get out. A wired bed? Outside of his control. He ambled to the bed, noticing jelly on top of it. A lab technician sat at the computer, eyes glued to the screen and his breathing labored just from sitting still. He needed to go to the gym.

Blake saw himself on the screen.

"Go on." Doctor Kendra raised her eyebrows at him.

Blake laid down. The jelly suspended him above the bed's surface, making him feel like he floated. It didn't stick to him, but it felt like bubble wrap. Another bed floated above him. Were they going to drop that on him?

He wasn't claustrophobic, but the bed made him squirm. He resisted the urge to leave and instinctively reached for his knife, which rested ten feet away in his pants.

"Are we ready?" She faced the technician.

"Ready," the man rumbled.

Blake shuddered. "Is there a safety word for this thing?" Everything felt cold.

"Yes." The technician snorted. "Peaches."

Blake faked a chuckle. *Take a deep breath. You've been in dozens of firefights. You've killed men. This is nothing.*

The lid-bed dropped over him. He closed his eyes as it sealed shut. Goo pressed against his face. He clenched his fists.

"Breathe," a computerized voice said. *Cortana?*

Blake didn't think he could. This was too much. He was getting out. He jumped up, bursting free of the bed.

Only he wasn't on the bed.

"Good," Cortana said. The voice echoed from every direction at once.

Blake looked up.

"What's going on? Are the lights out?"

"You're in the simulation. You're about to undergo several dream scenarios."

Blake pictured a physical Cortana smiling before plunging him into a pile of crap. "What kind of dream scenarios?"

"We'll record your responses and your handling of the situation."

What could they throw at him that he hadn't already seen in combat? He waited in the darkness.

Chapter 5

If Blake could glare at darkness, he would. He wanted to attack the dream with the aggression of a shark tearing into prey, but he was blind. He felt around for something he could use as light, but he captured air.

A mist descended, bringing illumination with it. He waved his hand, stepping deeper into it. It took a few steps before the mist lifted and he stood on a road. It felt so real—technology like this didn't exist. *An interactive dream?*

He closed his eyes and thought of Sophia and Clara. When he opened them, he hadn't moved. He pinched his skin, feeling the pain. Not dead. Not awake either.

He strode forward. The road went on for miles like an abandoned highway outside a small town. Breathing was tough. He swallowed several coughs, despite seeing no smoke, and came to a fork in the road. The fog continued on the left but disappeared on the right. Further down, he saw a small building with a light on. He laughed. His nightmare was a Brothers Grimm story. *What a screwed-up interview.* If he wandered into the fog. Would they think he was reckless? Or fearless? If he walked to the building, would he find more danger because he chose the brighter path, or less danger? If he took too long, would they consider him incapable of decision making? Or think he's someone who rolled with the punches? He hated psychologists.

The easy way usually went to hell on missions, and he had learned to roll with his instincts: Stick to the first decision and see it through; going back was only good with time travel.

Sixty feet away, a neon sign that sat above the building read *Diner*. Maybe five or ten people screamed like someone was torturing them. Good chance it was a critical situation if this was part of the test. He had no weapons, so it limited his response—they'd know that. He stepped off the road to hide his silhouette. A lightbulb hung from the entrance, casting a faint glow on the street. Not a single vehicle was parked outside.

A gruff man hollered as if barking battlefield commands. As Blake reached the building on the windowless side, he heard children whimper. *It's a dream. It isn't real.* He reached for the blade in his pocket, but it wasn't there.

A gunshot rang in his ears. The window at the front of the diner shattered.

Blake stalked around the corner to find a boy—maybe six years old—lying on the road, glass shards surrounding him. A deep black hole created a void where his nose and mouth should have been. Brain fluid dripped into the hole, like a broken water main filling a tunnel.

He nearly vomited. Thankfully, he had practiced gagging it down in Iran and Somalia.

Another gunshot.

"No! No! No!" a woman screamed.

Blake scanned for a weapon. Without one, someone could kill him as easily as the children. Was he supposed to play hero? What did they expect from this test? What were the rules of engagement?

He picked up a shard of glass, then continued to the entrance and peaked through the window. Bodies lay everywhere. Mostly childrens. Few moved. A woman wailed, cradling a child.

"Shut up! Just shut up!" The killer brushed at his baby blue buttoned-down collar shirt as if he could wipe off the blood spatter like dog hair. He stomped to the mother, a slight smile forming on his lips, his shoulders back and head high, like a too-good-for-you banker denying a loan, pointed the gun at her head, and pulled the trigger. Her head smacked the table behind her and snapped forward onto her child.

Blake had seen a lot of death, but the suddenness caught him off guard.

An infant lay still a few feet away from the entrance. A hole in its chest. Any of these kids could be Sophia. Blake smothered his rage. *Stay on mission. This isn't real.*

The cries of the living covered Blake's movement. He eased open the door. The killer hadn't seen him. Blake crept inside and hid behind a table. The rank of dead flesh and blood reminded him of Somalia. He took three slow breaths. He had to charge out at full speed, catch the killer off guard, and kill him.

This dream tech was incredible. It felt so real. Why wasn't this on the open market? Microsoft would love it.

Blake charged straight into him, but instead of the gunman's back, he met his dark blue eyes and the barrel of his gun.

***

Blake pressed his hands against his stomach and chest in the darkness, certain he was alive. He figured he had failed the test. The killer hadn't heard him; he had his back to him. No way could he have known Blake was there.

He blinked, and a different scene came to life. He sat in bed at home. Clara cried downstairs—the same shriek he'd heard when they lost Adam nineteen years ago to complications at birth.

Not Adam. I don't want to relive this.

He leaped to the door, ignoring his training and instinct to find a weapon first. He raced downstairs and into the living room. Clara sat on the floor with Sophia's lifeless body in her arms. *Oh, Christ.* Blood pooled on the floor.

The room darkened as Blake cried, and every muscle in his body tensed even as he collapsed. *Breathe and focus. It's not real, no matter how real it feels.* He wanted to escape the simulation. How? Another sequence came to life, but he didn't feel up to it anymore.

He needed to bury his emotions—lock them deep in the back of his mind. *Ignore and override.*

Thousands of dead bodies filled the scorching desert sands like the aftermath of a battle fought in the open. The bodies were a mix of civilians and soldiers, with many bodies partially shrouded in sand. In places, the flesh was burned away so severely that only skeletal remains were left, stark against the charred tissue. Guts hung out, limbs were torn from bodies. Blake vomited, unable to handle the acrid, sickeningly sweet smell.

You can't just freeze up. He walked through the desert with no destination in mind. His feet burned from sand buried in his shoes, and the sun pulsing at his back. He didn't want to feel the heat in his face.

A body stirred a hundred yards away. Colonel Grenil. He'd died on a rescue mission Blake aided in twelve years ago. The brass had asked a lot of questions about his judgment on the mission. They hadn't found him at fault. Was he in a zombie simulation?

"You left me to die!" Colonel Grenil bristled when he saw Blake. His skin flaked as he moved, and he snarled through teeth like decayed wood. Blake backed away.

"It was the right call," Blake said. He always thought Colonel Grenil would agree with him, even though he'd died.

"It's your fault!" he bellowed. "It's your fault!" Then he squeezed his arms around his splintered ribs and whimpered, gasping for breath as if begging for oxygen. "You left me. You could have saved me, but you didn't want to risk it."

Blake shook his head. "We had no chance. Anyone going after you would have died."

"Liar!" he screeched so loudly Blake covered his ears. The sight of him should have frozen Blake in place. *No.* Blake wouldn't abandon him again. He willed himself to move toward him.

Blake placed a hand on his shoulder. "I know you're in a better place."

Colonel Grenil smiled, but his moldy-grape eyes seemed to loathe him. His face twisted, and he pounced on him. Blake grabbed him by the chest to keep him back. Colonel Grenil snapped at Blake like a dog, drooling in anticipation of its next meal. Blake couldn't hold him back. *This is insane.* He tripped on a limb. Colonel Grenil landed on top of him, gnashing to tear out a chunk of flesh.

Work the problem, Blake. Work the problem. Could Grenil die again?

In one fluid motion, he grabbed his head and twisted his neck until the bones crunched. Colonel Grenil collapsed.

Blake stood as a dozen more dead soldiers lumbered to their feet and tottered toward him. He recognized most of them. Mike, Dock,

Brad, Hudson. Men he had served with that didn't make it home alive. He zigzagged through the sand and around them, tripping over several bodies but bounding back up before they grabbed him. They howled for him to stop. "Don't leave us to die again," they said.

Work the problem. To kill them, he'd need an explosion. A grenade might do it, depending on the dream world's parameters. A machine gun with unlimited ammunition would be nice, but this wasn't a dream he controlled. Even if it was, his machine gun would jam in time for the dead to pile on top of him.

"Why didn't you save me?" Corporal Armstrong bellowed.

"You watched me die. You could have helped," Private Perez cried.

Blake remembered them all.

A child cried out. "You should have stopped them. You could have hurried."

"We had rules of engagement," Blake said.

"My family," the boy whimpered.

"They were dead. It was too late," Blake said.

He bumped into James. Voided eyes stared into his soul where they once brimmed with compassion. Crusted skin peeled off his cheeks. Skin flapped where they'd cut into his neck. "You pushed them to kill me." James's voice was reduced to a wheezy shout.

Blake's hands trembled. "That's not what I was trying to do. I didn't know they would kill you."

"Yes, you did!" James gripped Blake's throat and pressed his thumbs in. Blake dropped back, and James fell with him. He used his momentum to throw his legs up and roll James over his head.

When Blake stood, gray, peeled fingers clasped his arms and legs. He fought to free himself. He thought about James accusing Blake of getting him killed. Did James mean it? Was that his dying thought? He was one of the best officers Blake had ever served with. He was Blake's friend.

Sharp objects pierced Blake's body everywhere at once, and he felt shrapnel hit him. A grenade must have gone off. Blake screamed, wondering if he was going to die. What was the machine, and what was reality? Fingers clawed through his skin. He felt like a million cold bayonets plunged through him and pried him apart.

Everything blinked dark and then returned in a blinding light. *Peaches.*

Chapter 6

DOCTOR KENDRA RETRACTED A needle from Blake's arm as his eyes adjusted to the light. *When had she put a needle in my arm?* It felt like a bee sting and went away just as quickly. He wanted to scream, to tell her to shove the project down her throat. But he calmed himself instead. His eyes felt raw.

Doctor Kendra scrawled a note on a clipboard. "You can go home. We'll analyze the results and phone you by the end of next week."

Blake threw himself off the bed. "What? The end of next week? Is that a joke? Do you know what I just went through? Do you know what I saw in there?"

"Yes, I'm aware. Are you?"

Blake wanted to strangle her. Then he tried to remember what he'd seen...and...he couldn't. "How did you do that?"

"It's not important." Doctor Kendra flipped the page over and scanned her notes. "You'll get all the information you need when we call you. *If* you get clearance."

Blake rubbed his arm when the bee sting jab started itching. His heart felt like a boxing glove against his breast, so he breathed deeply to calm it down. Wait. Wait to see if he'd passed a test he couldn't remember taking.

On his drive home, he tried to remember what he had undergone. Traffic was heavy, but slow, giving him room to concentrate. He turned off the cheap car radio that only emitted large bursts of static and focused on the last thing he remembered before he woke up. A day-long interview with Doctor Kendra then the hallway and lying on the bed and the cover dropping on him. Nothing after.

When he pulled into the driveway, the headlights spread across Sophia sitting on the front step, an infectious grin on her lips. The anxiety squeezing his chest let go.

Chapter 7

Blake pulled a bottle of water out of the fridge and sat on the couch. Strips of tattered leather poked his sides. Sophia sat on the far side of the couch with his iPad, playing RuneScape, a game with a virtual playground where she designed and built the world around her. At any moment, she'd complain about another app crashing because it couldn't keep pace with updates. Sophia's friends thought he'd be amazing at military games, but those weren't realistic—other than the graphics. Tactics meant nothing when you lacked personal control of the soldier. He struggled to aim. Every time he pushed the stick too hard, the idiot soldier threw his gun up in the air like a recruit.

"Building us a new home?" he asked Sophia.

Sophia smiled. "Yeah." She swept away stray strands of short black hair and returned to her game.

Blake missed his baby girl. Years ago, she ran to him and showed him whatever creation she'd worked on like her Popsicle-stick house. She was so damn proud of it. When he had smiled at her creations, her eyes sparkled, and she skipped away.

Then she grew up. Sophia still loved him, but she cuddled less and talked about boys more. She had friends in public school that he didn't like, especially Jess and Dylan. Her friends were rude to their parents and wore a month's supply of makeup in one day. Their personalities told him they'd grow up cruel. But they were still kids, and he hadn't the slightest clue how to change them. Attitude was inevitable. His neighbor, Derek, had a seventeen-year-old girl and said girls got tougher with age. Blake secretly wished Sophia would be the exception—daddy's little girl for life, even if he didn't always deserve her love.

"Do you want to go for a run with me and Dex later? You have to train for that little road race we entered you in," Blake said. Having heard his name, Dex stood and wagged his tail. He could outrun them both at a sprint or over distance. He had when Blake served on the teams. Belgian Malinois were born and raised with the military and ran for hours, maintaining all their motivation. Blake had become Dex's handler three years ago when Dex retired.

Sophia lowered the iPad. "Sure. Do you have time?"

He checked his watch. Eight thirty in the morning. He didn't have to be at the unit until ten.

"Yeah, I have time. Dex, do you have time, boy? Do you have time?"

Dex's tail picked up speed, and he bounded up and down like air-frying popcorn. He'd never stopped being a puppy.

Clara walked into the room, her hair disheveled, eyes narrow and piercing. She held a phone. Blake smelled burned hair but kept quiet. "Did you not hear the phone ring?"

Blake rubbed his eyes. *Doesn't she get tired of being angry at such trivial things?* "No."

Clara walked over and slapped the phone into his hand. "It's Doctor Kendra."

Blake swallowed, his throat dry. Eleven days since they'd tested him. He'd had bizarre nightmares, mostly with soldiers that had died in combat asking him to admit his mistakes or begging for help. "We didn't have to die," they'd said. He'd been there for all their deaths.

Every morning, he woke and immersed the memory deeper into his mind. He almost called Doctor Kendra to inquire about the side effects of whatever he'd gone through or the needle she'd pricked him with.

"Hello, Sergeant Powell," Doctor Kendra said.

"Hello, how can I help you, doctor?"

"We've gone over your results from your test. Unfortunately, we don't feel you're the right candidate for the position. Thanks." Her voice trailed off, and he imagined her letting the receiver crash down.

"Wait, that's it?" He sprang off the couch and marched upstairs to his bedroom. Every footfall was a shotgun blast on the steps. "I've been having dreams since your machine tested me."

"You told me you already had dreams. Is that relevant?"

"Soldiers and children that I've seen die over the years. I mostly dream of the moment they died."

Doctor Kendra spat a single laugh that stabbed Blake's eardrum. "It sounds like post-traumatic stress. Maybe you should see someone."

Blake gritted his teeth. *Isn't that why they sent me to you? To get rid of them, not cause them?* "But I've never dreamed about them until I went through...whatever that was. What the hell are you laughing about?"

"I'm sure you'll resume normal dreams in a week. Give it some time."

The phone clicked.

"Hello? Hello?"

That malicious witch! Blake slammed the phone on the ground. Plastic shards flew across the floor.

Clara and Sophia ran into the room.

"Dad, what happened?"

Blake shook his head. "A job I was hoping to get. I didn't get it. I shouldn't have broken the phone." He hesitated. "Come here." He held his arms out. Sophia ran into a hug.

Clara glared. "Are you going to replace the phone? You need to watch your anger. It's not good for Sophia to see this sort of thing."

Blake scowled at her back as she whirled around and stormed out of the room. Dex trailed in.

"It's okay, Dad. If they don't want you, they're crazy!"

Blake smiled, but his smile didn't reach his eyes. "How about that run?"

"Can we go tonight? Mike just texted me, and he wants to hang out before class. He's really cute." Sophia's eyes ignited.

Blake masked his irritation beneath a grin. "Sure. Tonight. I'll go to the gym instead. Sorry, buddy." He scratched the top of Dex's head. Blake might have asked Clara to come for a run if her mood wasn't volatile. It was easier to do his own thing.

***

He kept to his gym routine. Usually, he stopped to talk to the receptionist about how her college classes were going, but today he stuck with only saying hello to a select few on the way in and minimized the small talk. Normally he didn't think about his nightmares, so why was he doing so now? What had that machine changed? There had to be a way to get information.

He ran on the treadmill, mixing an easy tempo with four-hundred-meter repeats. As he went through the motions, he became angrier with Doctor Kendra. Each interval was faster than the previous until he could barely run three hundred feet and ripped the emergency cord out. He grabbed his towel and walked into the weight room. He paced himself with higher volume sets instead of going heavy despite how tempting it was with the young recruits working out nearby. Then, he switched to dumbbells and arm curls, but he still couldn't muster the proper mental energy to go hard. Life's stresses usually sailed off him in a cool breeze. He smelled burned rubber as the wheels of his mind turned.

"Are you done with that?"

Lieutenant Mitchell hovered over the dumbbells. The lieutenant rarely exercised with the regulars. It was strange to see him in fitness clothes and not in uniform with a freshly shaved head. Was he scrawnier? Blake hadn't seen him in months. He looked maybe a hundred and sixty pounds, soaked.

"Yeah." Blake blinked down at the dumbbells, panting. "I'm done."

The lieutenant crooked an eye and tilted his head. "Everything okay, Sergeant? You look a little...out of character."

Blake glanced in the mirror. Had he lost muscle mass? Lifting alone got the job done, but lifting with Delta pushed him to his max. He rubbed beneath his eyes like the dark patches were from a dry erase marker. When had so much white popped up on his head? "I'm fine. It's been a rough few weeks."

"My door is always open if you want to talk, Sergeant. We're a family, and we'll support you. There are plenty of resources available." The lieutenant tried a smile that should have reassured Blake.

Blake nodded at the floor tiles. No clue where that door might be and no intention of using it, anyway. "Thank you, sir. I'll be fine." He knew what a private conversation could bring—a trip to a psychologist and removal from combat. Permanent removal. Bad enough he'd said anything to Doctor Kendra. He had no desire to sit at a desk. He wasn't a goddamn pencil pusher, he was a trained lethal weapon. His brothers in Delta needed him like he needed them. He should be leading them into combat, not jerking off at the gym by himself.

Lieutenant Mitchell clamped a hand on Blake's shoulder, then moved to the incline press, matching Blake's weight. Blake counted the reps: fifteen, sixteen, seventeen. *What is he on?*

Blake left the weight room, further annoyed for doing less than the puny lieutenant. He ventured into the mat room. Dozens of mats lay back to back along the floor. Police Forces and Special Operations units came from all around the United States to train in the gym and learn from the high-level hand to hand combat specialists. Despite this, the mat room was empty and stank of anti-bacterial.

The door creaked open, and Lieutenant Mitchell walked in.

"Want to test your skills?" he asked.

Blake didn't want to be rude, but he felt too frustrated to fight. If he lost his temper, he might knock the lieutenant out like he had Wade when they sparred during team training. "No thanks," he said. "I was going to stretch and head ou—"

The lieutenant punched Blake hard in the stomach.

Blake folded forward and heaved to catch his breath.

"Are you going to defend yourself?" the lieutenant said. He pressed his lips together and flared his nostrils.

Chapter 8

BLAKE STRAIGHTENED AND TOOK his hand off his stomach. He waved, inviting the lieutenant to try again. *You wanted this. Don't complain to your superiors when you get your ass kicked.* The lieutenant lunged to deliver a right hook to the face. Blake diverted the punch, stepped inside, and shoved him back.

The lieutenant rebounded and kicked. Blake intercepted by kicking up. The top of his foot hit the lieutenant's hamstring, disabling the power and momentum.

"What are you doing?" Blake said. He wasn't used to officers picking fights.

The lieutenant flurried Blake with punches and kicks. Blake deflected most. A few connected but didn't inflict any damage.

"What the hell are you doing? Stand down lieutenant." Blake steeled his arms, planted his legs. *Time to put the lieutenant down hard.*

The lieutenant attacked again. Blake blocked the first three punches then moved close, ducked behind him and threw an arm around the lieutenant's neck for a headlock. The lieutenant dropped his weight and slithered out of the headlock like an oily snake. Blake hefted him up at the armpit and slammed him onto the mat. The lieutenant's head slapped hard, and his eyes bulged. Blake jumped on top and grabbed him by the throat.

"What's wrong with you, sir?"

"You can't throw a punch, Sergeant?" The lieutenant panted. "You Delta Force hit like Girl Scouts."

Blake laughed. The lieutenant joined him. Blake rolled off the lieutenant, hauled him to his feet, then punched him in the face, sending him back on his ass. "You're a long way from your desk, sir."

The lieutenant rubbed his jaw. "You interviewed for a position in my department."

Blake furrowed his brow. "What department is that?"

"Classified information. But you know that." The lieutenant sat up.

"That thing with Doctor Kendra? I was told I didn't get the job."

"Everything is a test, Sergeant. We've been studying your behavior since the test. Your dreams took a turn for the worse. Doctor Kendra told me about it. That was the point. We needed to see the effects on your personality. You need to be especially tolerant of post-traumatic stress to get the position. If you can't handle your own stress, how can you help others handle theirs?"

"So, what are you saying? I'm not immune, I failed."

The lieutenant smiled. "No, you didn't fail. Had you started drinking, drugs, hurting people, taking things too far when you should back down...those are failures. Being on edge isn't failure."

"Why are you here, sir?"

"To offer you the job. You maintained a level head. Your outbursts were...within the norm," the lieutenant seesawed his hand, "give or take."

"What happened to the other candidates? What did they do?" *Could they have lost their cool and hurt people? Had I been a serious threat to Clara and Sophia and didn't know it?*

The lieutenant's smile faded. "Most responded outside the norm. The government has searched for two years to find another operator. It hasn't been an easy search. When they recruited me, I thought of you, which is how your name ended up on the list."

"You could have called."

"Always thinking, aren't you, Sergeant? Another test. I read the results. It's not the same as knowing how you'll react when pushed. Let's call it a bonus test."

"How many times have you done this test and been wrong?"

The lieutenant laughed with a raised eyebrow and a bloody lip that would grow in the next few minutes. "Too many to count."

Blake smiled. Few officers stepped into the ring with an operator—especially when he's pissed off.

"What happens now, sir?"

"I'll pick you up at home tomorrow morning and acquaint you with your new job. You won't be reporting to your unit again. Don't worry, I'll take care of the paper trail. As far as everyone is concerned, you're still on leave. We'll discuss the rest tomorrow."

***

When Blake walked through the door, Clara was already a deep red with a clenched jaw. "What are you so happy about? Good time at the gym?" Clara slapped the butter knife in her hand down on the counter. "I made Sophia's lunch while you took *two hours*." She checked her watch. "Shouldn't you be at the unit?"

Blake updated her on what happened at the gym and the new job that would get him home every night. She'd wanted him home for years and he'd felt terrible missing out on so much of Sophia growing up.

Clara blanched, but she recovered and offered a light hug. She had to lean forward to connect. He pulled her hips close to his. Her body felt limp and distant. Clara had grown impatient the last few years. Each deployment had clawed between them, like a wedge that increased the distance until it was an unfathomable chasm, even when he returned home. She'd asked him not to tell her about the missions and the things he saw because it had become too much for her. She ignored the fresh scars. Blake worried it was too late to close the gap between them.

Clara returned to the kitchen, and Blake sighed and dropped onto the couch. *What's this job about? What keeps me in combat and gets me home every night?*

By late afternoon, Sophia walked into the house, eyes narrow and lips pursed. "What's wrong with you? Ugh, Dad, I don't feel like running anymore. I'm super tired." Her feet seemed attached to concrete weights, and she arched as if she wore an invisible lead vest.

"I got the job," he said.

Sophia shed the weights and vest and ran into his arms. "You'll be home every night? No more going away for months?"

"Well, I don't know the details yet, but yes, looks like it." He kept his grip tight on her. *This will be worth it. It's what our family needs.*

Chapter 9

THE NEXT MORNING, BLAKE stood in front of a mirror, checking his tie and service medals. He thought about wearing a suit. Maybe combats. In the end, he played it safe.

"Thank you," Blake said, walking through the kitchen. He took his polished boots from Clara and wolfed down a large breakfast of eggs, toast, bacon, and sausage. He wasn't sure how the day would go or when he'd have time to eat again. Eating in the teams was a luxury.

A horn blasted outside like a triumphant elephant. Clara and Sophia stood at the door with him. He hugged them both. Clara wouldn't meet his eyes and turned her cheek to him when he leaned in for a kiss. He sighed, choosing to believe that would change with time. This was only his first day on the job. A relationship strained over years couldn't be healed in a single day.

This was the first time the two had seen him off in years. Usually, he left for months at a time. His last moment with Clara was always a subdued fight before he walked out the door, and Sophia learned to keep her distance. He hated that.

"Ready to go?" the lieutenant asked when Blake slid into the passenger seat of the car.

"Ready."

A dozen miles outside Crimson Coast Command Base, they turned down an unmarked road headed to an old bunker several elite teams used for training. Blake hadn't trained there since he was a rookie. "We headed to the silo?"

The lieutenant nodded. "The silo and beyond. There's an underground operating base we use for this project. All the equipment you saw during your test is there. We bring some of the tech outside the base when we test recruits, but that's it. If things go bad, there's no trace of the equipment."

"Are you going to tell me anything about this project, sir?"

"Patience, Sergeant. You'll find out soon enough. No more killing bad guys in the field."

Blake didn't consider himself a killer. Sometimes a terrorist impeded mission success and needed to be put down hard. It's what soldiers did. He'd seen plenty of people freed from tyranny, and even if he didn't stick around long, the people he saved were grateful for the help. Mostly.

He watched the trees pass through the window and noticed a few farms in the distant valley. Horses and cows. He imagined farming would be backbreaking. And boring. The air probably smelled of gunsmoke after years of teams shooting in the area. "Anyone farming out there, or is it all a cover?" Blake asked.

The lieutenant smiled but didn't offer an answer.

A road sign read *Military Personnel Only. All others are required to turn around. Trespassers will be prosecuted under the National Interstate and Defense Highways Act.*

When they approached a one-story building and a three-level parking structure, Blake had immediate memories of joint operations with SEAL Team Six at the Silo. Delta and SEAL Team Six rarely trained together, but when they did, goddamn if they didn't thrive in competition. The teams alternated playing as the enemy to see who completed missions faster. No two scenarios were identical. They both had their strengths. Delta trained for autonomy. *I don't need anyone holding my hand to blow shit up.*

They slowed at a gate with six guards on duty. The lieutenant showed his ID badge to a guard named Gonzalez, and Blake did the same. Gonzalez glared down at a clipboard, while the other soldiers pointed their weapons at the car. *There aren't many places where fidgeting can get you killed.*

Gonzalez stepped out of the booth, returned their ID cards, and waved for the gate to be raised and the tire spikes to be lowered. "You're clear, sir. Welcome aboard, Sergeant."

They parked the car in the parking garage and walked to the main building. Weird that the garage was larger than the facility. The main building must have been a few hundred yards long and wide.

Blake and Lieutenant Mitchell marched into the facility, flanked by armed guards.

"Heavy security," Blake remarked.

The lieutenant shrugged. "Advancing technology in secret helps our country remain a powerhouse."

Right. Blake didn't care about politics. He was just the tip of the spear.

They walked down a narrow corridor. Lieutenant Mitchell was laser-focused on the steel door at the end, but Blake examined everything. Only mounted cameras, pivoting to monitor them, broke the monotony of white walls. They came to the steel door, and the lieutenant flashed his badge. A beep cut through the echoes of their footsteps, and the door unlatched. They stepped into a small room. The door behind them clicked shut. Fans blew what felt like arctic winds at them. Blake covered his head.

When the wind died, the lieutenant said, "They lower the room temperature so your internal heat rises to battle the cold. It's easier to detect any anomalies your body might have with the infrared scanner. You'll have to get used to it."

"So, I get to experience Canada every morning."

"Lieutenant Mitchell, Sergeant Powell, you're cleared to enter," a voice said from a speaker above their heads.

They entered a room with offices crowding them on all sides. Glass windows acted as a barrier between offices. Wasted resources. Nobody hovered over someone else's desk. No chatter of a typical office.

Eyes peered up at them but fell back to the computer screens as they walked by. A few officers nodded at Lieutenant Mitchell, and he responded with a chin bump. *An unusual amount of concentration. They must get a lot of work done.*

They stepped into an elevator with four buttons on the panel—G, BL1, BL2, and BL3.

"BL3," Lieutenant Mitchell said.

Blake pressed the button. The door closed, and the elevator dropped.

"If you yawn, your ears will pop."

How deep underground is this thing going? Blake's ears popped without the yawn—deep underground. It took about twenty seconds for the elevator to chime and rumble open. They eventually entered a room with four monstrous computers huddled in the center. Hallways veined out. They had at least four machines identical to the one he'd tested in.

"Sergeant." Lieutenant Mitchell snapped his fingers. "This way."

They walked to a machine with the lid closed. *Sausages in a bun.*

"Sergeant Powell, this is Colonel Marks. He's heading up the Genesis Project."

Blake clicked his heels together and raised his hand to salute.

Colonel Marks wore gym clothes and sweat dripped down the side of his face. "At ease, Sergeant."

Blake shook the colonel's soggy hand.

"Come here and look at this video, Sergeant. This is what you'll be working on." Colonel Marks swept a finger toward a large screen.

Blake walked over. "Sir?"

The colonel pointed his chin at the screen. Blake tried to ignore the rancid body odor. It smelled like someone had left an orange next to a radiator a few weeks ago.

A battle played out on the screen. Soldiers in a firefight. Many of them looked dead. The fighting continued until two soldiers remained. "It's okay. It's my time," one soldier said to the other—*like a bad movie*—and sprinted into an enemy trench. He threw a grenade, killing everyone, including himself. The other soldier sat down and placed shaky hands on his head, letting his rifle fall into the dirt.

"It's taken months to get this far," Colonel Marks said. "Remember one important thing: don't rush. It always fails. These things will take time. We're here to help soldiers overcome their personal demons. It's important."

"Should I understand what I'm seeing, sir?"

"Follow me, Sergeant." Colonel Marks led them to a small room with three round tables. Clean white countertops circled the far wall, and shelves hung above it. Someone had handwritten *Lounge* on top of the doorframe.

"The project is called Genesis," the colonel said. "The images you saw were memories. Nightmares. A soldier's post-traumatic stress."

"We go into those nightmares with the soldiers that dream them and shape the memory," Lieutenant Mitchell said.

Chapter 10

Blake's mind rang with a hundred questions at once, and he could barely keep track. *How does the technology work? Are we really going into someone's nightmare?* Working on PTSD didn't sound like a top-secret project.

The colonel smiled and signaled to sit at the table. "Doctor Michael Stillman wanted to help soldiers overcome trauma, so he created the Genesis Project with funding from the US military and partners. As the doctor dug deeper into the project, he used virtual technology to get a better insight into soldiers' dreams. He created interactive virtual technology so we could enter dreams from the outside and make minor adjustments. At first, the changes were too ambitious. Soldiers could tell the difference between their nightmares and the changes—dark times. But as the project continued, we discovered smaller changes over a long period had a better effect. There's no way for us to alter the dream entirely." Colonel Marks leaned back in his chair. "If you have questions, you can ask when I'm done. Speak freely."

Blake nodded. Everything the colonel said brought new questions, and he struggled to remember them. He pulled out his pocket notepad and pen to jot them down. Blake felt Lieutenant Mitchell's eyes on him from the other side of the table like a scientist studying a rat in a maze.

Colonel Marks continued. "We have high-ranking officers committing suicide. The cost of preventing that is astronomical, and most of the time, the soldiers revert to their depression. I've lost a lot of friends to PTSD. High-ranking officers and senior NCOs are brilliant tacticians. Losing them has detrimental implications in combat. Sometimes we don't recover. Imagine losing Patton before Vietnam." He issued a soulful sigh. "You'll have to learn about the soldiers assigned to you. Study their nightmares, then head into the nightmare as a member of the team and modify with subtle changes, like a buddy dying face down instead of face up, or guts still attached instead of splayed out like a spaghetti dish gone wrong. Your goal is to reduce their PTSD. There are some major psychiatric facilities designed to help soldiers with post-traumatic stress, but they fail. Too many soldiers need help, and there isn't enough help to go around. We work slowly right now, but we'll pick it up."

"Why is there so much security? It's just a virtual program."

"This technology under the control of the wrong people could do a lot of damage. What you'll see here doesn't exist in the open market. It's worth billions to the gaming industry, but we aren't there yet. We've lost a few operators who couldn't take what they were seeing. People aren't ready for this level of reality."

"Besides, the machine only reads the details of dreams to create scenarios." Lieutenant Mitchell raised an eyebrow. "We can use dreams, but we can't create things that don't exist. It wouldn't be profitable to other industries just yet."

"Wouldn't someone have to be hooked up for this to work? It's not like meeting in a game lobby on the Xbox," Blake asked.

"We hook them up to a smaller version of the Genesis. It feeds them the dream while they sleep. The real magic is in the War Room."

Colonel Marks slid a folder onto the table. "No rehearsals on this mission. Look at the file and let me know when you're ready to go. I'll brief you on the system, and we'll send you for clinical training with Doctor Kendra in a few days. Until then, your job is to get to know the general's case and review his nightmares. Make sure you're considering an operating plan for the dream. I want a briefing next week."

Colonel Marks and Lieutenant Mitchell walked out of the room and shut the door behind them. Blake had seen a lot of terrible deaths and gruesome cruelty, but spread out over months and years, not compacted into a day. If this job cost him his relationship with Clara and Sophia because he couldn't absorb the trauma, he'd walk away.

That settled, he flipped open the file, and a sheet of paper and two photos spilled out. One photo showed a four-star general. *No easy day.* General Marcus Talbert had seen combat in Afghanistan on five rotations as part of the combat arms. He'd fought in Bosnia when it was a hot zone. A classified portion detailed a mission in Rwanda and Somalia during the genocide. He'd toured in Colombia and Yugoslavia. Fought on the front lines of some of the worst battles in recent history, ranked as a captain for several. The file didn't mention PTSD, but Blake could only imagine how much it battered the general's psyche. How did Genesis deal with multiple nightmares? Did it tackle them the same way as singular ones? The onboarding process for this project sucked.

He flipped to the back of the file where he found several combat photos. Each photo saw changes in the general's body language and personality like a progress study. The first photo showed the general's glowing confidence, his tall and steely posture. He looked to have a knack for his duties. The last picture showed the general slouched, eyes cowering in deep pockets. His skin sagged, his face wilted. He looked twenty years older than he should. Blake reread the file, trying to memorize as much as he could. Most of the general's missions happened before Blake enlisted.

An hour later, the door squeaked open, and Lieutenant Mitchell poked his head in the gap. "Ready?"

Blake preferred action to preparation, especially when prep lasted all day, but he understood the need for rehearsals. His team sometimes spent weeks, even months, adjusting tactics to take down a target. Why wouldn't Genesis give him more direction? "Where do I go from here?"

Lieutenant Mitchell's eye gleamed. He showed an enthusiasm for this project. "Right into the thick of it. A primary nightmare is one that shows up at least once in every seven recorded dream sequences. General Talbert has two of them. You saw the details in the file? Staff process hundreds of dreams to mark them as insignificant or offshoots of the same primary nightmare. For example, he saw a child die, so other dreams have children dying in them despite not being the primary nightmare."

Blake nodded. "Who decides what dreams are important?"

"A team of analysts."

Ugh. "What if they're wrong?"

Lieutenant Mitchell opened the door more widely and stepped aside to allow Blake to pass by. "Let's go."

Blake shook his head. Just like military leadership: admit nothing, play stupid when everything goes to hell.

Lieutenant Mitchell led the way to the lab. "This is the War Room," he said. They stopped at a machine labeled Genesis III.

Lieutenant Mitchell smiled. "There's no easy way to break into this process. We could write a training manual, but nothing prepares your mind for entering the Genesis. Your training in Delta gives you more than enough combat experience, initiative, and strategy. That's why we considered you. It wasn't just about your resistance to post-traumatic stress." He clapped his hands together. "Here's a tip for later: If you fail, just change your approach. Oh, and be careful not to make things worse. We don't want him to cancel his treatments."

"Treatments?" Blake asked. "Is this a treatment?"

"Talbert knows he's part of a PTSD program that isn't available to the public or the average soldier. He worked with clinics in Landstuhl, Walter Reed, and the Warrior Combat Stress program. None of them offered enough time to be helpful. Those programs are like an assembly line. The general is also being evaluated. You can't live a nightmare without the individual present. Now, if you're done with questions, let's get you in the Genesis."

Blake wasn't done with questions, but he didn't think that mattered to Lieutenant Mitchell.

"I'll set the system for observation, so you won't be able to change anything. That will come after you've seen the dreams, worked with Doctor Kendra, and developed an approach."

Lieutenant Mitchell pointed at a small room to the side of the Genesis III. "Change in there."

After changing, Blake lay on the bed, recalling the squishy substance. The lid of the Genesis lowered on him, sounding so clunky he wondered what would happen if it snapped shut and they couldn't open it. He fought a desire to leap out of the way. *Toughen up. You're the meanest motherfucker you know.*

Chapter 11

BLACK. BLAKE HAD FELT that emptiness before. What came next? The beginning of the dream didn't take long—better than Xbox loading times. General Talbert stood in front of Blake, taller than expected, with two bars on his shoulder. They stood atop a wall looking down at a crowd. Women and children screamed at him—at all the soldiers on the wall. Their shrieks spat venom. Blake had seen protests before. They often got ugly. He waited for this one to follow the pattern.

A large building adorned with American flags stood behind him. An embassy. Gunfire erupted. He spun, prepared to return fire but realized he didn't have a weapon. He reached to pull the pistol from the general's side, but an invisible wall blocked him. This felt too real, and they'd left him exposed. He dove behind the wall's overhang. Why weren't the soldiers returning fire?

A menu appeared at the left corner of Blake's vision, like the pause menu in a video game, but the simulation hadn't stopped. The only option available was exit. The customize and settings buttons had a dark shadow and didn't respond to Blake's touch.

Blake pinpointed the origin of the shots. A group of men at the outside perimeter of the riot held AK-47s, muzzles pointed at the sky. General Talbert marched across the wall. He shouted orders at the soldiers to hold their fire. Several soldiers had their fingers on the trigger, waiting to squeeze. Why hold back? They must be terrified if they're a sneeze away from killing someone.

"Sir, are we going to do something?" a soldier shouted from below. Blake peeked at his uniform: Sergeant.

General Talbert shook his head. "Hold your fire. We have our orders. They aren't targeting us. Shooting at them risks retaliation."

The sergeant grimaced and returned to the sandbag pillow box near the embassy entrance.

"Who are you to kill our people?" a woman screamed. "My husband is dead because of you! Murderers!"

Blake smelled feces and rot from the crowd. It crawled up his nostrils and made him dry heave. It had been real at one time. Real for General Talbert. His nightmare, his reality.

General Talbert ignored the screams as if he knew trying to justify American involvement in their country would anger the crowd more. He did the only thing he could—kept his men from shooting.

The terrorists in the back of the crowd inched forward. A corporal on Blake's left squeezed the trigger within millimeters of the pin popping forward. A weapon was bound to go off.

Gunfire erupted, but it wasn't aimed at the soldiers, and it didn't come from them. A young child, maybe seven years old, looked up at Blake, panicked. His head snapped back when a bullet punctured his back. He dropped. The woman who screamed earlier was crying for help. Several rounds cut her down as she danced like a marionette.

So much yelling. Everyone tried to break free from the crowd, but the shooters blocked their escape. They killed everyone. The carnage reminded Blake of why he'd become an operator: defend those who couldn't defend themselves and put a bullet in the cruel bastards that preyed on the weak just to further a political cause. How could anyone murder a little boy because they wanted Americans to get drawn into a gunfight so they'd break the treaty? That little boy and his mom could be Sophia and Clara. Blake balled his fists. He couldn't count the bodies, many stacked on top of each other. He swallowed hard. *What brutal shit men are capable of.*

General Talbert ordered his men not to return fire. Blake wasn't sure he would have obeyed that order. His dad would have. He was a soldier in every sense of the word.

This scene would give any soldier PTSD. No wonder it messed the general up. He could have stopped the murders. Those people could be alive. Even if it meant a dishonorable discharge and prison for the general, that seven-year-old boy could have walked away. Now General Talbert had to live with it.

A rifle leaned against the wall a few feet away. If Blake could reach it, he could change what happened.

The gunmen laughed. They fired at the air, teasing the soldiers.

Blackness. The dream ended. Blake groped around. *Can I get locked in a loading area? Do nightmare sequences freeze?*

A different sequence started. General Talbert sat beside Blake in a Humvee. Sand and dust arced up the tires as the driver sped through the desert. General Talbert's eyes were ringed with dark circles like tattered laundry. He must have lost twenty pounds. A silver eagle sat on his shoulder. *He's a Colonel now.*

Bodies filled the ditches beside the road. Villagers pillaged the dead. What were they looking for? Weathered stone walls stood on the other side of the bodies, ready to crumble.

From the general's file, Blake assumed they were in Rwanda during the genocide.

Their driver slammed the brakes. Tires squealed. They kicked forward. Their seatbelts constricted their chests in a cold ache. "What's going on, Corporal?" General Talbert said.

The driver leaned out the window with a shrug in his shoulders. "I can't see anything, sir. Both trucks are stopped up ahead."

The general picked up the radio. "Convoy One, this is Convoy Three. Come in."

Silence.

"Convoy One, this is Convoy Three. Come in."

"Convoy One, stand by."

"Convoy One, this is Convoy Three. Why have we halted?"

Silence.

"All convoys, this is Convoy Three. We are dismounting to check on Convoy One. Eyes sharp."

Dismounting a vehicle in a warzone wasn't in the book. Where was Convoy Two and what did they see? Blake peeked around, trying to get eyes on Convoy One. They were around the bend on the left, and a boulder blocked most of them from sight.

All eyes from Convoy Two stared straight ahead.

Everyone but their driver stood outside, weapons at eye level, searching for a target. Enormous boulders surrounded them. A choke point in a canyon was a textbook ambush with high ground advantage going to the enemy. The general heard nothing when Blake told him to get back in the Humvee.

The general sucked in a breath and expelled it in notches. "Sams and Marila, cover the high ground. We're moving in a stack. Walker, you take the front. I'll move as number two."

They formed a single file and walked toward the second vehicle. When they reached it, they knew why nobody moved. Convoy Two was dead. Blake would have screamed ambush if he could. Gunfire erupted from everywhere at once. Bullet holes filled two soldiers. The general sprinted to the second light-armor vehicle and leaped inside. He pulled a body on top of him. The reek of blood and the metallic gunfire mixed with the cacophony of death. Blake followed the general into the truck, impervious to the bullets flying, although he was sure he'd die.

The general stared at the face of the sergeant whose body saved his life. The soldier's eyes popped open, and the general gasped. Blake jerked back and quickly recovered.

The dead sergeant said, "I was still alive. I could have survived. You used me to save yourself. Murdered me. You abandoned your men. I was still alive. I'd be holding my wife right now if it weren't for you. You left them to die. Fuck the bars you've earned on our backs."

The general cried. "There was nothing I could do. You were already dead."

"You saved your own life. You could have helped the men outside. The ambush was your mistake. Your men should be alive, or you should be dead with them. Coward."

The general slouched to the first aid kit under the seat and wept.

***

The Genesis opened. Blake coughed out the smell of dust and death. He felt cold sweat. He hyperventilated, rolled over, and smacked onto the floor. Aches blitzed up his palms where he braced himself, hunched over cold tiles. *It's not real, it's not real, it's not real, it's—*

Lieutenant Mitchell hovered over him.

"Those are the two nightmares?" Blake asked between huffs.

"Yes, those are the nightmares. Theories?"

Blake frowned. "I need more than a second to think."

The lieutenant nodded. "Sure, I'll give you some time. Report back before the end of the day at seventeen hundred. I'll drive you home. I imagine you can get yourself here tomorrow."

Blake changed back into his uniform. His mind was already working. He found his notepad and pen in the lounge, still sitting on the table.

"Did you requisition that?" A man with large dark eyes and short brown hair smiled.

"It's an old habit of mine. I like to steal small accounting supplies and sell them on eBay for profit. I don't suppose you know where I can find a calculator?"

The man's smile grew. "I'm Captain David Guarnere. You can call me David."

"Blake."

They shook hands. David gripped his hand tightly enough for Blake to wince and tighten his own grip.

"You're an operator here?" Blake asked.

David nodded. "Longest currently serving."

"Any advice?"

"Make mistakes, then I'll help you out. There's no point in teaching you to do it right. You won't get it. Think of your first few sequences as rehearsals, even if we don't do those around here." David winked. "You screw up, you adapt, you execute again. Hopefully better. Kind of like the SEALs. You're a former SEAL, right? Team Six?"

Blake paused. "I've been around a few teams."

"We'll talk again later," David said. "You better get to work fixing your client. I've got one of my own."

Chapter 12

Corporal Anthony Hodge stood outside Senator Alex Fredrick's home, hidden in the trees. Only a sliver of moonlight kept the shadows at bay. He bobbed on his heels with starving impatience, squinting into the dark interior. How many hours had the senator been gone? A small forest stood sentinel around the mansion, secluding it. Impossible to protect without an army. Anthony had used a rope and hook to scale the wall.

He fingered the knife on his hip, rubbing the vinyl cord wrapped around the hilt. He had found the knife on the ground beside his best friend, who had his throat cut during an op. He promised himself the senator would suffer. Slowly. And he planned to collect on his promise. If it meant his own life, he'd give it up—he had nothing left to live for. First, the senator needed to confess on video so Anthony could post it online and show the world the truth.

Anthony fished around in his pockets for a cigarette. He couldn't light it, but he needed something to focus on. Resigned that no nicotine was coming and finding no relief in its paper form, he played with his knife. How many innocent soldiers had died because of the senator?

His veins pulsed when the front gate rumbled open and a car rushed around the corner, headed for the house. The car swerved up the driveway and stopped at the front door. Doors swung open in synchronization, and four bodyguards stepped out. The guards scanned the trees. Their surveilling eyes missed Anthony. They weren't really looking. They relied on the lazy pattern of their search, not the persistent detail required to spot Anthony.

The senator stepped out of the car and searched his suit. No finger print access for the prick? Anthony tightened his grip on the knife. The bastard wore a ten-thousand-dollar suit. White lines trailed his hairline on both sides, probably to make him look older and wise to his constituents. The senator lived a good life, smoking crack and drinking too much wine while Anthony's friends were dead and their families mourned the losses.

The senator stepped inside the house. Anthony cursed that he wasn't already inside, but he wasn't trained to disarm the alarm. It wasn't a home security system run by an apathetic joe-blow company. This system was high tech, with a live video feed when someone armed or disarmed it. Anthony had roughly ten minutes to dart inside before the senator's guards performed their perimeter sweep, went inside, and rearmed the system.

He pulled a Beretta 92 fitted with a silencer out of a holster tucked behind his back, glad he bought the hollow point nine-millimeter rounds—security had vests on and he couldn't shoot them all in the head.

Anthony stalked toward the guards. From a distance, one guard spotted his shadow melt across the pavement. Anthony stepped back to draw them in. His heart steadied. The adrenaline that usually crackled in him before an operation was gone.

The guard drew a pistol and pointed it at the bushes. He tossed his chin over his shoulder. "Ed, I need a light." The others took out their pistols and crept toward the bush. Anthony was nearly out of time. He took aim, held his breath—and fired four times, back to front. Each bullet killed its target. Anthony knew it without watching them drop.

He stepped over the dead bodies, entered the house, and eased the door shut behind him with a soft *click* of the latch. Elaborate paintings of old senators and a chandelier decorated the foyer. Wealthy degenerates killed anyone and threw money at their guilt. No consequences.

To his left, he heard a door snap shut. He stalked toward the sound, pistol raised, only a subdued crick to mark his steps. The guards were dead. It had to be the senator unless someone had gone to sleep very early and woke only now.

"Ben, can you—" Senator Fredrick turned the corner and lurched to a halt when he saw Anthony.

Anthony pointed the Berretta at his head.

"Take whatever you want."

Anthony smelled urine and balked. Murderer and a pussy. "I intend to. Get back in the room." Anthony shoved the senator into the room he'd just come out of. His other hand gripped the senator's shoulder. He dug his fingers into the senator's flesh.

"Is anyone else in the house?"

The senator didn't reply.

"If I'm caught by surprise, whoever else is in the house is going to die."

The senator closed his eyes. "No, nobody else is in the house. Did you murder my guards? They're all dead?"

Anthony nodded. He pulled the knife from his pocket and slammed the hilt into the senator's head. The senator collapsed to the ground. Blood trickled down his face.

"Do you remember this?" Anthony turned the knife over in the light.

The senator blinked to clear the blood from his eyes. "What? Remember what?"

Anthony couldn't stop himself from hitting the senator four more times in the face. "Can't remember?"

The senator wrapped his arms around his head.

"Are you so far removed from your sins that you don't remember the lives you took? Is that what it means to be a politician? Murder whoever you want and forget them like you forget what you ate for dinner?" Anthony pulled his cell phone from his back pocket and pressed record. "Confess to the murder of Corporal Jason Emit, Sergeant Sam Malcove, and Captain Angus Geraro. You murdered them in Afghanistan. Treason. Treason against my brothers. Treason against the United States Rangers. Confess!" Anthony punched him in the face.

The senator shook his head, trying to crawl backwards. "Confess to killing who? Your friend? A soldier? I'm sorry, but I didn't kill anyone. I haven't served in the military in twenty years. Please, you have me confused with someone else."

Anthony slashed the knife across the senator's arm. The senator's sleeve fell open to reveal a tattoo with the word *Ranger* on his forearm. Below the name was a skull with a knife through its head. *Death before dishonor* was written below the skull. "I remember that tattoo. I remember your face. And I remember my men dying. Death before dishonor. That's what you swore."

The senator looked at the tattoo as if it was poison stamped into his arm and he wanted to rip it out.

"In Tora Bora, they set you up with our Ranger detachment. You wore a lieutenant's uniform, and you snuck behind them and killed them, one at a time. Three of us died. I saw you. The only reason you got away was because you threw a flashbang at me and ran. Don't you fucking lie to me."

"Please, please, please." The senator shook his head, and his breath hitched. Whatever urine he held back pooled on the ground. "I didn't kill them. I have a wife and three children. It's terrible that you lost your friends, but I didn't kill them. I've never been to war."

Anthony shook his head. "I'm disappointed in you, Senator. You won't see your family in hell."

The senator didn't move. His lips quivered, probably half-starts of the lies he thought might save him.

Anthony smashed the phone against the wall. "For killing innocent soldiers—befriending them, then murdering them—I sentence you to death." Anthony slammed the knife into the senator's heart and stared into the senator's eyes as he bled out. "You should have confessed," Anthony whispered. "Now you'll burn in hell where nothing and no one can save you."

Chapter 13

Six months and Blake had only one client: General Marcus Talbert. He'd asked Colonel Marks for more clients to work with, at least a few with less severe PTSD. There was a panel that decided on fresh cases, he was told, and they didn't meet often. Despite the years the project existed, someone important on the panel didn't want too many soldiers involved. The project was too new, and the more soldiers involved, the more public the tech could become.

Blake made a few tweaks in the general's nightmares under the tutelage of Doctor Kendra, whom he met weekly via Skype. She reported how the General felt after the adjustments to his dreams, how his family life was impacted by the changes, and an overview of how she felt he was doing based on their appointments. Blake had also spent a few weeks with Veteran Affairs, learning how to help soldiers overcome PTSD.

The changes he made were big enough for the general to return to active service on a part-time basis. Colonel Marks felt the general would be ready for combat in another year—solid results. Becoming a general took twenty or thirty years, if ever. Getting a trained soldier back was a hell of a lot better than training a new one.

Blake worked the dreams in minute detail. He changed the embassy dream by adjusting the faces of the crowd. The woman glaring at

Talbert in the eye as she died changed to her glaring at the men behind her. A simple thing made the biggest differences. Blake didn't know the general's current assignment and had never met him to see what kind of difference he'd made. But it had taken months to get the woman looking back consistently.

In the Rwanda dream, Blake made larger changes. At first, they were wholesale changes—having the general not pull the sergeant over him—then smaller, like the general pulling him over face up. It took a long time to change the memory, but with the sergeant's head facing up, he couldn't look at the general to taunt him.

Blake headed to the War Room and stared at the Genesis III. He'd planned a new strategy for the general today. A huge step forward would hopefully wipe the nightmare clean enough to knock it out of the top ten. He ran his fingers down the side of the machine as if it were a treasured sports car.

"We need to talk," Colonel Marks said from behind him. "Now." Colonel Marks usually showed calm in the six months Blake had been with the project. Blake brushed aside thoughts of what the personality shift could mean. He'd dealt with officers throwing their weight around his entire career. Colonel Marks would probably tell him to do something different in the general's nightmares. Maybe he wanted to give him hell for being late yesterday.

General Talbert should be waiting in the Genesis for the session to start, but Blake had a feeling this overrode the general's time. "Yes, sir. Is this about Lieutenant Mitchell? We usually ride in together, but he's been on radio silence for a week."

"On me, Sergeant. We canceled your client today."

Blake paused, then followed the colonel into the senior officers' wing. *What the hell is going on?* Clients didn't get canceled. Changes to their patterns could set them off. When an operator was sick, another operator sat in on the nightmare to prevent the cancelation.

A plaque on a glass door exhibited Colonel Marks' name. Books overweighed every shelf. Most looked military. "Nice library, sir," Blake murmured. A small desk with a computer sat off to the right. A framed photograph of Colonel Marks with a woman and two boys sat next to the computer. The air felt thick and tasted like a cigar shop.

"Beautiful family." Blake smiled.

Colonel Marks glanced at the photo and grunted an agreement. His face darkened. "Have a seat." The colonel pointed at the metal folding chair.

"Brought out the big china?" Blake sat, hoping the chair didn't collapse. Two mugs sat on Colonel Marks' desk. The mug with the most stains read, "You can run, but you'll just die tired." Had Colonel Marks been a sniper? The other mug read, "Chaos coordinator." Long sentences followed, but Blake couldn't read them without leaning in.

"The only way to make sure people don't stick around too long is to give them a chair not worth sitting in."

"I won't keep you then, sir. What can I do for you? Why was my client canceled?"

Colonel Marks shifted his weight with a frown. "Have you heard of a Corporal Anthony Hodge? He served close to you in Afghanistan. He would have been a SEAL then, but he's also a former Ranger."

Blake couldn't remember every soldier he'd met. "Sorry, sir. I can't say I can put a face to the name. Even if I could, we didn't share any special moments. He didn't serve on my team."

"He's being held in our facility."

"Being held, sir? As in, he's a prisoner?"

"Our unit is handling the interrogation for now, but JAG is en route."

"Why would we be handling an interrogation of a—" He must have been part of the Genesis Project, and something went wrong. They probably cleared Hodge as fit to return to civilian life or active duty, but then he screwed up. "I'm afraid I don't know him, sir."

"He's being charged with first-degree murder. He killed Senator Fredrick in DC."

Blake's spine turned to ice. He waited for Colonel Marks to offer more, but the colonel paced his desk then pretended to scan the books on his shelf.

Colonel Marks hooked his hands behind his back and blinked in thought. Finally, "Follow me."

They made their way through the facility and outside, walking through a forest trail officers walked daily. *They make big decisions on these trails.* Blake breathed in the clean air. He spent so long with artificial air he forgot how nice nature felt. Leaves painted the forest in oranges, reds, and yellows. Blake loved autumn. Six months in the same nightmare, laboring for microscopic adjustments to take permanent shape. How long could he keep it up? He could have handled a larger workload and wider variety. Genesis felt real, but physical missions that changed every time he went out, real danger...*that* was what he loved.

"I want you to speak with him first, Sergeant," the colonel said as they tramped through the forest. Wet leaves shushed under their steps.

Blake held his breath. "Why would you want me to talk to him? I'm not a senior and I've had only one case. I really should get back to General Talbert. Not to question your intentions, sir, but shouldn't we wait for JAG?"

"Normally." The colonel sighed. "But I need inside eyes on this. Eyes that have seen what the Genesis can do. A mind that understands it. That recognizes PTSD. First Sergeant Martin was one of the first operators in the program, but in some ways, he is the least qualified and doesn't have the combat experience. He isn't a meat grinder. Captain Guarnere is away in training. This is important, Sergeant. Genesis can't slow down." The colonel led them into a large clearing. A narrow river surged in front of them, dwindling from sight to the south.

"You were a Ranger before you moved to Special Forces. You'll have a brotherhood with him. Look, this information is classified, Sergeant. Corporal Hodge was with the Genesis Project for years and was one of the first successes. We need to know what set him off. And we need to know if this can happen again. Suicide rate is high in soldiers with PTSD, but the murder rate isn't. I'll give you as much time as I can."

"Who was his operator?"

"His operator was the very first person to operate on the Genesis. A civilian. His name was Doctor Charles Minton, close friend of Doctor Stillman, the project's creator. After four years of operating, he couldn't handle the nightmares. He hung himself." Colonel Marks tossed that into the conversation as easily as he would mention his weekend plans. "After that, we started recruiting from the military. When regular soldiers didn't do well, we looked for operators. Few men can see and do things in combat without mental scars."

Blake watched the river flow. He had an inexplicable urge to jump in and float away. It wouldn't get him home, though. *I should take Sophia and Clara on a vacation and sit on a beach. They'd love that.* Sophia loved him being home every night, but the mental fatigue weighed on him so heavily he'd fall asleep on the couch in the middle of a board game. Clara wanted more than him being home. Quiet weekends together hadn't improved their relationship.

"I can talk to him, sir. But I'm not qualified for interrogations. Not legal ones. Are you sure about this? This will piss off JAG."

"You'll have to trust my judgment, Sergeant. He'll open up to you. You'll report directly to me after speaking with him, and you'll say nothing to anybody. If you're questioned at any point, you will disavow any knowledge of the corporal and get in immediate contact with me. Understood?" The last word slapped the air like a judge's gavel.

Blake knew the routine. "Hoorah, sir."

The colonel handed Blake a piece of paper, telling him to take his time before returning to the office, and marched away. Blake should have asked more about the history of the Genesis Project. In the six months he'd been there, he learned about Doctor Stillman, who they fired for classified reasons. He'd created the technology then handed it over to the military. Blake suspected that wasn't exactly how it went, though.

Blake looked at the paper. BL2. *Basement Level Two.* Corporal Anthony Hodge. Why did this paper look like a death certificate?

Chapter 14

BLAKE STARED AT THE river before heading back to his office, imagining the bodies of the men he'd killed floating down the river. Operation Sanitation came to mind—Echo team had killed several unarmed people near a water supply line because one of his men got into a scuffle about who was dumping chemicals in the water supply, and Blake had no choice but to protect him. The leader pulled a knife. Blake reacted on instinct. *They shouldn't be dead.* When the people saw their leader drop dead in the water, they attacked, choosing to follow their leader in death. The bodies trickled down the river, face down and gray, just as he imagined now. Blake hadn't thought about them since the mission, and he wasn't sure why the memory bullied itself into his brain now. Blake exhaled, tore his eyes from the river, and turned back toward the building.

Blake shared an office with three others, each with their own desk. Two other desks sat vacant and lonely. The room resembled a police precinct in a small town.

The name Corporal Anthony Hodge glared back at Blake from a Google search result as if provoking him to a staring contest. Nothing related to Senator Fredrick. When the local police arrested him, they kept his name confidential. The police did small favors helping the military save face. But the name would escape secrecy eventually. Politicians would scream for the military to release the details.

Blake clicked on the mouse and opened the Navy Personnel Command search center. Operators had access to the all-military personnel files for required research. They needed to know their clients and any soldiers involved in their nightmares. The search for Corporal Anthony Hodge turned up three hits, three separate soldiers. Only one served with the Rangers and transferred to Special Operations. Blake made note of the personnel file number.

Hodge had a typical military life, speckled with several tours in the combat arms with the Rangers. He was currently on assignment parading at Naval Base Coronado, California, a known SEAL training base.

He had earned two Silver Stars, a Purple Heart, and several other decorations. Silver Stars aren't easy to come by, especially with the Rangers, which is the only place he could have received it. Special Forces no longer documented war medals because of the confidentiality of missions and the need to deny their involvement. Thus, Anthony could have a dozen other medals. In Delta, the commanding officer had brought Blake into the mess, handed him his medal, and bought him a beer. Medals ended up dropped subtly in their file with a vague reference to their service at the end of their career.

Anthony's file shined with all the good things Blake expected in a Navy SEAL file. Very few official charges. A couple of drunk-and-disorderly references. A note about time away for a psychological review. Nothing about the project.

Blake sighed. He ran a search through the Genesis Project folders for the last name Hodge. One file popped up documenting the nightmares and adjustments made to them. They were all conducted by Doctor Charles Minton years ago, as the colonel had said. Blake reviewed many of the documents near the end of Anthony's treatment, and they showed positive results. Although there were dozens of setbacks, nightmares were tamed to being the odd bad dream. Signs of PTSD shrank to bothersome nuisances. *So, what happened?* Had the nightmares crept back into his dreams until the work with the Genesis fell apart? Even if that were true, why would he kill the senator? Corporal Hodge had nothing recent in his file.

Blake exhaled through puffed cheeks. Time to speak to the corporal. He threw himself out of his chair and marched through the compound.

When he reached basement level two, he barged into a sterile room with a waiting area and a desk on the right. Just like a hospital reception room. He passed ten empty seats to get to the desk. An imposing Plexiglas wall stood between him and the receptionist, who wore military fatigues with a golden oak leaf. A major, a high rank for a front-desk employee.

The major's head reflected the dull white of the room's lights, like he'd recently shaved it. Veiny muscles bulged as he hit the intercom button in front of him.

"Can I help you?" His lower lip hung boredly.

"Sergeant Blake Powell to see Corporal Anthony Hodge."

The major tapped away on his computer. He sat back in his chair and waited for something to happen. Nearly a minute passed.

Blake scanned the room. "Is everything okay?"

The major stared at the screen. He picked up the phone and muttered into it. Blake couldn't hear what he said. He glared up at Blake, then down at his computer. Finally, he placed the phone down and pressed the intercom button.

"You're cleared to speak with him, Sergeant. You'll have twenty minutes. When I buzz you through, remove items from your person and step through the metal detector. If you don't pass the detector, you'll undergo a search. If you refuse to be searched, you cannot speak with the corporal. Any questions?"

Blake raised an eyebrow. "No cavity searches, I hope. I didn't bring a change of underwear."

The major stared at him. He blinked with not even a crease of a smile. "Do you understand?"

"Understood, sir." Twenty minutes wasn't a lot of time.

A buzz and snap unlocked the door, and Blake stepped through. He felt as though he'd walked into a single-lane airport security terminal. A closed door waited at the end of the terminal.

The security check went as expected. He removed his shoes, his belt, and his military cuffs. A beady-eyed private said he'd get them back on the way out. He stepped through a silent metal detector. A female sergeant waited for him, the fabric of her combats taut against her solid physique. "Follow me, Sergeant."

She led him to another door. What were they thinking when they built this floor? *During an escape attempt, make sure the enemy is likelier to get lost than to escape.*

"He's through this door. You'll be able to speak with him for twenty minutes. I'll get you when your time is up. If there's a problem, I'll also get you. If you resist or delay, we won't permit you to return, and we'll escort you out of the holding area."

"Understood."

Corporal Hodge sat at the far end of a table, hands cuffed to the chair and feet chained to the floor. Seeing him alive and moving loaded Blake with memories. Corporal Hodge had been on sniper detail on a joint operation with Delta many years ago, long after he'd left the SEALs. Blake knew exactly who Corporal Hodge was.

Corporal Hodge's tongue ran along the inside of his gums. "You here to kill me?"

Chapter 15

"Why would I want to kill you?" Rhetorical. Blake knew why. Even though Blake didn't remember the name, he recalled his face. He'd served with Anthony during Operation Tangle in Afghanistan. Blake was already with Echo team then. Anthony had been a sniper with SEAL Team Alpha and provided overwatch for the first phase. Echo team had entered the building and took the objective: grab two high-ranking terrorists and kill enemy forces. Snipers picked off anyone exiting the building that wasn't American or in bindings.

The mission had unraveled. Echo team entered the building, and instead of finding trained militants, they found armed children. Most of them looked younger than fourteen years old. Echo team shouted repeatedly for the children to lower their weapons and take a knee. Instead, the children opened fire. Echo team killed most while some fled. The snipers didn't fire. They were on the radio demanding to know what was going on. They had seen the children fleeing and made a judgment call not to shoot. Outside, a child had pulled an AK-47 out of the sand a short distance from the entrance and shot Corporal Frank Targeron. Franky. Anthony killed the boy.

The debrief ended in shouting and punches. The mission left acid in everyone's mouths. Eighteen children dead. Nine surrendered. Mission failure. They never found the targets they'd been after.

Anthony had taken his hesitation to kill the kid hard. Blake heard he took a leave of absence from the SEALs.

"Are you there, Sergeant?" Anthony tried to wave at him, but the shackles constricted it to a hand flap. The chains jangled along the steel of the table.

Blake nodded. "I'm here, Corporal."

"I'm glad it's you they sent to kill me. It should be one of our own." Anthony spat a single laugh devoid of mirth. "You get why I did what I did, right? You'd want justice for your brothers too."

"I'm not here to kill you, Corporal."

"So, what are you doing here?"

Blake studied the corporal for a second. Something didn't quite sit right. "Do you know where you are, Corporal?" Blake sat on the opposite side of the table.

"Doesn't every holding cell look the same? The tour sucked, and they bagged me to transport me here. Why, where am I?" Anthony scanned the cell: a bed, a table, a toilet. Not much to look over.

"Does the name Genesis ring a bell?"

"Genesis. Genesis." The corporal pursed his lips. "The group that helped me with my dreams. I remember the shrinks. Doctor…"

"You aren't going before a panel…at least not yet. I'm here because my team needs to know what happened. Let's cut the shit."

"You know what happened, Sarge. That's why I'm here."

"You killed someone. A non-combatant. That's a trust we never break. That's what separates us from terrorists."

Anthony pounced, but his handcuffs snapped, recoiling him back into his chair. "He deserved what happened to him. I thought you'd understand that."

Blake caught a trickle of scotch in the air. Despite that, Anthony seemed sober. "Where did they arrest you?"

Anthony sat back, waited a breath, and smiled. "A bar half a mile away from the senator's home."

"You weren't running?"

"Not from justice. Never. I did what they trained me to do."

"And how is killing the senator part of your training? You had orders to kill him? Operating without orders—that's terrorism."

Anthony placed his hands on his lap. "I served with him in Afghanistan. They attached him to a Ranger unit—we were clearing a cave in the Tora Bora mountains. He murdered my team one at a time. The government *officially* said it was an ambush by Al-Qaeda members, but I saw him. I saw that pig, Fredrick, cut their throats." He spat on the floor.

Blake leaned back in his chair. If he wasn't full of it—and his face made Blake believe he wasn't—the details of the operation being leaked could cause chaos. *The senator looked fit, but taking down a unit of Rangers?*

"You're sure it was the senator? When did this happen?"

"I dream about it every night, Sergeant. Things were foggy after the war until I found some help." He nodded in a tilt as a conceding gesture. "Well...really...they found me. They helped clear some of the fog. A few months ago, the fog completely lifted. I remember the incident like it happened yesterday."

"Who helped you? What was their name?" Corporal Hodge hadn't been in a Genesis in years. Who was he referring to?

"I was in a hospital. Local psycho ward. Nothing special. Just someone to talk to. Got me thinking about the specifics of that day. Asking for details, you know?"

"Why didn't you report what you remembered up the chain? They would have handled it legally and internally," Blake said.

Anthony thrust a thumb at himself and spoke through his teeth. "*I had to handle it to make sure he paid. I wanted him to confess. Bastard wouldn't say what he did, even when he knew he was dead. If I got it out on social media, everyone would know. A viral video like that, politicians would think twice about getting away with anything in the military.*"

"This isn't going to end well." Blake shook his head.

"No, it isn't."

The door creaked open, and the female sergeant stepped in. "You're out of time. You'll have to request more time up your chain of command. Let's go, Sergeant."

Just perfect. Right when Blake started to get answers. "Is there a recording of our conversation?"

Her eyes bounced off the top right corner of the room and straight back at him. "No."

He chuckled to himself. If the wrong people heard what Corporal Hodge just told him, he'd be dead. They'd want to preserve the senator's reputation and keep the link to the military under tight guard. One dead corporal. Not too big a price to pay.

The sergeant led Blake to the elevator and stared him down to make sure he didn't slip back in before the door closed. He returned to his office and paced the room. *Twenty minutes.* He swatted the wall. *Twenty goddamn minutes to talk to the corporal. What did they think I'd accomplish in twenty minutes?* He needed to find out all he could about the senator and what he was doing when Corporal Hodge served in Afghanistan. If the senator hadn't been in Afghanistan, Blake would report to Colonel Marks and let him take it from there. *If the senator did kill those Rangers...*

Blake sat at his computer. He found his hands had curled into fists so tightly his fingertips bit into his flesh. He searched for Senator

Alex Fredrick. The senator had a stint in the army, but nothing in Afghanistan at the same time as Corporal Hodge. But, that didn't mean the senator wasn't in that part of the country, it just wasn't public record. *This is FUBAR. What would the senator gain from killing Rangers?* The idea of the senator in Afghanistan for a political mission that turned into murdering Rangers sounded absurd. But Anthony was convinced it happened—Blake saw it in his eyes. Could the memory be fake? Is that how the Genesis had been involved? *Impossible.* The Genesis couldn't implant memories. It could only adjust the memories that were already there. If it wasn't real, how did it get into his memories?

Blake was getting nowhere. He thumped his desk.

He returned to the colonel's office and knocked.

"Come in," the colonel coughed.

Blake walked in, stood at attention, and saluted. "Here to report on Corporal Hodge, sir."

"Not a very long conversation, Sergeant?"

Blake shook his head, his arms tensed. "They gave me twenty minutes. I got what I needed, I guess."

"Anything longer is more than you offering him some food as an old friend of his."

Nice cover story for JAG.

"Was it enough time to find something?"

"I don't know, sir. Corporal Hodge thinks Senator Fredrick was in Afghanistan with him and his men and killed a bunch of them." Blake studied the colonel's ice cold stare. The corner of the colonel's mouth twitched.

"Did you confirm it?"

"No, sir. I haven't seen the senator's manifest at the time of the incident, and it's not available to the public. But I believe Corporal Hodge believes it."

Colonel Marks massaged his forehead. "This must be his imagination. A blending of reality and a nightmare. Maybe he saw the senator on television before he fell asleep and dreamed it up." He picked up a glass of water.

"Sir, is it possible that Doctor Minton changed the memory to include the senator?"

The colonel had to close his mouth to keep from spitting up water. When he recovered, he said, "We alter memories all the time, Sergeant. That's what we do. But Genesis doesn't allow us to insert anyone unrelated. And why would he wait this long to act?"

"So why are his memories so suddenly clear?"

The colonel slammed his glass on his desk. "That will be all, Sergeant. Thank you for taking the time to speak with him. You are dismissed."

Blake left the office more confused than when he entered. It was after midday, and someone had rescheduled General Talbert for treatment before nightfall. Blake still had time to implement his new plan.

Blake checked on the senator's whereabouts during Corporal Hodge's deployment. He googled Senator Fredrick's office and phoned it.

"Senator Fredrick's office. How can I direct your call?" The receptionist sounded so robotic Blake thought she was a computer.

"Hi, I'm writing a news story for K1 News about Senator Fredrick concerning his time in Afghanistan. Can your office help me with some details? I'd like to know the dates he went and what he did while he was there. I have a few witnesses that have opened up about it, but I'd like to hear his side of the story."

The receptionist took so long to respond and was so eerily silent that Blake wondered if she was still there. "I'll have to check into this and get authorization. The senator isn't in at the moment. Can you leave a name and number I can reach you at?"

"My name is Derek O'Hare. You can reach me at..." He considered, jaw hanging open, and then gave her his actual cellphone number. This better not implicate him.

"Okay. We will be in touch soon."

Doubtful. "Great, thanks." He ended the call.

Chapter 16

BLAKE RUBBED HIS FOREHEAD to smooth out the wrinkles. General Talbert had a relapse when Blake tried to remove the child from the nightmare by pulling in other faces to cover the boy, but General Talbert honed in on him like a hawk hunting for prey. One of the men in the crowd stabbed the boy several times while he watched. The general woke up howling, the boy now center stage in his mind, according to Doctor Kendra's after action report. Security waited with the general until he composed himself. They told Blake the general thought Security was the enemy from the simulation and lunged at them. The general looked like he'd been tortured and left for dead when they found him. When the general left, he was still ranting about what they had done to him.

Blake needed a drink. He drove to The Saloon, a rundown watering hole soldiers frequented. The Saloon was an informal mess hall mixed with NCOs and officers. Nobody saluted or followed protocol. Everyone wanted a break from work-related stress. Arguments broke out, but nothing progressed beyond a scuffle. Dull compared to Echo team—they brawled as a rite of passage.

Blake leaned over the bar, elbows on the mahogany, the leather padding that used to cushion arms was now cracked and inelastic.

He looked into the clear gold of his lager but only swirled it in a lazy whirlpool. He didn't sip.

"Rough day?"

Blake knew the cracked voice behind him without looking. The odors of musk and cigars that accompanied it were hard to mistake. The bar stool beside him squeaked as the padding barely fought against Colonel Marks' weight.

"Security sent me the video of General Talbert." The colonel signaled the barkeep for a drink. The barkeep knew the colonel's usual and nodded. "I'm sorry I added the unnecessary distraction of Corporal Hodge to your day. I'll need your report by morning."

Goddamn reports. It was standard procedure when a client lost his mind in the middle of a session—although it almost never happened to other operators. This would prompt regular visits with Doctor Kendra. Blake finally took a sip of his beer and snorted. How unqualified he was for the Genesis Project. He wasn't a shrink. Healing memories wasn't a soldier's job.

"Want to talk about it?" Colonel Marks received his drink and a napkin.

Blake glanced around. Several soldiers hovered nearby. Two whispered a private conversation, and a third watched television.

"No, sir. Thanks." Blake paused for the snap of two billiard balls. "I'll get you the report first thing tomorrow."

"This place could use some work."

Light fixtures almost broke free of the ceiling. Grooves cut so deeply into the bar it was a miracle it hadn't cracked in half. Fist-sized holes and beer stains decorated the walls. Blake missed Wade and James. They'd come to The Saloon, drink, share stories, talk about the crap in their lives. He'd lost that with the project. David had become a good friend, but it wasn't the same.

"You don't talk much, do you?"

"I'm not much for small talk, sir. I'm just trying to complete the mission you assigned me." Blake sipped his beer, pretending the colonel wasn't there.

The colonel placed his mug next to Blake's and left the bar.

***

"You don't look so good." Clara snorted when Blake walked in the door. "And you smell like booze." Her eyes crawled up and down him.

"Had a setback. No idea what went wrong. I have to fill out the paperwork by morning." Blake crept to a slow stop. He cocked an eyebrow. "Everything okay with you?"

"You could've called to say you wouldn't be home for dinner," she said, raising her voice. "We waited here stupidly for you."

The table held a plate of food hidden under a microwave lid. "I'm sorry." Why hadn't he taken the time to call? He hadn't even thought about it, he was so used to operating on his own schedule.

"It's fine." Clara threw her hands up. "You're always more concerned with the goddamn boys than you are with your family."

Keep quiet. You'll only make it worse. "I'm going to see Sophia. Thanks for dinner." He headed upstairs and eased Sophia's door open a few inches. Sophia was already asleep. "Goodnight," he whispered.

He had no energy to fight with Clara, so he headed to their room and plopped onto the bed. Within seconds, he plummeted to sleep, welcomed by the same nightmare—the general's nightmare.

"You could have saved me," the sergeant said, looking down on him from inside the Humvee. The sergeant's face morphed, slowly...gradually...twisting into...

Corporal Hodge?

Blake thrashed up from his bed to find a dark room. He calmed his heaving breaths, wiped his clammy forehead, and found Clara standing at the door, eyes like saucers. She wielded her alarm clock like a weapon, leg braced.

"What's going on?"

She set the clock back on the table and sat on the bed. Her fingers inched toward him just short of contact.

"Just a dream." Blake swallowed.

"You didn't have dreams like this before. Never. What are they doing to you?"

Blake wasn't sure. Side-effects of the Genesis? "It's fine. I'll be fine." He gulped in another breath, lungs so greedy for oxygen he couldn't breathe quickly enough. "I'll talk to Doctor Kendra." He lay down, closed his eyes, and fell asleep. He dreamed of the woman in the riot screaming for help. The boy that stood beside her had saucers for eyes. He was so small. Like a little Sophia. *Screw the Rules.* He partially squeezed the trigger, blocked by a lack of strength. *Shoot, you piece of junk.* The iron sights found the terrorists, but the bullets wouldn't come out. He watched her body dance as bullets tore through her body, cutting her in half. *Jesus Christ.*

He woke again, tightly gripping the bed sheets.

"Blake, what the hell is going on?" Clara screamed, hand to chest.

Chapter 17

Blake lay back on the pillow, feeling his cold sweat on the sheets.

Clara breathed heavily beside him. "Does anyone know this is happening?"

Blake hadn't told command about the dreams. They seemed harmless—a face here, a voice there. But they had degenerated a few weeks ago.

Clara recoiled, clutching a clump of the bedsheets in both pale hands. "Oh God, you haven't, have you? You aren't on Echo team anymore, hiding a little injury so they don't stop you from deploying. This is different. I'm not okay with this. I don't think I can sleep now. Not in this bed."

Blake searched her eyes, her ghostly cheeks, her quivering lip. Had his thrashing frightened her this much? The only time he had seen her this terrified was a few years ago when her mother had a health scare. He bit his lip. "I'll sleep on the couch."

Clara inched to the edge of the bed as he grabbed his pillow and slinked out of the room. Thousands of soldiers lived on the streets because the system couldn't look after them. If he reported the nightmares, he might be one. They'd remove him from Genesis and from military service. *I should have stuck with Echo team.* Echo team had spent eight years together in some of the most dangerous places on

Earth, making the world safer. But he thought of Sophia without him every night, again, and clenched his teeth as he staggered downstairs.

Corporal Hodge. What would happen to him? Blake and Hodge both knew how the job affected soldiers, how it caused nightmares. Corporal Hodge came home wounded mentally, and Genesis helped him. But then what? How did he jump to killing a senator? Because the senator killed American soldiers? Farfetched, but farfetched theories were usually true. If the senator wasn't there, how did his face haunt Hodge's nightmare? Adding memories wasn't something the Genesis could do. Even if it could, why the senator's? What was the link? Moderate level government officials like senators were easy to kill. They had security but nothing special. So why risk the Genesis?

Blake reached the stairs, keeping close to the wall to avoid the creaking wood. Dex left his bed and followed, nails clacking the hardwood floor. Blake could creep up on a target, but he couldn't sneak downstairs in his own home.

On the couch downstairs, he listened for footsteps, but thoughts of Clara's troubled face spun in his mind. He sprang up and paced, lay on the couch, sat, paced, sat...Finally, he fell asleep.

He throttled awake when someone touched his shoulder. He leaped for someone's throat, but—it was Sophia. He stopped himself. Dex barked. Blake's commotion hadn't gone unnoticed.

"Sorry, sorry. I'm awake," he said. "Sorry."

"Dad, why are you sleeping on the couch?" Sophia's index fingers twiddled around each other.

He smiled. "I had a nightmare. And there's a lot on my mind. Don't worry. Everything is fine."

She looked him over, brow raised. "Your dark circles are as deep as Santa's bag. Are you and mom going to split up?" She was definitely her father's daughter.

"And you look like you lost a fight with a hair dryer." He smiled. "Your mom and I are fine. It's just some work trouble, that's all. I've had a tough time sleeping."

She snuggled into his arms. He leaned closer and breathed in the scent of her hair. If he could, he'd keep her here forever.

"Heading to work today or taking the day off?" Clara stood behind them in her nightgown, chestnut hair sprayed in all directions, much like Sophia's. He'd rarely seen her without makeup.

He grabbed his pillow, which had tumbled onto the floor when he'd kicked awake. "I'm heading to work. Colonel isn't giving me any leeway on the report."

Clara's head dropped. *Does she want me home?* They talked more, but it felt as if she did it at gunpoint.

"Do you need me here?" he asked.

She tugged a breath in through her nostrils. "I was going to make breakfast, that's all. Like we used to. If you're going to work, you should leave soon. It's fine." She crossed her arms. A spatula shiny with cooking oil peeked out from under her right arm.

Blake dropped his pillow on the couch. He sensed he'd be sleeping there again. He bit back a retort. He didn't have the energy to deal with another argument, but there was no getting around the report.

Sophia noted the exchange and dragged her feet to the kitchen table. "I'll eat."

Blake sighed. The moment had gone so fast.

A light knock came from the front door, breaking some of the tension in the room. When nobody moved to answer, the knock deepened.

"I'll get it," Blake said, almost grateful for the respite, although it would be waiting for him when he returned.

"Ready to jet?" David grinned, too happy for a guy going to work. "Is that bacon?" He pushed Blake aside and lunged into the kitchen, giving Sophia a tight hug and kissing Clara on the cheek. It seemed Clara appreciated David's kisses more than his.

"Go ahead," Clara laughed sweetly. "One slice."

David snatched one slice, waited for Clara to turn her back, then grabbed another. Sophia pointed at him, shaking her head. "Secrets between spies," he said to Sophia as he strutted by. He stopped to whisper something in her ear and she laughed, and accepted a half hug as David moseyed back to Blake.

Blake smiled, feeling little of the happiness. David made it look so easy to elicit smiles from them and Blake failed at every opportunity. Even now, his mind drifted back to work and he felt helpless to stop it.

***

Blake stared at his computer in his office. Sometimes he wished it would do the work for him. He needed to report what happened yesterday with General Talbert. *What* had *happened?* How had he seen the boy? Why did he focus directly on him?

Colonel Marks burst through the door, hand clutching the doorframe, shoulder still in the hallway. "Sergeant, the report is going to have to wait. We have an emergency session in the boardroom on the first floor—now."

Blake followed Colonel Marks to the elevator. "Is this regarding Corporal Hodge? Is he okay?"

Blake expected to hear that Corporal Hodge was dead. Killed by accident. Maybe dressed as a suicide.

"Navy Special Warfare transferred a SEAL to our unit. He strangled his wife to death in his sleep last night." Colonel Marks studied the digital numbers on the elevator as they ascended to one.

Blake's body felt like an electrical conduit. "Damnit."

"He's on lockdown until our evaluation. The Genesis is analyzing him now."

The elevator door dinged open on the first floor and they made their way to the boardroom. Seventeen officers milled around a large rectangular table in a few conversational pockets. Blake didn't have time to listen in—the room shot to attention when they saw Colonel Marks.

"Room!" Lieutenant Stormont shouted.

Chapter 18

"At ease, gentlemen," Colonel Marks ordered. "Sit down."

Colonel Marks went to the head of the table.

"Up here, Sergeant. You're point man on this operation."

Hold on. After what happened to the general? They want me to take the lead on this? Blake joined Colonel Marks at the head of the room, hands folded behind his back.

"At oh two forty-two last night, a Special Operations SEAL team assaulter, Senior Chief Petty Officer Patrick Wilburg, killed his wife," Colonel Marks said. "He strangled her. From what we know, it was an accident, and he was hallucinating from a nightmare when he killed her. The nightmare comes from an operation conducted about a month ago in Guatemala. We don't have further details, but we know the nightmare is ugly." Colonel Marks scanned the soldiers in the room as they gathered their thoughts. After a ten count, he shifted his weight. "There are no reports of instability on his file...until Guatemala. The coroner's report confirmed strangulation. Senior Chief Wilburg didn't deny the charge. He's being held in seclusion here at Genesis and isn't saying much. He claims he woke up from a nightmare with her body in his arms."

Blake shook his head. "Sir, did you say Guatemala? I know the government sends SEALs everywhere, but the US isn't operating in Guatemala."

"It's in the report. You'll learn more inside his dream. He's a long-time vet in the SEALs, and the brass wants him returned to active duty. They believe they can get a plea under section sixteen for automatism—claiming the chief wasn't criminally responsible on account of a mental disorder. They want him back in the field." He lifted onto the balls of his feet. "This is why we created Genesis."

Each officer in the room smiled and nodded at each other as though they had struck gold—a chance to validate all their hard work. Pencil pushers and stakeholders with budget implications. Generic military haircuts, clean shaven and immaculate uniforms. They looked like they were stamped out of a template. The only disparity was the wrinkles on some faces and the number of bars on their epaulets.

Colonel Marks cleared his throat. "Questions?"

"What's the ETA on the report?" Major Graham's broad mustache moved independently of his lips.

"Tomorrow. The Genesis needs at least twenty-four hours to compile a database of nightmares."

Colonel Marks regarded Blake, his expression clear that Blake would be the one providing the report.

The officers grumbled. Colonel Marks didn't take his eyes off Blake. "This takes priority." Another implied order.

"Copy, sir. One more question, if I may." Blake waited until Colonel Marks nodded. "Has he ever been part of the Genesis Project, sir?"

"No, he is not one of ours."

"Colonel Marks, what happens if the nightmare doesn't match the story? What if the chief just killed his wife?" a clean-shaven Major

Lokey asked. He looked far too baby-faced for the number of bars on his uniform.

"We'll deal with if it comes up, Major. We classified this case level three. That's top secret even to those with top secret clearance to the Genesis. Innocent until proven guilty, Major. Let's hope he's innocent."

As Colonel Marks left the room, the officers glanced at each other uneasily.

"You better get going, Sergeant," Major Lokey said like a command.

Blake didn't move. He waited as the other officers bumped past him out of the room. Some scrutinized him but didn't say a word. They knew what he was doing, and they wanted no part of it.

"Did you hear me, Sergeant?"

Blake turned to look at Major Lokey. "I did, sir. Thinking about the assignment, sir. Don't want to rush into anything."

Major Lokey glared at Blake, issued a final breath, then marched out. The major was going to step on a lot of toes before he was done.

Blake headed for his office, expecting to do research on Wilburg before heading into the Genesis. Colonel Marks halted him in the War Room with a hand up. "Let's get you into the dream. He's prepped."

Blake flinched back a step. "Already? I haven't done any preparation for this operation. I thought we were waiting for data to be gathered."

"Things are moving fast, Sergeant. You aren't trying to change or adjust what happened. This session is observation only. Genesis will already have at least his most recent nightmare catalogued. If we want to study more of his nightmares, we will later."

"All due respect, sir. I haven't been here long and I—"

"General Talbert was a warm-up. This is reality. It's your job. Get in the damn machine, Sergeant." Colonel Marks cracked his knuckles against his thighs, his face red. "Now."

Blake pulled his gown over his head. The material clung to his skin thanks to the moisture from his sweat. The colonel never looked that angry.

"Do your job, Sergeant" Colonel Marks glared at Blake down his nose as if it were the barrel of a rifle. "Or I'll find someone who will."

Blake glanced at the colonel one last time before the lid shut on his face. He tugged an involuntary gasp at the cold jelly that congealed against his nose.

Chapter 19

Blake waited in the dark and planted his feet to regain equilibrium. Deep breathing didn't help. What kind of nightmare made a soldier strangle his wife to death without even waking up?

He'd heard of soldiers slamming an elbow into a wall or grabbing someone hard enough to bruise them in their sleep. In those cases, the soldiers woke up quickly. He'd never heard of murdering someone while asleep. That required at least two minutes of strangling. To most people, that might not sound like a long time, but it's a world of time.

The darkness faded, and color blossomed slowly, like someone easing a dimmer switch. Blake stood in a forest, oak trees standing like guards around him. The air tasted muggy, and he held back a cough.

He blinked at a flash to his right. A camoed soldier hunkered three feet away. Any further, and Blake wouldn't have seen him move.

The menu popped up but offered nothing but an exit option. Colonel Marks hadn't cleared him to change anything. Observation only.

Two men stood on Blake's left, equally invisible. They wore no insignia. One of them must be Senior Chief Wilburg. With enough prep time, Blake would have known all three men. He didn't like flying blind.

The three slid forward in a line. Each step looked purposeful. They didn't so much as snap a twig.

He followed them through the forest. A building crested a hill. The building grew as they approached, blocking out the moonlight. Chunks of mortar had crumbled from the first-and-second-level siding, and rain had rotted the wood.

Several hovels appeared a few hundred feet away as they reached the summit. He tried to imagine what part of Guatemala had such archaic housing. Straw topped the hovels like untamed hair. The big bad wolf could blow these homes down with a wheeze.

The middle soldier was the radio operator. He handed the radio to another soldier who pressed it to his mouth as they snaked through the trees. "Eagle, this is Mouse. We've located several hiding holes. Request permission to proceed." For now, Blake was going to assume the speaker was Senior Chief Wilburg.

"Roger, Mouse. Charlie Mike."

Blake determined from the lack of doors that they approached the rear of the building. The wall had only small windows. They formed a single line against the wall. Blake stood at a distance, giving the three soldiers room to operate. He listened for ranks or callsigns, but they gave up nothing. SEALs didn't chat much during an assault if things hadn't escalated.

As they stalked along the wall, Blake peeked into a window, but a film blanketed it. He squinted to pick out any characteristics of the room. A bed, an armchair. Was this a bedroom, or maybe a hospital recovery room? Nothing moved inside.

The soldiers reached the corner. The lead man checked around the corner using a mirror on a stick. He gave the thumbs-up. They repeated the drill at the next corner.

Blake followed them to a paint-peeled entrance where a rusted door rattled from the wind. The foulness of bacteria and feces battered him so hard he recoiled two steps and choked. The revolting flavor hit like the butt of a rifle. He'd smelled something that bad only a few times in his career.

The team slipped into the building and halted sharply. "What's going on?" Blake whispered, then remembered they couldn't hear him. Wide shoulders and backpacks blocked the view in front of them. When they advanced, Blake saw the revulsion...and the source of the stench. Bodies. Men, women, and children mounted on the walls like hunting trophies. Blake twisted away and puked.

"Fuck," he whispered, his eyes crawling up the mosaic of corpses.

Nails driven into the heads of the dead were all that held them upright. He couldn't see any other trauma. Had these monsters nailed their victims up alive? He'd seen a lot of nasty shit...but nothing so cruel as this. This was inhuman. He joined Delta to stop bastards like this. Was this real? Could Wilburg's mind have conjured this horror out of nowhere?

The team stalked forward, clearing each room as they moved. Dead. Everyone was dead. Fifteen rooms with nothing but death and decay, with bodies nailed to the walls.

Blake struggled against vomiting again, searching for the knife in his pocket. He swallowed back searing rage. What was the point of this kind of evil? He should be in the field, fighting these terrorists. Civilians didn't get it. Friends told him to leave the military. They questioned what he did. "What right do you have to take someone's life?" They'd never seen what he'd seen. Babies killed in their mothers' wombs. Women gang-raped. Boys and girls executed because of the shade of their skin. If there was one thing in his life he'd never regret, it was killing those monsters. If there was a god, and he wouldn't let

Blake into heaven for what he'd done, then he'd take his place in hell. He'd never repent.

They slinked upstairs. A sign read, *Maternidad.* The monsters had spared no one the same gruesome treatment. They cut mothers' stomachs open, and babies dangled lifelessly from umbilical cords.

The team needed to burn this place. Tears ran down his cheeks. He gripped his rifle so tightly his arms shook. The children's bodies reminded him of Sophia; if she'd been born in this town, she'd be hanging dead here. He prayed these tyrants had killed the mothers before cutting their babies out.

The dream dragged on. The carnage overtook all four battle-hardened men, and each threw up while they cleared the rooms.

Something behind Blake cracked. He whirled around to see a man dressed in a mix of American and rebel camouflage. A knife hung loosely in his grip, blood dribbling from the tip.

When the rebel saw Chief Wilburg, he froze like a rabbit in the shadow of a hawk. Chief Wilburg tackled the rebel and squeezed his hands around his throat. If Chief Wilburg felt half as awful as Blake did, he'd be in his red zone, incapable of releasing until the rebel stopped breathing.

Blake would have shot the monster, but he was sure the choking felt satisfying.

"He's dead, Chief."

That confirmed which soldier was Senior Chief Wilburg...unless they'd deployed multiple chiefs on the mission. Blake understood why this nightmare had translated to accidentally killing his wife.

The room clicked into darkness. He was alone in the machine, waiting for the Genesis to let him out.

Chapter 20

BLAKE STEPPED OFF THE platform and changed into his uniform. He tried smoothing out the wrinkles on his shirt and pants but couldn't. His mind drifted back to the hospital nightmare, and his stomach did the same. He turned and threw up in a garbage can.

"That bad?" Colonel Marks stood behind him.

"Yeah." Blake clutched the edge of the garbage can to keep from spilling to his knees. His tongue tasted bile. "That bad."

"I'll need a report. Now." Colonel Marks slapped his hand against the doorframe.

"Roger, sir." Blake breathed deeply, wiped his mouth with his sleeve, and strolled to his office. He burped acid fumes from his stomach. As he wrote his report, he felt something nagging, something...off. Why would a rebel return to a slaughter by himself? Rebels traveled in groups. They relied on mob mentality for the perversions they enacted. So why had the guy returned alone? And why did he seem terrified? The guy should have fought back, screamed for help, or ran like hell—anything but wait to be strangled to death. Blake added his thoughts to the report. The comment would get him pulled into Colonel Marks's office. He sent the email anyway. While he waited for the inevitable phone call, he tapped his pen against the table. Two soldiers had committed murder in less than a week. A senator was dead and now a wife in equally suspicious circumstances. Chief Wilburg had nothing to do with the Genesis though. But here they were, processing it. What did that mean?

The phone rang. "Hello?"

"Sergeant, it's Colonel Marks. I'd like to see you in my office."

"On the way, sir."

Inside the colonel's office, three officers waited in chairs. The loud-mouthed pup Major Lokey, Lieutenant General Hall with a thick goatee and a stomach so large the buttons on his already extra-large shirt threatened to pop, and Colonel Baker, cleanly shaven with deep-set eyes.

Blake brought himself to attention and saluted. The space where Colonel Marks had placed the photo of his family now lay empty.

"You wanted to see me, sir?" Normally, the rank structure was relaxed, but Blake had a feeling this wasn't one of those times.

Colonel Marks's elbow rested on his desk, and his head leaned into his hand. He'd aged in a few hours. When he looked up, Blake saw wrinkles on his uniform. It was going around.

"We read your report, Sergeant. An awful thing. Is there a reason you didn't include a recommendation on the case as in your other reports?"

"There hasn't been a lot of research on Senior Chief Wilburg. The rebel, the guy at the end of the dream, feels out of place."

All three officers scowled.

"Am I not expected to give my opinion, sir?"

The colonel's face turned crimson. *Today's military doesn't have thinkers. Should I report what I know they want to hear? The guy killed his wife, for Christ's sake. The least we can do is make sure it was the accident he claimed it was.*

"We need you to write your recommendation based on the facts, not your suspicions." General Hall's voice sounded hoarse as if he needed to clear his throat.

"Tell me what you want me to write. And I'll write that." Blake's eyes were rifle sights that leveled at Hall. "*Sir.*"

Major Lokey jumped to his feet, inches from Blake's face. His breath smelled like onions when he huffed so closely that Blake felt it on his cheek. "Is that insubordination, Sergeant? Do you need to spend some time in confinement?" Another huff. "It's available."

One more step forward, and Blake would give them a reason to confine him.

"Relax, Major." Colonel Marks padded the air. "Sergeant, let's talk about it before I send it up the chain just in case you want to reword it. Based solely on what you saw, which is what is in question, do you believe he strangled his wife by accident because of the dream?"

Blake tracked Major Lokey's steely eyes until the major sat, and then he looked at Colonel Marks. "Based on the dream that I saw—and on that only—yes, it's possible he confused the nightmare with reality. He strangled the rebel as the dream ended. But, assuming his hands were on his wife in the same timeframe, she would have been choking for roughly thirteen seconds before he woke up. That's plenty of time for him to have realized what he was doing. It takes two to four minutes to strangle someone to death. Even if she passed out, he knows CPR. That's a long time to hold on to someone's throat after waking up."

"You're speculating again, Sergeant," General Hall said. "Just the facts."

"Yes, it's possible he killed his wife since the dream ended with him choking the rebel."

They all nodded, having finally heard what they came to hear. Blake could have strangled them. He just needed the right nightmare of his own to lean on. *Goddamn military bureaucracy.*

"That will be all, Sergeant. Send me another copy of your report with the facts only. We'll hold on to Senior Chief Wilburg for further assessment."

Blake clicked his heels together, saluted, and left the room. The energy he'd first felt walking down the hallways at Genesis had long since faded. Every time he blinked, he saw the bodies of the mothers cut open, the babies' lifeless bodies dangling. Would he be the next soldier charged with killing someone innocent because of a nightmare? *Could I hurt Clara or Sophia? Are they in danger?*

Echo team made actual change, killing assholes like those, but he hated the idea of not seeing Sophia every night.

Blake returned to Colonel Marks's office. He threw open the door without knocking, saluted, and said, "Colonel Marks, I'm requesting permission to return to Echo team."

Chapter 21

"This isn't a good time, Sergeant." Colonel Marks's eyes slowly found his. He dropped the pen he held, leaned back in his chair, crossed his arms, and glared at Blake. "Getting out of the Genesis Project is not simple. It's not like transferring units. You should know that by now, soldier."

Blake ignored the tone. "I would appreciate you getting to the transfer request when you can, sir. I'll fill in the paperwork and have it on your desk by the end of the day."

"We'll talk later, Sergeant. I'll find the time to stop by your office." Without a goodbye, Colonel Marks picked up his pen and returned to his work.

Blake clenched his fists, firming his position of attention. The steel of the knife in his pocket poked his thigh.

Colonel Marks curled his lip and raised his eyes from his work but not his head. "Anything else, Sergeant?"

The other officers glared at Blake. Blake felt their judgment through their eyes.

"No, sir."

His request took less than a minute to brush off as if he'd asked for ammunition at the gun range. *Request heard. Now leave 'cause it doesn't matter.* He'd said what he needed to say, and he would make it happen. Leaving Sophia for operations sucked, but one day she'd be gone and he'd be left with the pieces of his life. Sophia might hold it against him, but he needed to get back in the field.

He headed to the holding area to check on Corporal Hodge and let him know he couldn't help him.

He walked to the security door and turned the handle. Locked. Without busting through bulletproof glass to press the buzzer, there was no way in. Long minutes passed before someone came. The red-faced Major Bingham brushed invisible lint off his shoulder as he sat down in his booth, huffing as if he'd run a set of stairs.

"Hello, Major Bingham." Blake said with a friendly smile.

The major frowned. "How can I help you, Sergeant?" He didn't look up.

"I'm here to see Corporal Hodge."

"You aren't authorized to see him." Bingham flipped through the notebook as lazily as a magazine. He licked his fingers to flip the next page.

Blake's voice matched Bingham's own tone. "Did you even check the computer to confirm that?"

Bingham rapid-blinked and sighed. He finally looked up and pressed his palms together at his lower lip. "I don't need to. I know who's authorized. He's popular, and you aren't on his list anymore." He raised his eyebrows as if to punctuate his statement. "Goodbye, Sergeant."

Blake wanted to punch through the glass and grab Bingham by that scrawny neck. "Can you tell me if he's doing okay? He asked me to check in on him."

"He's great. Loving the food and digs, I hear."

What an asshole. Blake marched out, returned to the main floor, and passed through the War Room. Peter Young's head hid under

Genesis III. Blake zeroed in on him with stomping feet and a need for answers. "What's going on?"

Peter jolted and smashed his head against a panel. He rubbed it and unleashed a breathy curse. He crawled out of the machine, put a small chip in his pocket as he stood and stared down at Blake as if to squish him. His head, as smooth as a snow globe, reflected the ceiling lights like a mirror ball.

"Don't worry. Your head isn't any larger than it was before you slammed it."

Peter smiled. "I c-c-could use my head to s-s-quash you, and there's nothing the military c-c-could do about it."

"Officially." Blake cocked his head. "You never know."

Peter's smile faded. "I-i-i-t's not good to talk like that with e-every-thing going on." His eyes shifted. "S-someone's always listening."

Blake bit back a laugh. "You think they're listening to you? Is it a top priority to kill the only guy that can splice the red wire and connect it to the other red wire?"

"A-a-an engineer in a place like th-th-this hears a lot of things he isn't supposed to. If they t-torture me..." He shuddered and dropped his voice. "I-I won't last long."

"Everything okay?"

Peter was a civilian employee. One of the very few the government had contracted to work on the Genesis Project. He wasn't technically governed by the military and couldn't be court-martialed like a soldier, but anything could happen in a top secret project. Because of his lack of military experience, he also seemed prone to paranoia. When Blake first met Peter, he needed drugs to calm down. David explained it was his personality, and he did his best work with his high on life.

Peter's eyes crept around the room, scaled the walls, double-checked the door. He leaned in. "It's n-nothing." He plastered on a smile that didn't even reach his cheeks.

"You sure?"

Peter nodded deliberately.

Blake left—he had his own problems—and stood in the hall with the empty feeling of having answered nothing. If Genesis III functioned properly, everything else could wait.

Back at his desk, he opened a personnel search tool and typed in Wilburg's name. It didn't take long to get seventeen hits.

Only one ranked as Senior Chief.

The chief's profile was so squeaky clean it would have been a filler episode in an already boring television series. The chief was practically a boy scout. No offenses and no complaints. An innocent guy who saw some terrible things and unknowingly killed his wife because he didn't get help in time.

"S-s-sir, there is something I want to talk to you about." Peter stood at the door, hands stuffed into his pockets.

"You don't call me sir. I'm just a sergeant."

"S-s-sergeants s-s-should have more respect than o-o-officers, sir. You've earned it."

Another argument he didn't feel like having. "What's up, Peter?"

Peter scanned the office as if expecting hands to stab out of the shadows and drag him away. He leaned in so closely Blake heard his breath notch. Who did he think was listening in this office? His eyes still creeping, he said, "Sir." He pressed his elbows at his sides and slouched as if to shrink away. "Th-th-th-there is something you should know about the Genesis."

Blake wanted to block his ears. "Peter, I think you should stop talking now."

Peter gulped. "I..." He leaned into the screen. "W-w-why are you looking at Lieutenant Zackery?"

Lieutenant Zackery? Blake glanced at his screen and then back at Peter. "Who?"

"L-l-lieutenant Zackery. O-on your screen."

Blake did a double-take. The name in the search was Senior Chief Patrick Wilburg. "He must have a lookalike. This is Senior Chief Wilburg."

"No, I'm p-p-positive that's Lieutenant Zackery. It l-l-looks just like him. I talked to him f-f-for months when he w-was here. Maybe a year ago. M-m-months before you."

Blake shook his head. "That's impossible. Chief Wilburg has never been part of the Genesis Project." *Then... wait. Could he have been under a different name? Someone would have noticed the photos of Wilburg and said something. Especially Colonel Marks.* Blake punched Lieutenant Zackery in the system and came back with nothing. "Do you have a picture of Lieutenant Zackery? Or his file?"

"It s-s-should be in the archives, y-yeah. You need a-a-authorization to get in the a-a-archives."

No easy day. He'd have to explain to Colonel Marks why he needed access. Could he trust Peter? "Are you sure, Peter? The name isn't in our database."

Peter squinted at the screen. "Th-th-that's strange. Y-yeah, I-I-I'm sure he existed, even if he h-had a twin. I remember the file s-sitting out on the Genesis when I worked on it. He s-s-stopped to say hello twice a week at n-n-nine o'clock when I got my second coffee. We passed each other like c-c-clockwork. M-maybe I'm wrong."

Blake studied Peter's bushy brows and narrow eyes and leaned in close. He smelled alcohol. "Have you been drinking, Peter?"

Peter jumped back like he'd been struck. "U-unrelated."

Blake shook his head and looked at the clock. Eleven hundred hours. "It's early for drinking."

Peter slouched, and he turned to slink out of the office.

"Peter, wait. What were you going to tell me?" Blake saw a momentary spark of hope, but it died as quickly as it appeared when Peter stole out of the room.

Blake spent the next hour thinking. How could he get into the archive without raising suspicion? It wouldn't be a problem in any other government building, but here security was clamped down as firmly as a bear trap. He'd have to find Peter and ask who the lieutenant's operator was.

Blake walked toward the colonel's office to ask for clearance but turned around twice. He curled a fist to smack a wall but resisted. He was usually good at solving problems, but how could he avoid sparking the colonel's anger? Chasing phantoms for Peter might piss him off. Instead of talking to anyone, Blake found everything on Senior Chief Wilburg that he could, then shifted his focus to Corporal Hodge. *If the Genesis connects them...*

Chapter 22

BLAKE SHIFTED ON THE sofa. His lower back ached from the wait. Despite the appearance of the comfy leather couch, it felt horrible to sit on for twenty minutes. Cold pain zapped up and down his spine when he shifted.

"Why are you here, Sergeant?" Doctor Kendra clicked her pen, her eyes pinging around her notepad.

"Orders," he said.

"Can you elaborate? I can't help you if you don't talk to me."

If he talked to her, he'd lose any shot at transferring back to the field. He might lose his job. "I'm good. Colonel Marks requested we have a session because of a transfer request I made back to the teams."

Doctor Kendra's eyes finally left her pad. "You want to leave the project?"

"Yes."

Doctor Kendra nodded and scribbled something. *She must be halfway down the page, and we haven't said anything to each other.* "Why do you want to leave the project?"

"Not so much leave the project as return to my unit in the field. I feel like I make a bigger impact there."

"Colonel Marks mentioned there are some big cases pending that you're involved in. You don't think that's a big enough impact?"

Blake rolled his eyes. Next, she would ask him on a scale of one to ten how much impact they both had on him. Then they could balance the positives against the negatives. He didn't have time for this.

"Holding a weapon inside a computer through the same sequence a hundred times isn't the same as being a door kicker."

"Door kicker." She nodded, though her attention seemed elsewhere. "What age do door kickers usually retire?"

"There's no set age."

"Okay." She raised her eyebrows with a smug smile as if the matter were settled. She knew she'd made her point. Few Delta operators served in the field after twenty years, and Blake was coming up on his twentieth. The hours were grueling, and the job was hard on the body. Blake felt it more every year. He used to drink and sleep each mission off, recovered after only a few hours. Not anymore. "So you prefer the violence of combat to the violence of helping someone recover from trauma?"

Doctor Kendra's problem—and every operator knew it—was that she manipulated every situation until she got the answer she wanted, which included you doing whatever brass wanted you to do.

"Yes," Blake said. "Given my choice, I'd think that's obvious." He studied her for a reaction, but her mannerisms were as indecipherable as a foreign script. She continued writing without a flinch or a tick and even picked up speed. Blake would bet she played poker on the weekends.

"How are Sophia and Clara? When last we spoke, things weren't quite what you'd hoped they would be."

"They're fine. Sophia is growing. Clara hasn't opened up any further. I tried to talk to her, but she's always so goddamn defensive. She's living in the past when I wasn't around, and now that I am, it feels like she doesn't want me there."

"Have you spoken with some of the guys in Echo team?"

"We go for beers once in a while. They're mostly on missions."

"So, you've lost both families."

Played into that.

"How is your relationship with Captain Guarnere?" she said.

"Good. We get the families together and have some drinks. When we step away from the wives, we talk about the missions."

"The nightmares," Doctor Kendra corrected.

"The nightmares."

"Are you having any of your own?"

Blake bit his lower lip. "No, no nightmares from my own missions." Clara wanted him to talk about the nightmares. She'd be furious if she overheard him talking to Doctor Kendra about returning to the teams. He wasn't jeopardizing his shot at getting in the field to report nightmares Doctor Kendra couldn't help him with. If they let him get back to the field, he'd be fine. The nightmares would go away, he'd be where he should, and life would go on. Better for everyone.

Doctor Kendra put her pen down. "No Genesis related nightmares?"

"Nothing impacting me." Blake answered so quickly and so resolutely, it was almost an interruption.

"You'd be the only soldier who has worked with the Genesis and not been seriously impacted. That's why we have follow-ups. Even unscheduled ones like this. *Especially* unscheduled ones when a soldier makes requests like leaving the unit." She leaned back, looking relaxed for the first time. "Tell me about them."

"The nightmares don't impact me."

"And I wrote that down for your file, Sergeant." She steepled her hands in front of her mouth. "Now tell me about them."

Blake scanned the room for a recording device. She wouldn't be dumb enough to use something obvious. Even if it wasn't legal to record him without permission, if the wrong ears heard about his nightmares, it could dismantle his career.

"Let's go for a walk." Doctor Kendra stood. "So you feel comfortable." She extended her arms and rotated to show she didn't have a wire. Could he trust her? He'd never completely trusted anyone.

They walked through the center and outside through a field. Blake led them through the middle of the grass to keep away from hidden recorders.

Doctor Kendra waited until the rev of engines in the compound's parking lot faded to purrs. "We're outside of earshot. There's nobody listening. It's safe to talk to me. Colonel Marks doesn't need to know anything right now. Let me help you."

"You want to know about my nightmares?"

"You're having nightmares that are impacting your life?"

He swallowed hard. He should tell, shouldn't he? *Screw it.* He'd better not regret this later. "Yeah. Not my own. The ones I've been working on. General Talbert's nightmares. Senior Chief Wilburg's too. All Genesis stuff. It's sticking with me. It's lodged in my psyche."

"What role do you play in the nightmare?"

"What do you mean?"

"Are you a spectator? Are you a soldier?"

He hadn't talked to Clara about that. She'd assumed the nightmares played out in his mind, even when he was off duty. "In the worst of the nightmares, I'm the enemy, killing people or soldiers." He heard their howls even just saying that.

Being on the enemy's side of the nightmares disgusted him. Clara would have been too. Doctor Kendra, however, just scratched her nose. He thought she'd be mortified.

"What do you think it means, being the enemy? Do you believe your subconscious is suggesting something?"

He shook his head. "Nothing I want to know. I've never thought of treason or betrayal if that's what you're wondering." He cracked his knuckles. "Never."

She chuckled. "That's not what I meant." She placed a hand on his forearm. Her skin felt like satin. He should have pulled away, but he didn't even flinch. He let her keep her hand there and made no gesture of his own to acknowledge what she'd done.

"Dreams have a way of sending us subconscious messages. Do you remember our training for identifying stress markers in nightmares? Operators assume the markers are related to the most gruesome moment in a nightmare, but what if there's more to the nightmare that you can't see? Are you keeping an open mind as we'd practiced?"

He finally pulled his arm away, but he disguised the move by stuffing his hands in his pockets. "I think so. How am I supposed to know? I didn't go to school for this. A few weeks of training, and I'm supposed to know how to help these guys?"

She took both his hands, sliding them out of his pockets. He felt powerless to stop her. "You're the only one who understands what they're going through. If I tried to help them, I'd feel the gruesome violence, but I would miss the details you're trained to pick up. Not to mention, I couldn't keep reliving those moments. I wanted to. I tried." She smiled, and a touch of sadness reflected in her eye. "Keep an open mind, Sergeant. Nobody knows what you men are going through. Not your wife, not your daughter, not me." Up close, her soulful brown eyes penetrated his defenses.

"I guess so," he said.

She released his hands and walked. He missed her touch. What had she done to him? "Colonel Marks wants me to find a medical reason to have your transfer declined."

Blake swiped at a mosquito. "I know. *Is* there a reason?"

"We should see each other more often." She met his eyes, a smile hinting at the edge of her lips. So slight, Blake wasn't sure he saw it. "So you can work through the nightmares. I know you're struggling with it, but I don't believe there's a reason to decline your transfer request." She reaffirmed their eye contact. "Are you sure it's what you want?"

Blake started to wonder the same thing.

Chapter 23

That night, he ate dinner with Clara and Sophia. Sophia hadn't stopped talking about a new computer game. Something about swords, slashing, spells, and wizardry. But Blake's thoughts trailed to earlier in the day. Colonel Marks should have met with him about leaving the Genesis Project, but he hadn't. He'd left it to Doctor Kendra. Blake hadn't seen Peter or any of the high-ranking officers from the meeting, either. Were they discussing how to proceed with Chief Wilburg? They had the report reworded so they could recommend Wilburg for the Genesis Project to fix him up and return him to active duty. But he'd already been in the Genesis—according to Peter. *He's dangerous. Does Chief Wilburg know how dangerous he is? Or does he think he's doing what's right?*

His arm was being shaken.

"Dad, are you okay?" Sophia was gazing up at him.

He shook his head to clear it. "Sorry, Sophia. What?"

Sophia dropped her fork. "You haven't said a word. I just told you I was having a baby."

Blake blinked at Sophia. "What?"

"I was kidding, Dad. You aren't listening to anything I'm saying."

Clara hid a snicker behind a napkin.

"Sorry, Sophia. There's a lot going on at the office." It was all he could think to say. *Focus up. You're supposed to be at home with your family.*

Dex sniffed his hand and rumbled. He was hungry. Sophia rolled her eyes.

"Is everything okay?" Clara said.

Blake thought about telling her he wanted to transfer back to Echo team, but he didn't have the energy to fight with her. "A few projects aren't going my way. That's all."

The way her eyes locked on to him told him she knew he'd fed her bullshit.

Clara and Sophia cleared the table. Blake hadn't touched his meatballs. *What happened to Corporal Hodge and Chief Wilburg?*

He walked to the computer in the living room. Searching for Corporal Daniel Hodge on Facebook returned a profile, but Blake couldn't see his picture without being his friend. He wouldn't accept the request.

His mind kept buzzing with thoughts of Doctor Kendra's touch. Had she meant anything by it? He'd never felt hands so soft. Is all of her skin that smooth? What did she mean by her smile? Or had he imagined it—

Stop it. He rattled his head. *Focus up.*

Back to his mission. He searched for Senior Chief Wilburg—no success. An old school soldier like Chief Wilburg didn't spend time online. A couple of articles popped up, referencing his name on Google, but a quick read showed this wasn't the same Wilburg. He doubted the chief was involved in paper mills or worked for the City of Toronto in Canada. For the hell of it, he searched for Lieutenant Zackery. No Facebook profile or website. Blake clicked on an image and—shocked like he'd been tasered during basic training—Senior

Chief Wilburg looked back at him. It wasn't a resemblance. It was a duplicate. Blake found his hand had crept up to his face.

Clara's footsteps clicked up from behind. "Who's that?" She rubbed his shoulders, her hands tougher than Doctor Kendra's. She pressed a kink into Blake's shoulder, and he winced. He turned his head up and found her smiling. She looked so beautiful when she smiled. Too bad she found reasons to frown so often. *Or was it just me that made her frown?*

"I'm not really sure."

She grunted and regarded him with a crooked eyebrow. "You aren't sure whose photo you're looking at?"

"I'm doing a little research on someone at the office. This is a picture of someone related to him. They look very similar." No. They looked *identical*.

She nodded slowly, doubtfully. "Are you going to come to bed? Or do you want to watch something with me? It might take your mind off work."

"No, thanks. I need to do some more searching. I'll come to bed soon." Blake tilted his head back to see her. "Sorry. This will be over soon and you'll have my attention." He hoped he wasn't lying. She'd never understand there were soldiers that needed him; lives that depended on him.

She slapped the back of his chair. "Really? Do you know how many hours you've spent on that computer since you left the teams? If you want to be here with us, be here with us. You're a ghost every night. Get some help if you need it." She huffed away, her footfalls booming up to their bedroom. She shut the door with a sharp *clack*.

He didn't have anyone to talk to like he did in the teams. The guys drank beer and shot the shit about their wives, kids, porn...everything. The Genesis needed a brotherhood, a team, instead of a group of individuals working together. David was great, but the bond of battle was different. And it would be helpful if Clara laid off him just a bit. He might have sat down with her if she didn't always find a reason to argue. Sure, it's his fault he worked so much, but she hadn't bothered coming to him the last six months when he was as bored as a security guard in an empty lot.

Blake gritted his teeth, finding concentrating nearly impossible. He sighed and headed upstairs, deciding to get a round of arguments over with early so there was time to get some sleep afterward.

Chapter 24

Barking snapped Blake from a worthless sleep. He recognized the warning. Dex didn't know he was retired and still fell back on his instincts.

Move. Blake kept a Glock nine-millimeter in a combination safe beside his bed. He moved on instinct: unlock the safe, grab the pistol, load the magazine, pull back on the action to chamber a round. Eight seconds.

His bare skin froze him. Clara's eyes sprouted widely when she saw the pistol. She covered her mouth and pulled up the bedsheet.

Blake put a finger to his lips. "Get dressed."

He yanked on pants and headed for the door, Clara's drawers slamming open and shut behind him.

Clara rushed out the door and pressed against him. "Stay close," he said into her ear, keeping his eyes trained on the stairs.

Dex sat vigilant at the top of the stairs. Blake gave him the single file signal. Dex crept down the stairs, leading the way. When Blake didn't follow him, Dex waited partway down the stairs facing the bottom, hackles raised and legs tensed to pounce.

Blake listened for rustling. Was someone down there?

Sophia's room was opposite the staircase. Blake stalked to her room. The door creaked, and the reek of unwashed socks and wet clothes made him flinch. Good thing Dex knew his smells.

Sophia sat up in bed, eyes cloudy, covers pulled up to her neck. "Dad?" She gasped at the gun in his hands.

"Shh." Blake raised a finger to his mouth. "Grab a sweater and follow me. Stay close."

Sophia rushed out of bed, threw on a hoodie, and followed him to Dex. Clara stood behind Dex.

"Let's make our way downstairs and call the police," Blake whispered.

Dex padded down the stairs and sat at the front door. Every time the step creaked, everyone cringed. Dex didn't growl or bark. The military trained him to sit when detecting explosives and lay down when detecting a human. *Change of plans.*

Blake handed Clara her cell phone. "Go back upstairs. Lock yourselves in the bedroom. Call the police. Dex, come."

Dex followed Blake to the back door, sniffing along the way.

Outside, the cold air gave Blake goosebumps, and the grass chilled his bare feet. Clouds blocked the moonlight from spotlighting him. He tightened his grip on the Glock, knowing he was at his most vulnerable outside. A mist descended as he ghosted forward.

"Blake? What's happening?"

"Clara?" Blake whirled up at the open second-floor window.

"Is everything okay?" she said.

"Lock the back door and wait for me." Should they run to the neighbors? No. He discarded that idea. Someone might be waiting to intercept. With the house locked, at least he would hear a door or window shattering if someone tried to break in. Dex smelled explosives, but if the enemy intended to detonate it, they would have already.

Blake kept tight to the house. He weighted each step cautiously to avoid breaking a branch. He smelled forest pines—no sign of anyone else.

Dex led him to the front door. Blake had his finger beside the trigger, nervously scraping the trigger guard. The forest stretched for a hundred yards before breaking at the neighbor's house.

Dex sat facing the door. A package lay on their porch. Tracks from Blake's car led up the driveway to the garage.

Down the road, red and blue lights flashed. If the enemy was close, they were nearly out of time.

Blake tensed as military police cars screeched to a stop at his driveway. They tainted the pine air with exhaust fumes. Blake dropped the Glock and raised his hands.

"Are you okay, Sergeant?"

Corporal Finnigan.

"Yeah Josh, I'm good. Dex smelled explosives. Cardboard box on the porch." Blake threw a thumb behind him at the package. "I'm just retrieving my firearm from the grass." Confident that Corporal Finnigan was aware, he stooped to pick up his gun, and tucked it behind his back.

Corporal Finnigan stepped back, eyes on the box. A coffee stain trailed down his uniform, glaring as brightly as his bald head. "We'll call the engineers." He hesitated as if he were asking Blake if that was the right thing to do. Explosives were uncommon in the area.

"Good call, Corporal. I'm going to get Sophia and Clara out."

Blake led Clara and Sophia to the neighbor's then walked the perimeter. Whoever had placed the explosive didn't stick around. Why the hell would someone put an explosive on his porch? He didn't think they'd armed it. They'd know Dex would sniff it out. They probably counted on it.

After the perimeter check, Blake headed to the front lawn. A pair of soldiers stood beside Corporal Finnigan. The darkness hid their rank and unit. They wore the green suits of bomb squad specialists. Before Blake asked any questions, they headed for the cardboard box.

"They're going to place a blast box on top of it and blow it," Corporal Finnigan said.

Chapter 25

"Why?" Blake frowned. "They don't know what's inside. Don't they have robots to disarm it?"

Corporal Finnigan shrugged. "Blast box is safer. They bolt it down and detonate it."

What if the bomber wanted me to see something inside the box? They would have known about Dex if they'd done their homework. *It's not armed. It can't be.*

"Hey, guys, hold on a second." Blake hustled to the porch and filed between the engineers before they secured the blast box.

They yelled for him to stop and then panicked back to their cars when he didn't.

Blake felt his pulse in his neck. The world became muffled, and shouts sounded as if they were spoken under a pillow. Blake pulled out his knife. His lungs ached. He'd been holding his breath. After a quick gulp of air, he slit the tape, securing the lid to the cardboard box. He ran his finger through the box's flap to feel for wires connected to the explosive. Not armed. Blake gently opened the lid and peeked inside at an antipersonnel mine, Model M16. Unarmed.

Blake threw his hand up. "We're clear."

A collective breath went out from onlookers hiding behind trees and vehicles.

"Have you lost your mind?" Corporal Finnigan sprang up from behind his squad car.

Blake wasn't listening. He plucked a piece of paper out from beneath the mine. In careful handwriting, it said, *Blake.* He threw a glance over his shoulder, disguising it as a sneeze, and then slipped the note in his waistband.

"How did you know it wasn't armed?" Corporal Finnigan asked.

"It made sense. I have to...take a piss." Blake didn't get inside. Several police cars screamed down the street to his house. Military Police had probably paged them. Colonel Marks stepped out of his black BMW in a ruffled Run for Life T-shirt and jogging pants. His biceps filled the sleeves, veins popping. If not for the pancake hair, he'd be an impressive sight.

"Sergeant, on me." Colonel Marks snorted.

"Sir, I have to take a piss."

"What happened?"

"Stupid-assed Delta shit happened. We're lucky to be alive," one engineer said behind Colonel Marks.

Colonel Marks' eyebrows raised. "What's he talking about?"

"Someone placed an unarmed mine at my front door. Dex sniffed it out. We called the police as a precaution. I didn't see anyone around."

Colonel Marks' eyes narrowed. "You called the police as a precaution? After you realized someone put a bomb on your porch? Jesus Christ, Blake. Who did it?"

Blake shook his head. "I didn't see anyone. Just the box. Dex didn't sniff anyone out. They probably left right after dropping the box. Unless the engineers saw something."

Engineers with mine detectors searched his property. They swept left to right to left like beach bums looking for fallen change.

Whenever the machine bleeped, they decorated the ground with glow-in-the-dark green chalk.

"Probably my bicycle," Blake yelled.

The engineers glared at him for disrupting their typical day of eating vending-machine potato chips and talking about the latest explosive tech to hit the market. They probably completed loads of training and simulations, rarely employing the skills. Clearly, the two on Blake's porch hadn't spent much time clearing mines: chalk covered the ground. A good gust of wind could erase all their work in a chalk storm.

"They don't like you very much," Colonel Marks said.

"They were going to use a blast box to destroy the contents. I thought something might be in there for me. A message maybe. A warning. So, I opened the box myself."

"What do you think the intention was?"

"No idea, sir. Maybe it's random." *Random if we don't consider that I'd been investigating Chief Wilburg and Lieutenant Zackery.* "I'd like to check on my family, sir." He slapped his thigh to call Dex to him. Dex bounded up the lawn.

"Of course. I'll get the reports from the MPs and engineers before I leave. We'll launch an investigation. You'll have an officer stationed outside your home at night until we know more."

"I appreciate that, sir." But did he? Would the officer be protecting him...or spying on him?

He jogged to Derek's house, the note crinkling in his pants. Derek answered the door in a housecoat and holding an umbrella.

"Defending my family with an umbrella?" Blake said.

Sweat trickled down Derek's head into the already large sweat stain on his shirt. The room smelled like the local men's hockey locker room. He scanned the street and slapped Blake's shoulder as a cue to enter. "Yeah, yeah. Get in here, you sumagun."

"Thank you so much for taking them in." Blake stepped in.

"Of course, of course." Derek shut the door after another quick scan. "Is everything okay? Did they find the bastard?"

"Nope. Nobody. Just a box with some harmless explosives."

They walked down the narrow hallway to the kitchen. Blake had never been in the house. Black marble countertops sat atop oak cupboards. A small island in the middle of the room had stools and a small selection of alcohol. The fridge tucked into the corner looked as if it opened into a butcher's meat locker. The parties they could have. *What does he do for the military? A contractor? Maybe a doctor?*

"Beautiful home," Blake said as if it were no big deal.

Sophia ran and bounded into his arms. His ribs groaned. He kissed the top of her head and sniffed. "What's in your hair?"

She smiled. "Lilacs. It's a spray in the bathroom. I asked if I could try some in my hair. It makes your hair soft." She pulled his hands into her silky hair.

"Nice," he cooed with exaggeration.

Clara walked over and joined the embrace, sliding her hands under Sophia's arms. She held on for a long time. He twisted his belly so they wouldn't ruffle the paper.

"I need to use the washroom. And do you have an extra shirt?" Blake said.

Derek clicked a finger gun toward the door. "Down the hall you came from, on your right. I'll get you a shirt."

Blake walked into the bathroom. They called it a powder room, but it was more like a locker room. Blake locked the door and pulled out the note from his pants. *What the hell was that smell? Did Derek air out his hockey gear in here?*

Chapter 26

BLAKE READ THE CRYPTIC note, this time noticing the downward slant in the writing, likely indicating a depression or decline.

The note read:

For your eyes only.

Your search won't end well.

Think of the families.

They fought for something.

Think of the destruction the truth would produce.

They need us.

If you persist, there is only darkness in your future.

Blake put the note on the vanity. He hardly recognized himself in the mirror—more shadowed lines on his forehead, sandbags beneath his eyes like General Talbert, and a scruffy beard that itched. Where was the boy that left home at eighteen, fearless and determined to change the world? He had become a soldier. The killing didn't bother him. The lack of meaning did. His youthful spirit died somewhere overseas in the dirt. Now he felt distant and heartless—Clara wouldn't argue. The Genesis hadn't helped.

No. Not completely heartless. He had Sophia. He loved her as he had loved no one else. And the enemy had invaded his doorstep, threatening his family. If they put a note in the box, they knew what

Dex would do. They knew he'd push past protocol and do what he wanted. Who would know how he'd react?

"Blake, are you okay?" Clara tapped against the door. "I have a shirt here for you."

Blake analyzed himself. He would decide on the fate of the note later. He cracked the door open.

Clara's eyes narrowed. "What are you doing in there? Is everything okay?"

"I'm fine. I needed a few minutes to shake things out. Clear my head. Are you both okay?"

"I suppose so. Maybe a little shaken up. Sophia is good. She's having fun with Bridgette playing Lego. She doesn't understand what happened. Neither do I." Clara tried to wedge the door open with the shirt. "Open the door. What's wrong with you? Take the shirt." She shoved against the door, but he propped his foot against it so it wouldn't open further.

"Thanks." He took the red-and-black flannel shirt. He could have worn it for hunting if the red was brighter. It looked like a grandpa hand-me-down. He fastened the snaps then folded the note and placed it in the chest pocket. The stench of cigarettes bled through the shirt.

When he walked into the living room, conversations ended.

"Would you like something to drink?" Sue grinned.

"Sure, I'll have a beer if you got one."

She headed for the fridge, her long blonde hair gummed up with hair products.

"Here you go. One cold beer." Sue handed him the can. "Are the police still at your house? What's going to happen?"

"It's fine. The police are investigating to make sure it's safe for us to go home. Maybe a prank."

"A prank?" Clara threw herself to her feet. "Someone thinks it's funny to leave explosives at our front door?"

Blake raised his brows at her, signaling for her to calm down.

She raised her voice instead. "This isn't like leaving a bag of dog crap so we stomp on it. They could have killed Sophia! What if it went off?" Her hands shook.

Blake pulled her close and wrapped his arms around her. She kept her arms in front of her as if she were protecting herself. How could he make her relax? Definitely not with the truth.

He brought her ear close to him. "Maybe you should go to your mother's for a few days. With Sophia. Until this blows over or at least the investigation is over."

She tore out of his grasp. "This isn't something we need to talk about right now."

He sensed her struggling to keep calm, her fists clenching and unclenching. Her breathing quickened like a bull working itself up before it charged.

Derek and Sue pretended to read the newspaper on the table.

"What's going on, Blake? Why would someone want to hurt us?"

Blake wasn't ready to share what he knew, which wasn't anything useful. "It could be anyone. I've done a lot of things in my career that pissed people off." Vague as the note was, he knew it was related to the Genesis. "But the package wasn't armed. We were never in danger."

Most of the neighbors knew he served in the military. Still, people moved in from the Army, Marines, Navy and Air Force, so nobody knew specifically what unit he belonged to. The cover story was that he worked for Intelligence and Combat Support as a Civil Affairs Specialist. He identified critical requirements needed by civilians during missions or crisis situations. His primary responsibilities included research, coordination, conducting, and helping write civil affairs documents while enabling the civil-military operations of the supported commander. It was a mouthful, and people's eyes glazed when he rattled through it—the perfect cover story. It sounded dull, and it explained his constant absence.

Sue and Derek watched him, probably wondering how he'd made enemies. Their eyes returned to their papers when he glanced their way.

Blake chugged the last of his beer and clanged the can on the counter. "Call your mom and see if she's up for company. Please. Until this investigation is over, at least."

Clara fumed. She looked at Sue.

"Yes, of course. Call her if you need to." Sue pointed down the hall. "There's a phone around the corner in the dining room on the right."

Clara stormed around the corner.

Where the hell was Sophia? Blake felt the paper in his pocket, swearing it called to everyone, drawing their attention. He needed to think. Sue and Derek needed a reason to leave the room.

Clara returned a few minutes later on soundless steps. "We're going to stay with my mom." Her eyes ticked up to him, as if to say, *Are you happy?* "I'll tell Sophia. Are you okay if we spend the night here? We'll go in the morning."

"Of course, of course!" Sue laughed. "Stay a day. We love having you over." She yawned. "Let's all get to bed. I know I'm exhausted."

Perfect. Everyone would be out of the way.

Sue stood so quickly she almost knocked her chair over. "There's a spare bedroom down the hall and a couch in the living room. That should be enough to keep the three of you for a few hours."

It didn't take long to set up the beds with blankets and pillows. The police came by to tell them the house was safe and they could return in the morning. Blake let the officer know they'd spend the night at

Derek's. He didn't say anything about Clara and Sophia heading to her mom's. He didn't want anyone to know.

He stared at the ceiling but couldn't sleep. The prospect of nightmares kept him from closing his eyes. *Should I destroy the note?* No. He'd put the note in the fireproof safe at home in the morning. Although Clara knew the code, she wouldn't go into it. It held vehicle information, life insurance policies, and paperwork they almost never looked at.

***

The sun crested the horizon like a single eye creaking open in the morning. *Did I sleep at all?* Clara slept beside him, breathing like an assisted-living machine. Despite their night, she would sleep a good portion of the morning—she slept under any circumstance. She would have made a good soldier.

He lifted the wool blanket. Clara stirred. He rolled off the bed, landing like a cat on his feet. He threw on his stinky shirt and dress pants and wandered into the kitchen. It was empty. He left through the front door.

When he approached his front porch, he found the wood planks yanked out and snapped apart in a frenzied search for more explosives. Goddamn engineers. He walked into the house and cursed. They'd thrown the couch cushions around, emptied drawers, and upturned lamps. Were the engineers paying him back for getting in their way? The floor creaked behind him, and he spun, fists clenched.

"They did a number on the place." An MP stepped around books and fragments of a plant pot to stand closer to Blake. "Didn't mean to startle you. My shift watching the house."

Blake had never seen the man before.

"Get any of their names? I'd love to have a word." Blake recoiled from the MP's cheap cologne, maybe Old Spice. He didn't have the heart to tell the guy no women ever vroomed over the smell.

"Have a girl with you in your car?"

The officer's eyes narrowed, then he burst into laughter. Blake chuckled at the officer's squeaky tone. He sounded like a teenager.

"I'm Corporal Radcliff. John." He extended his hand. "Get into a fight with an ashtray?"

"Something like that. Blake." He grabbed John's hand and shook. "Engineers did this?" He swept his hands around the room to indicate the chaos.

John shrugged. "I would guess as much, but I came on duty only a couple of hours ago. Not much communication for soldiers, right? Didn't see the need to enter until I saw you walking up to the place."

Blake wandered down the hall to his study. He had to sidestep a pillow and a toy left on the floor. John waited in the main hall as Blake punched in the code to the safe and opened it. He took one last look at the note, memorized it, then placed it inside.

Should he tell Colonel Marks? No. Colonel Marks would do anything to protect the Genesis, including interrogate Peter like a radical digging for answers.

He locked the safe and returned to the hall. John sat on a wooden chair he must have grabbed from the kitchen.

"Any idea why someone left the mine here in the first place?" John's heel rattled off the floor.

Blake shrugged and blew out of puffed cheeks. "I don't know."

"Why trash your house?"

"I wish I knew that too." Blake felt the weight of the pocket-knife in his pants. He headed upstairs to change into a T-shirt and jogging pants. Colonel Marks gave him the day off, and he was going to make sure Clara and Sophia made it to her mother's before he did anything else. Blake headed back downstairs and heard Clara and John talking.

"Thank you, John. We appreciate you keeping an eye on us. Can you wait outside so we can clean up and feel normal again?" Clara sounded so pleasant that Blake barely recognized her.

"If you need anything, you know where to find me." John's steps petered out through the door.

Blake descended the stairs. "I didn't think you'd be up so early, given the circumstance."

Clara's eyes fell on him. "I didn't want to, but since you left Derek's, Sophia wouldn't stop asking about you. She doesn't want to visit her grandmother. She wants to come home."

"It's not safe here. You know that. This is one of those times I need you to listen and not argue."

She threw her hands up. "All I do is listen! I'm tired of listening. I'm sick of you spending all your time in your head. You're not here even when you say you will be." She narrowed her eyes like a sniper squinting through a line of sight. "Do you even love me anymore?"

He wanted to ask her the same question. He averted his eyes to look out the window. "I don't know."

Chapter 27

Continuing his investigation might have consequences for him and his family. Blake wanted Clara and Sophia far away until it was over; he'd put his foot down if Sophia protested. Dying himself didn't scare him—Sophia or Clara dying twisted his stomach like a coiled spring. Bile rose in his throat. He closed his eyes and saw Corporal Hodge begging him for his help, to not leave him for dead. How many of his brothers would turn into killers if he walked away? Would someone kill Clara next?

Blake's eyes shot open. "You need to go. It's not safe."

"You don't love me?" Clara retorted, apparently wanting to continue their fight. "It's fine. I stopped loving you a long time ago." Her fingers balled into fists. She picked up a glass from the floor and hurled it at him and it shattered against the wall.

Blake smacked the wall with an open palm. "I said you're going. That's final." *How can you not understand how dangerous it is here for you both?* He didn't want to get rid of them; he wanted to protect them.

Clara's lower lip curled. "Tell that to your daughter." Her words sliced like shards of glass, thrown in anger, still embedded in the wall behind him.

Sophia stepped out from the living room. "Dad? What's going on?" Her eyes scanned the chaos on the floor around them. She looked poised and ready for a fight.

God damn it, Clara. Why did you make me say that when you knew she was here? He wanted to punch a hole through the wall, but not with Sophia there. "Take it easy, Rocky. You're going to your grandparents for a few days. Maybe a week or two. There will be no discussing it. Clear?" He made sure his words had weight, but he smiled at her and winked.

Sophia crossed her arms and puffed her chest. "Unclear, Dad. You taught me that a Powell doesn't back down because they're scared. They fight. They can't bully us out of our house. I know you're not scared. You aren't scared of anything. And—"

"There is one thing that scares me, Sophia." Blake eased his hands onto her shoulders. "Losing you." *Don't get teary-eyed right now.* "When you come home, you can hang the American flag outside the yard and march the perimeter to your heart's content. For now, your mission is to go to your grandparents and protect mom."

"I don't want to go!" Sophia tried to shake out of his hands.

Blake sighed. At least she was acting her age. "It's not for long. You're going."

***

Packing took an hour. After they'd left, Blake plopped on the couch, a lead ball in his gut.

His cell phone rang. He expected the caller to be Sophia begging for one last chance to stay home and stand against oppression, but when he glanced at the caller ID, it said *Private Number.*

He tapped the answer button and barked, "Yeah?"

A female answered as robotic as a voice synthesizer. "Hello, this is Marsha, a secretary with the senator's office calling. May I speak to Derek O'Hare please? We're returning a call regarding your article."

"Sorry, you have the wrong—" *Wait.* Derek O'Hare was the false name he'd given to Senator Fredrick's office. He massaged his forefingers on his temples and grunted out a "This is Derek."

"I'm responding to your inquiry about Senator Fredrick's time in Afghanistan. I assume you know the senator lost his life recently."

All too well. "Yes, I heard. I would appreciate any details you can give me. We're working on a short autobiography piece."

"Certainly. We can provide what information we have. The senator was in Afghanistan from June second, 2009 until June eighth, 2009. He was working with the Red Cross as a promotional piece for his re-election. During this time, he helped unload trucks, read stories, and played soccer with the local kids. He was doing his best to bring attention to the need for relief and positive reinforcement for the kids there."

Typical political answer. Probably read from a script. Assuming that was the only time he visited, he wasn't the killer. Big surprise. So, who killed Hodge's men?

"Are you there, Mr. O'Hare?"

Think. Think. Blake needed a follow-up question that might expose a lie. "So, he wasn't involved with the United States Military while he was there?"

"Yes, they would have been part of his security force. He stayed on several operating bases and visited the troops."

"Do you know if he took any medication while he was there? To prevent him from getting sick or fight off something he had caught?"

The caller scoffed. "I don't like where your line of questioning is going. He's dead, and you want to run his name through the mud? It's clear how he died. You'll have to call someone else to find trash on him for your newscast. All you journalists are the same. You're probably the reason he's dead—your stupid stories with a complete disregard for the facts. Don't call here again." The phone clicked off.

Blake glared at his phone, not quite believing she'd hung up on him so abruptly. She must have been under a lot of stress.

He drove into the office late that afternoon. When he passed through security, he discovered the janitor emptying trash bins in the office. The admin staff had already gone home for the night, but Blake found David beside the Genesis, hunched so close to his monitor that its blue glow reflected off his skin. They might have an hour before orders came to leave.

"Hey, Blake, what are you doing here?" David sprang out of his seat so fast it rode its squeaky wheels into the desk behind him. He clutched Blake's sleeve and guided him into a corner. "I heard what happened. Are you okay?"

Blake nodded. Did he smell beer hidden behind peppermint gum? "I'm fine. But there's something we need to talk about." Blake scanned the room to ensure nobody was listening. As dark as it was, no one sat at the glow of any other monitors. He glanced up at the dark globe on the ceiling—a hidden security camera. "But not here." He jabbed his head in the direction of the elevator.

They both walked outside to the waterfall where Colonel Marks had first told Blake about Corporal Hodge.

David leaned in, his hands shaking. "What's going on?"

Chapter 28

WATER TRICKLED DOWN THE falls. Fortified trees stood against the moonlight, casting shadows like rank-and-file soldiers huddling in for a closer inspection. David listened to Blake beneath a canopy of trees. Blake told him about his concerns with the Genesis and how it was the common denominator in both murders.

"I need you to help me get into the archive. There are files in there on Lieutenant Zackery that I think are central to all of this. Even Corporal Hodge's file should tell me a lot."

"What do you need me for? Ask Colonel Marks for access. If there are soldiers killing people because of our machines, he'll want to know about it."

Blake waited for wind to gust through the trees. After another quick glance to check for eavesdroppers, he cleared his throat. "He asked me to step away from the case. I can't go to him with what I know yet. If I get the information I need, I'll take it to him—after I make a few copies. It's too early, anyway. I don't have proof, and you know how Colonel Marks is about the archive."

"About personnel files?" David asked. "You mean how they're confidential, and it's a federal offense to break into a military archive to look at confidential files?"

Blake smirked. "Yup. Do you remember what happens when a Delta Operator is captured behind enemy lines? The government disavows any knowledge of us. Do you know why? Because it's a national offense for us to exist in most of the places they send us. But they send us because we're needed."

"I don't know what to say, Blake. This is just...different."

Blake nodded. "We've known each other for only six months, so I get you don't completely trust me. But you know what kind of operator I am by now. You know what kind of *man* I am. We shared a lot of stories. A lot of family barbecues."

The wind picked up, and goose bumps ran down Blake's legs. Crickets chirped in the cover of the trees.

David gulped. "What do you want me to do?"

"You've been here for years. You must have case files that you look up in the archive. I need you to get access to the archive and then leave your access card at your desk. If they catch me using your card, they can't hold you accountable."

David placed his hands in his pocket. "And you don't think the explosives at your home had something to do with this investigation? That it wasn't a warning to back off? Where are Clara and Sophia?"

"They're both fine. Safe. Far away." Blake shook his head. "Look, I'm nearly certain the Genesis played a role in the murders. I hoped it was a coincidence until the explosives. I was thinking of backing off before that. Handing off what I knew to the colonel. But now, I can't do that."

David threw his hands to his temples and clutched his hair. "You're willing to risk your family for this? Do you really think there's a safe place to hide from people who do this kind of thing? They're probably watching your family right now. You should take it to Colonel Marks and walk away."

"The colonel doesn't want to know. I need proof. I could ask Peter, but I can't trust him to keep his mouth shut."

"Then how do you know you can trust me, goddammit?" David said. "Maybe you aren't meant to be a hero. You're not fighting a war, Blake."

"If the Genesis is prompting soldiers to kill innocent people, then the project needs to end."

David paced the small alcove, muttering to himself. Finally, he spun on his heel to face Blake. "Okay, I'll help you get into the archive, but if you don't find anything, that's it for me. And if you get caught...I can't help you." He wasn't sold on the idea. He'd agreed to it, though, and that was enough for Blake.

They returned to the War Room. Blake waited in his office, staring at the wall but not looking at it, lost in thoughts of the possible consequences. He drummed his fingers on his desk. Stood. Sat. Tapped his foot. Stood. His head jerked up at the sounds of feet—*who was here at this hour?*—and he saw Peter stroll by. Peter glanced at him and then away. He picked up his pace so quickly he almost tripped on his heels. Blake snuck into the hall, feet in wide arcs like a cat burglar. He trailed Peter, keeping in the shadows afforded by cubicle walls and pillars.

Peter's journey ended in the computer lab. He jammed a screwdriver into an unused computer terminal. Blake stole into the lab behind him and scurried to a pillar—his foot fell on a discarded screw and rolled against the column with a clunk. *Focus up!* He was trained better than that.

Peter cut his breath short and glanced around the room as if to check on a noise. Why the fear? Was he fixing the terminal...or was he there for something covert? Satisfied no one was there, he slid a panel off the computer and laid it on the desk. He inserted a small chip into the computer and then slipped the panel back in place. Blake almost stepped out from behind the pillar to demand what the hell that was, but he couldn't jeopardize the chance to take the chip. He snuck back into his office and drummed his fingers to the tune of "I'm a Little Teapot," a song Sophia had loved for a long time. When Peter walked by, Blake focused on his computer.

"H-h-hello, sir." Peter stood at the doorway. His hands hung behind his back.

Blake feigned calm and leaned back in his chair. "What's up, Peter?" He tried to keep his voice even despite the rush in his lungs and his chest.

"About th-th-the Genesis Project..." Peter swallowed back the saliva of nerves. "I-I was mistaken. I th-th-thought something was wrong with the m-machine, but it turns out i-it's fine. I w-wanted you to know that so you w-wouldn't worry."

Blake nodded. Had someone said something to him? "Okay, thanks Peter. I appreciate you following up."

Blake decided not to press him. Not yet. Peter acted more strangely every day, but Blake sure as hell wouldn't find out why by asking. He watched Peter walk down the hall toward the elevator. Before he reached the elevator, Peter walked out of view.

"Everything okay?"

Blake's heart skipped a beat, but he acted perfectly calm when David appeared in the doorway. He sucked in a long breath. "I'm good. Do you have the pass?"

David bunched the corner of his mouth. "No. He wouldn't approve it. Colonel Marks said there was an investigation going on, and a lot of it involves the archive. There are dozens of people working in there. Apparently, Corporal Hodge caused a lot of backdating." He shrugged. "Sorry."

Blake examined a scuff on the wall. If Colonel Marks found evidence, Blake could let him deal with it. They would shut the Genesis down, and the threat would go away. But what about Wilburg—Lieutenant Zackery? If the colonel was investigating Corporal Hodge, knowing there might be an identity issue in another case would be helpful. First, Blake wanted to know what Peter had hidden in the computer.

David cocked his head. "You stared at the wall for a full minute and have nothing to say? What do you want to do? Drop the idea? Tell Colonel Marks? I think you should tell him." He rotated toward the door. "I can go with you. We can ask him to keep it between the three of us."

Blake lowered his voice. "I think I'll keep it between us. We aren't involved in what he has going on, officially, and I don't want an armed bomb on my front porch."

"Does anyone else know there's potentially something wrong with the Genesis?"

"Assuming my computer isn't being monitored...Peter knows something. Anyone who might be involved with Corporal Hodge's case knows. I told Colonel Marks the story Corporal Hodge shared, so also anyone he told. I don't know, David. It could be loads of people. Probably a dozen. There's you. We can't ask any of them."

David scratched his clean-shaven chin—not even a shadow yet. "Pick one person. The most likely person who would want to keep it a secret and is willing to threaten us."

Blake's mind tumbled through all variables. Too many. "I don't know."

David threw up his arms. "Well, I'm getting back to work. I have a few cases to review that are coming in tomorrow morning, and it's getting late. Take care, buddy, and let me know if you need anything.

We can talk more later. Barbecue at my place Saturday?" He smiled. "Think about it. If so many people know what's going on, why only threaten you?"

"Roger. Have a good night."

Blake strolled through the office searching for Peter. When he didn't find him, he headed for the computer and unscrewed the side panel. He scanned the room when the screwdriver clacked against the screwhead, then slid the panel off, set it on the desk, and clicked on his phone's flashlight. A small chip rested inside. It would fit into the computer's microchip slot. He grabbed the chip, turned back to his office and found Peter standing in his path, staring at him.

Chapter 29

BLAKE SLID THE CHIP into the same pocket he kept his knife in. Peter's eyes trained on that pocket. "What's going on, Peter?"

Peter's large hands clenched to tight fists. He blocked the path to the door. Blake would have to go through him. He rolled his eyes down, then up at Peter to assess the roadblock. As large as Peter was, Blake had no qualms about the outcome of the fight.

"W-w-what's in your p-pocket, Blake?" Peter's pupils dilated.

Blake crossed his arms. So, Peter was willing to fight. "Do you want to tell me what I have in my pocket?"

Peter suddenly looked exhausted. "D-d-don't p-play g-games with me. It's n-n-not for your e-eyes. You c-can't access it, a-anyway. It's encrypted."

Blake nodded. Sweat dribbled down the side of Peter's face. "Then you won't mind if I look at it."

Peter stepped aside. "I'll g-go with you."

He didn't enjoy having his back to someone he didn't trust breathing down his neck. He listened to Peter's steps, measuring in case he needed to react. Worst-case scenario, Peter could pummel him, but Peter couldn't justify killing him.

Blake clicked the chip into the microreader. Peter leered at him, one hand on his shoulder and one on the desk. The stench of beer wafted out of Peter's pores like rot from a dumpster.

The computer whirred awake in a song of blips and beeps. A screen popped up, requesting a program to read the files. Blake browsed; all were AES files, but the computer didn't recognize them. What was an AES file? He had expected a password request.

Peter held out a hand. "I'll t-t-take that b-back now, thanks." The sweat on his head made it shimmer in the light. A sour odor joined the stench of beer, making a nasty concoction. It was funny how fetid someone smelled when you didn't like them anymore. Blake kept his eyes glued to the computer. Should he force Peter to open the files at knifepoint? His hand slid int—

"Hello, Sergeant. Peter." Colonel Marks stepped into the office with a stack of paper in his hand. His uniform was wrinkled beyond what an iron could press. He spoke through a yawn. His steps wobbled, and he rubbed the space between his eyes. Blake couldn't decide what was more pressing: Peter demanding the chip back—which likely contained damning information about the Genesis—or the colonel calling him out on trying to get David to access the archive on his behalf.

Peter stiffened like his muscles had seized all at once. Colonel Marks dropped the papers and helped him sit, talking to him soothingly. With one eye on the colonel, Blake copied the files onto his hard drive and shut the window. He whirled around and smiled. "Hello, Colonel." He glanced back. The computer had finished copying.

"Peter, take a minute. I need to talk to Sergeant Powell. It's confidential."

Peter didn't move.

"Peter? Are you all right? Can you give Sergeant Powell and me some privacy?"

Peter came to life as if a puppet master had reared back on his strings. "I'm okay, sir. I w-was grabbing something from Sergeant Powell and h-had a distracting m-memory." Peter lunged at the computer and ejected the chip. He tucked it into his pocket, and stepped out of the office, giving Blake such a wide berth that he almost rolled along the walls.

The colonel watched Peter leave. "Strange."

Blake nodded. "Very strange." He had taken care of one problem. Now, he needed to get rid of the other problem. "How can I help you, sir?"

Colonel Marks sat on the plastic chair and wiggled with a wince. Blake smirked.

"Touché," Colonel Marks smiled.

"What can I do, sir?"

The colonel picked up a stack of papers and threw them onto Blake's desk. The top document was called Transfer Request Form.

Colonel Marks tapped the stack. "You'll need to fill that out to request a transfer from the Genesis. There are a lot of confidentiality agreements." Colonel Marks' lips twisted. "Unfortunately, with the investigation pending on the explosive at your door, this request won't be processed for several months. Even then, it may not get approved."

Blake had heard that story before with other officers. He'd never serve with his men again. "You don't intend to approve the request, do you, sir?"

"There aren't a lot of men that can do what you do, Sergeant. Avoiding PTSD in our staff has taken a terrible toll on soldiers. There are only three of you operating right now. We wish we had more to meet the demand. Letting you go would put us at a great disadvantage."

"The world would be a safer place if I was serving with Echo team, trying to stop major threats to this country."

"The world would be a better place," the colonel raised his voice, "if our generals were in the field preventing the deaths of hundreds of our soldiers in the very fight you're referring to. Don't forget the value of what we do here." He leaned in. "And do not belittle it. Every high-ranking officer that comes through here and goes back into combat is saving hundreds of lives that an officer with lesser knowledge or balls couldn't. You're saving the lives of all the men who would have to follow someone with less experience in battle."

Blake waited silently. Would the colonel believe he might not be cut out for it, or would he think Blake was making excuses if he told him about the nightmares?

Colonel Marks tugged at his uniform jacket as if to hand-iron it. "I have to get home. Joyce doesn't react too well when dinner gets cold. Put in your paperwork." He gave up working out a sharp crease. "Take a few days off with your family. You've been through a lot. Even if you're one of the craziest SOBs I know, you're still human." He left the room.

Blake wanted to smile but couldn't. He could arm-curl sixty pounds but wasn't strong enough to lift the corners of his lips.

Alone at last. Blake researched the AES file type, which turned out to be a basic encryption program he could download on the Net. He couldn't install it on his workstation because it would get flagged. He needed a coding key, too. He copied the files onto a USB drive and turned on Isaac's computer. Isaac hadn't been to the office in months.

The login asked for Issacs's credentials. He knew the required username—a combination of the service number, the last name, and the first three letters of the first name. *What are they?* Blake searched the drawers with fitful crashes and found Isaac's dog tags in the middle drawer. Now…what was Isaac's password? He searched his drawers again, finding no clues. A family member or kids might do the trick if he had any. He studied Isaac's dog tags again. The religion listed was Catholic. He tried that as the password. Incorrect. *Idiot, as if that would be the password.*

He pulled apart the USB drive until only the chip remained. His laptop came apart with a few screws, and he placed the chip inside. Security wouldn't notice the stowaway. The mission would end if they did.

Two security guards stood at the terminals. One sat in front of a screen, monitoring items running through the scanner. The second officer watched Blake approach with disinterest. His pack felt like a hundred pounds.

"Out for the day, Sergeant?" the guard said.

"Out for the day," Blake said, slowly placing his pack on the conveyer belt while breathing deeply to avoid sweating. The pack headed for the scanner. If they realized what Blake had done, assuming the drive contained top secret information, it could mean five years in a military prison. Would they notice the extra creases on his forehead or his deep swallows?

The guard took too long with his bag. He could practically feel the guard zooming in on his laptop and spotting the drive chip. "Going for drinks tonight?" Blake said. "I hear there are some good lookers on Thursdays."

The guard behind the scanner looked up and smiled. "I'll be there. Need a drink after today."

"I'll see you there," Blake said, stepping through the backscatter and reaching toward the scanner to pull out his pack. The guard nodded and started up the belt. Shouldering the pack felt like taking a big weight off his shoulders.

His only option to get the files decrypted was a friend of the family, a nerdy hacker who had broken into National Bank's internal servers eight years ago and wired trace amounts of money to his account from millions of other accounts. Apparently, this kid is the reason they changed their security protocols. He'd walked into the bank like a teller, reached the servers, and simply plugged in the program that gave him access. Nobody questioned him on the way out.

Chapter 30

BLAKE PULLED INTO AN Esso station and snatched up the receiver at a phone booth. The military was known to bug personal cellphones. Even third-party apps could be tracked.

Eyes combing the parking lot and gas bay, he kept his voice hushed like an inmate sharing secrets with a guard. "Hi, is Clara there?"

"Dad!" Sophia shouted into the phone.

Tears welled. "Hey, baby girl. How are you?"

"Pissed off."

He loved the advanced vocabulary they'd paid for in private school. How many twelve-year-olds said "pissed off?" She needed a new role model. Then, he thought back to when he was twelve and told his dad to go fuck himself. Different relationship.

"Is Grandma treating you well? Let me know if she isn't, and I'll send my goons."

Sophia scoffed. "You're more scared of Gramma than the bad guys."

He chuckled into the receiver. "True enough."

"Dad, the food tastes like cardboard. I don't like it."

"You're going to have to tough it out, Sophia. Listen, I really need to talk to your mom, okay? I'm not at home, but this is very important. Can you let me talk to her for a little?"

The tone died. Had she hung up?

He heard her cheeks droop in her drawn-out words. "Sure. Whatever. Mom!"

The phone on the other end knocked against something. Then Clara said, "Hello? What happened?"

Blake pulled the phone away and stared at it for a moment, expecting her face in the receiver. "I need to ask you something, but I can't tell you why. You remember Billy? Angela's son? The one that went to prison for a while?"

"What?"

"Clara, it's important."

"We haven't seen Angela in years. Billy? Was that his name? He was a computer science guy, right? Why? What's going on?"

"I can't explain. Do you know where they live? Have you been to their home?"

"Blake, I want to know what is going on. I know I said I didn't want to hear about it, but things have changed. Someone wanted to kill us."

Blake thumped a loose fist on the phone booth pane. "Listen to me Clara. Do you know or not?" The less she knew, the safer she was.

"Hold on. I have to check my contact info." Clara paused but returned a moment later with the address. "You're chasing something, aren't you? You're not backing down. Anything for the goddamn team. Forget what we're going through."

"I'm sorry. I have to. I love you."

"You don't." A click ended the sentence.

"Hello? Clara? Hello?" Blake thumped the receiver against the phone box in case it needed a kick. "Hello?" Nope. Clara had hung up. *I'm sorry, Sophia. I love you both.* No matter how badly he wanted a normal life with his family, threats existed everywhere he went. He'd never have a career selling cars or checking bags at the airport. He wasn't built for it.

He drove to the address in two hours with help from Google Maps. When he arrived, he pulled the chip out of the computer in his pack and got out of his car.

Neighboring houses had missing front doors, roofs with shingles flapping in the loose wind, and walls that looked like grenades had eaten chunks out of them. It reminded him of Bosnia. If he fell asleep in his car, he'd wake up searching for his rifle. Billy's house didn't look more appealing. The front door hung on cords, and the siding reminded him of launching M40s to infiltrate barricaded houses. What were the odds that the thirty-year-old still owned a computer? It didn't look as though he owned a home.

He ran his hand through his hair. But where else could he go? Nobody would expect him to go to Billy's house. He walked up the sidewalk over fractures in the cement pads large enough to warrant a *Watch Your Step* sign with weeds poking through. Instead of a doorbell, he found a gap in the siding the size of a mouse hole. He knocked on the wall, careful not to knock it down. No answer.

"What! Who is it?" someone shouted like a brick through the spider-web-cracked window.

"Angela?" Blake said to the window. He squinted to see through the threadbare curtain.

"Who's askin'? You a cop?" Her voice sizzled with alarm.

Angela was thin and smart. While usually dressed down for any occasion, she could do well with the right motivation. Unfortunately, her next fix was all that motivated her.

Blake cleared his throat. "No, I'm not a cop." Would that really work to convince her? "It's Blake. We used to hang out with my wife

Clara and my daughter Sophia. Billy would come over with you and show us the computer games he was building."

A gasp. The voice lost its acid and spoke now with sugar. "Ohhhhh, Blake! Come on in, darlin'."

Blake took a deep breath, pushed aside the wavering door, and walked in. When he let go, the door cracked back against the frame with no spring to cushion it.

The interior looked as rough as the exterior. He passed through a kitchen that might have a sink or stove buried under the dishes and garbage. Flies buzzed. The smell of mold and animal dung dug up old memories of crawling through sewers for exfil. Blake listened for bleeps or clicking from a computer. At the end of the hallway was an open door on the right and another on the left.

"Hello? Come on in. Did you hear me? Come down the hall. I'm not comin' to you."

Blake crept down the hallway. Each step creaked as if he might break through the floor. *Am I in the Temple of Doom?*

He ended at a room as worthy of a chemical shower as the kitchen: ashtrays brimming with residue, needles thrown everywhere, a cracked end table, a lamp with no shade, a couch weathered down to threads as inviting to sit on as a haystack, and a stench like whatever had defecated in the kitchen had come here to die. More flies circled.

Blake cupped his nose against the reek, barely able to withstand it. "Hello, Angela." She sat on the couch. The back of her head faced him, bobbing slowly left to right like a buoy. She faced a television broadcasting *Drugs Inc.* What a coincidence. Shopping for ideas?

She turned to face him. *What the hell?* Angela's skull was so caved in she looked like she'd died, only her brain hadn't realized it yet. Her skin was blotched with liver spots. Her fingernails were rusty brown and chipped. Her teeth were like an exhumed corpse's, and her eyes were cloudy. Ribs rippled through her skin, even under the stained sundress. Time had kicked her with both feet.

"How are you? You got any meth?" *She must be jonesing.*

He should have felt sorry for her. She was family. But he'd seen too much in his life in situations where people had no other choice. Women were raped and murdered for no more reason than the color of their skin. This woman had a chance and had thrown it away.

"No, I didn't bring any meth. I actually came to see Billy."

"That little f—" She threw herself against the couch in a fierce coughing fit, phlegm gargling with each hack. When she recovered, she raised a bony finger at him. "That little bastard is downstairs. He don't let me in there anymore since I met Dale. Snob probably hides the meth on me and hoards it. He keeps to himself. Barely comes out for dinner." Even across the room, her breath reeked like the bark of a diseased tree.

"Can I go talk to him?" *You don't look like you've had dinner in months.*

"Whatever, man. You got no meth, right? Then screw off. I don't care." She waved him away.

Dale must be quite a winner. Any hope of discovering a computer hacker in this house had disappeared. Finding Billy alive would be a bonus.

Down the hallway, he found a small room filled with open boxes, clothes strewn on the floor, books torn apart, and shards of plastic sprayed across the walls and floor. This was an episode of *Hoarders: Next Level.* A door leaned on one hinge at the far end. To reach it, he stepped over a surfboard, squashed a stuffed animal, and skipped over a cardboard box that crumbled when his toe caught the edge. He nearly fell but caught his balance on a garbage bag filled with clothes. The door led down a set of stairs into what looked like a dungeon with a rectangle of dim light showing cracked concrete. He tested the water-rotted first step with his toe before committing his weight. He didn't want to find the bottom of the staircase before he meant to. He repeated the process at each step. The moldy stench petered out the closer he got to the basement, replaced with Febreze. He found a closed door at the bottom with a sliver of blue light trying desperately to escape.

Blake rapped a knuckle on the door. "Billy?"

A crash of activity as if someone were preparing to make a break for it and then, "Wh-who is it, who's there, what do you want?"

"It's Blake Powell. We met years ago, with Sophia and my wife, Clara. I need your help with something. Can I come in?"

Footsteps thudded toward the door. Chains and bolts clacked, and the door creaked open half an inch. An eye appeared like a scared cat peeking out from the darkness of a crawlspace.

"Is she there?"

"No, she's in the living room thinking you are holding out on her."

"Okay, phew. Come on in." The door swung open, and a clean shaven, short brown-haired man looked out at him with curiosity.

Blake stepped in.

Chapter 31

Blake walked around a large U-shaped table that gobbled up most of the elbow room. A disarray of computers stood atop or beside one another. Screens and laptops beeped in Morse-code rhythm. Diagrams, charts, graphs, and a poster of a hot rod smothered the walls. Olive paint peeked out between the charts. The pungent bite of Febreze scratched his nostrils. What stood out was the plain closed door on the far left of the room.

"Hey, Blake!" Billy radiated pride, noticing Blake admiring the room like someone might admire a vintage Aston Martin. His hand shot out like a harpoon striking a shark, and they shook. Blake tightened his shoulder to brace against Billy's sharp tugs.

There was no chair for a guest. Billy probably hadn't received a lot of company.

"It's great to see you, Billy. You look...happy."

Billy sprang away and held his palms out as if to shove Blake back. "Hey wait, aren't you a cop? Aren't you? Right? A cop?"

Is he on meth, too? "I'm a soldier. Not at all the same. Right now, I'm trying to help people who suffer from the effects of war."

"Okay, okay, cool, okay, cool-cool-cool, okay." Billy nodded, hugging himself and scratching at both of his arms. He bobbed from his right leg to his left and back. "So, what are you here for? Here for?

I mean, it's cool to see you, but...it's cool to see you, but it's kind of strange, strange that you're here."

Blake held up his chip. "I have some files I can't access. I need someone with expertise to help me out." He left the question hanging in the air as thick as the Febreze.

Billy's eyes and neck twitched, then he returned to scratching his arms. His head kicked to the side in an unheard drum rhythm. "Hmm. Okay, okay, got it, okay. Well, you know that sounds suspicious. Yeah, kind of suspicious. Suspicious. A soldier needing some help? Secret files? From me? Why not the government? They don't have computer whizzes at your disposal?" His finger proclaimed in the air. "Hah! They're too dumb, aren't they? Yeah, they're too dumb." Billy spun around twice, enthralled, a cartoonish smile on his face. "The government only trains the Taliban for shit like this, I bet. Yeah, shit like this must go to the Taliban. How else can they so easily take down our systems?" As Billy described the Taliban, he wrapped an invisible towel around his head. "Oh, you don't know, do you? How the damn Taliban have computer people that totally screw with the world? Oh yeah, they screw with the world. And Americans just keep outsourcing. Because it's only an invasion of privacy under some stupid act if it happens in house. Know what I mean? Yeah, you know what I mean." He sniggered so enthusiastically he almost gobbled on the spit.

Blake had no idea what the hell Billy was talking about, but he nodded anyway. Could he trust Billy to keep his mouth shut?

"No, they aren't very smart. But this is very important information. Can you keep it a secret? Can you help me out? Just between the two of us, right?"

"Do you have any meth?"

The question shouldn't have disappointed Blake, but it did. "No, I don't have any meth. Do you need help scoring some?"

"Shit, yeah, man! Can you help me out? Can you hook me up?"

Blake didn't want to lie to him, but he needed help more than he needed a clear conscious. "How about you help me out, and then I'll see what I can do? No promises. No obligations."

"God," Billy preached, "this man asks for deliverance from his problems and wants to give nothing in return. Nothing!" Billy laughed and raised both arms into the air, staring at the ceiling straight into Heaven. "Lord, should I grant it to him? Yes? He's an old friend—family, kind of—that's true. That's true." His hands dropped, and his eyes fell on Blake. "On your word that you'll try to get me some meth." He put his hand out.

Blake saw the same fog in Billy's eyes as in Angela's. He couldn't help him. Billy needed a treatment center, but Blake knew the odds of recovery. He'd figure it out later. He shook his hand and placed the chip into it, then clutched Billy's hand with firm eye contact, "Keep the files on the drive." He waited a beat...and let go.

Blake followed Billy waddling to one of the larger computers. A flap beneath his heel made his shoes sound like flip-flops. He jabbed the chip into the computer, opened a program, and tapped away.

"AES? That's it? You come to me with AES encryption issues? That's almost insulting. This is like asking me if I can help you change your diapers. Hah. Yeah, change your diapers. I ain't wiping the shit off your ass, though. Whatever's in here, man, got that? Got that? Ha ha, you got that?" Billy stood and rubbed his hand up and down his ass to imitate wiping.

Blake contrived a laugh to humor Billy. Billy clicked for over an hour before he opened the file. Blueprints popped up, numbers and codes attached to each print.

"Not bad. Little slow. Yeah, slow. Took longer without the unlock key. Where the hell is this? Looks like some Area Fifty-One shit. Coding to unlock something. Pretty tough to read without launching, but it needs a sister device. No idea what device that is." Billy leaned in for a closer look, and in his state, he bopped the monitor with his forehead. "You stole this shit, didn't you? Yeah, you stole it. Shit, some army guys are going to bust my door down. What the hell, man? Why did you bring this shit here? People die over shit like this. Oh shit, I hope nobody can tell we accessed this." Billy shot to his feet and gripped his hair in fistfuls. "Ah shit, we're in so much shit. Shit. Shit."

Blake pushed Billy out of the way. How and why would Peter have access to these files?

"We're in trouble." Billy grappled past Blake back to his keyboard. "Wait, I don't see a tracker here." *Click, click-click*—thousands of keys pressed in unison. "That's weird. Someone was already trying to get these files out of the system. Transferred them. The tracker is disabled. You didn't just take it off a government computer? Right, no. No, you didn't take it off a government computer." Billy jumped to his feet and paced quickly enough to burn a hole through the rest of his shoe. His eyes never left the computer screen. He scratched at his arms with manic speed.

Blake shook his head. "No, I didn't. I took it off a disc someone else made. I needed to know what was on it for security reasons. Is there information about a man named Corporal Hodge? Or Lieutenant Zackery? Maybe Senior Chief Wilburg?"

Click-click-click. Billy had an incredible reading ability, and Blake couldn't keep up.

"It's all coding. No names."

"No names? Soldier's ranks?"

"Nope. No, nothing. Wait. A key code. To a room."

Blake followed Billy's reedy fingers to a list of key codes with override numbers. *Archive.* He'd never been to the archive but knew they equipped it with card access. "How old is this?"

Click. Click. "The file is a few days old—at least the copy. Yes, the copy. Originals? Three years old."

He memorized the codes. If the file was a few days old, the keypad had to exist, and the codes might work. Otherwise, why make the copy? What would happen if he used the codes? What was Peter up to?

"What do you want me to do with this? Yeah, what?"

Blake took Billy by the shoulder to stop him from jittering. "Leave it on the chip, and I'll take it with me. Don't copy anything. Pretend I was never here. You know what will happen if the government found out you saw this, right?"

Billy's eyes darkened. "Yeah, not good. No, not good. Yeah, bad." Billy's fingers convulsed over the keyboard, and he pulled out the chip. He paced the room with it clenched in his hands, as if contemplating his next move.

Blake gripped Billy's clean-shaven chin. "You got it? Keep quiet. Just between you and me." If not for Billy's drug problem, he could probably make something of himself.

It had been a long day, and Blake didn't want to make any impetuous decisions. Plenty of those on his record. He hoped to be rested and clearheaded before he decided what to do with the chip.

He arrived at home at one in the morning to find darkened windows at his neighbor's home. Nobody roamed the street. A police car was still parked outside his house. A shadow waved from inside the car, and he waved back. The darkness masked the identity of the officer—they all looked the same with a beret on.

Blake eased the door of his car shut so the sound didn't snap down the street at this hour. He walked to his front door and heard a growl.

He perked his ears up. "Dex?"

The low rumble grew louder.

"Dex, heel." He couldn't see Dex and didn't know it was him. Behind him, the squad car rumbled to life and drove off. *Where is he going?*

Blake edged toward the house, hand at his hip where his knife hid. Yesterday's footprints and holes in the dirt hid any clue if someone had been by. The trees surrounding his home waved in the cool breeze—he could have used Dex's help to sniff out intruders. But if Dex was growling, something was wrong.

Blake ghosted around the house. His patrol took ten minutes, but he didn't uncover anything out of place. He reached the back door and grabbed the handle—

Dex's growl rose into a snarl. Something was wrong. Blake had to enter on the second floor.

He grabbed a ladder covered in leaves. He'd left it beneath an oak tree to build a treehouse for Sophia. He planted the ladder in a dip in the ground against the house and climbed to Sophia's bedroom window. "I hope you ignored me when I told you to lock your window, baby girl," he said to himself. He yanked up, but the window didn't budge. He thumped his head against the pane. "Damnit, you listened." Sophia never listened.

After a quick descent to grab a fist-sized rock, he cracked the window like an egg, big enough to put his hand through.

He released the latch, used the rock to clear the shards, and crawled through. He hadn't cleared everything. A hidden shard sliced open his forearm and he clutched it to slow the bleeding. Blood dripped onto the carpet. He sipped air through clenched teeth. With his free hand, he wrapped his shirt over the wound. He crept down the hall to the bathroom, wiped some of the blood, and cleaned the wound. Dex bounded up the stairs. "Dex. What's up, boy?" Blake stepped into the hallway.

Dex rounded the corner snarling at Blake. The last time Blake had seen that posture, he was wearing a bite suit.

Chapter 32

Dex's teeth were bared, his tail high and turned out.

"Dex, no!"

Blake retreated into the bathroom. Dex dug his claws into the floor and jammed his head into the doorway, preventing Blake from slamming the door shut. *He's not slowing down.* Dex muscled through the door, skidded on the tiled floor and slammed into the vanity. When he recovered, he sprang as if propelled, leaping for Blake's throat.

Blake stumbled back. "Heel!"

Blake threw up an arm, blocking Dex from ripping out his throat. Dex bit down and yanked him to the floor. Pain surged through his arm, so excruciating his ears sang and his vision paled. The blood set Dex off, and he pitched his head from side to side, trying to separate his new toy from its captor. Blake grit his teeth and kicked out at Dex's hind legs.

Blake grabbed Dex's snout with his free hand and threw a leg over him as if mounting a horse. He locked a chokehold around Dex's throat to prevent Dex from shaking his head and rupturing an artery.

Dex released Blake's forearm and skittered back so fast Blake collapsed against the tiles.

"Dex. Heel."

Neither side had an advantage, but Blake was fading. "Dex. Enough!" Blake kicked away, and his blood spattered the walls. He needed a door between them.

Dex leaped. Blake aimed his next punch down Dex's throat, and Dex jumped right into it. He dropped onto the floor, clawing at Blake's forearm. Blake buried his fist in Dex's throat.

This isn't Dex. They did something to him. This isn't him. I don't have a choice. Blake threw his leg over Dex and rolled onto his back, forcing Dex's paws into the air. Dex tightened up with legs flailing. His energy faded. Before the life went out of Dex, Blake released him. He crawled out the door and closed it.

Blake never cried. His father had beaten him when he didn't fall in line and told him to never give himself completely—it opened him up to attack. Never compromise your decisions, he'd said, as if different perspectives were insignificant regardless of their source. A real man had no self-doubt. It was for pussies. *Fuck Dad and his bullshit lessons.*

Chapter 33

A LOUD BANG ON the front door, followed by, "Police! Is anyone home? Blake, are you there? This is the police! Blake?"

Blake wiped his dried eyes and turned on the hallway lights so a rookie cop wouldn't shoot him in his own home. Dried blood opened fresh wounds, and he grit his teeth. Dex whimpered in the bathroom, but Blake knew he couldn't check on him yet. He needed to be sedated and brought to a professional to determine what the fuck happened.

"Blake? Are you here?"

Blake grunted away the sorrow swelling in his throat. "Up here." His words cracked like a heavy smoker.

"Coming to you. Hold your position."

Blake didn't want to move. He rubbed his legs to increase blood circulation—the floor had been cruel to his joints. A pistol peeked from the staircase, followed by Corporal Radcliffe's blue eyes. His thick frame rotated with his head, left to right, as he cleared the room.

"Jesus, Blake, what happened? There's a lot of blood here."

"Dex." Blake blinked, holding back tears. "He tried to kill me."

"What? Why?"

"I don't know. When I got home, I heard him growling. I thought he was warning me. So, I climbed up the..." His words sounded thick. Could Radcliffe understand him? "I climbed up to the second floor.

Dex attacked me. He ignored my commands. I had no control over…"
He cracked his heel against the baseboard. *Did those monsters mess with Dex's brain? Drug him?*

"You need to get to a hospital. You don't look good. Why couldn't—"

"I…I couldn't…I couldn't control him. How did they get to him?" Blake bit his lip. He wanted to ram his fist into the wall. "How did they get into my home with you watching?" Blake's legs felt like lead.

"I don't know. A different squad was on duty last night. I'm on day shift. There weren't any officers when I arrived, so I came in to check."

"Go. Find out," Blake said, trying to sound authoritative through the pain. "And call a base vet. Dex needs to be sedated and have a tox screening done."

"I'm going to call an ambulance, and then I'll look into it."

Blake fell back. He waited a long time in the emptiness, listening to Dex's labored breathing, wishing he could open the bathroom door and Dex would pop up and slather his face with happy kisses.

When the paramedics arrived, they marched up the stairs, sounding less military and more like gangly piano movers hitting everything. The first paramedic must have weighed one fifty, and most of that was in his height.

"I need a phone." He glanced at the medic's nametag: Browning.

"Later, sir. We need to get you to the hospital first."

The second paramedic was a large female, the lifter of the two: five-foot-ten, maybe two hundred pounds. She was Cuddy. He gripped her sleeve. "Please. I need a phone."

"At the hospital."

Browning helped Blake up by his armpits. Blake's arm snapped up, and he dug fingers into a pressure point on Browning's clavicle.

Browning opened his mouth in a ghostly, silent scream and took a knee.

"I need a phone." Blake crouched beside him. "Now."

"Jesus, Blake. Let him go." Radcliffe offered him his cell phone. "Use mine. I haven't heard anything yet from the night watch, but I'll let you know."

If Sophia and Clara were home, they'd be dead.

"Thanks." Blake released Browning and took the phone. It rang repeatedly with no answer. Blake gritted his teeth, frustration mounting. Bile rose in his throat, and he swallowed it down hard. The phone kept ringing—a stark, unanswered echo in the chaos—as the paramedics carefully brought him down the stairs and into the ambulance.

The phone clicked. "Hello?"

Blake's heart was clambering, but he felt an electric shock of relief at Sarah's voice. "Sarah? It's Blake. Are Clara and Sophia there?" He tried to hide his concern. He covered the receiver with his palm and waved at the paramedics. "Turn off the sirens."

"Blake? Is everything okay?" Sarah was barely audible over the commotion on Blake's end. Not a good time to be soft-spoken.

Nothing's okay. "I'm good. Something has come up, though, and I need to speak with Clara and Sophia. Are they there?"

"They're swimming in the lake. I'll go get them, but it might be a bit. Did you want to call back in ten minutes?"

Blake winced when his forearm flared up. "I don't know if I'll get another chance to call." The paramedics wouldn't let him stay on the call when they reached the hospital. Browning glanced at the bandages in a bin on a shelf, then at Blake and his partner.

"Can you see them swimming from where you are?" Blake said into the phone.

"Yes, I'm watching Sophia run off the dock right now. Are you sure everything is okay?"

He smiled. "Yes. Do me a favor. Tell them I love them both and we should gather up what we have and go on a vacation together to a nice cool climate."

"I'll tell them. You sound exhausted. What's that noise in the background?"

"Thanks, Sarah. Tell her exactly that, okay? Can you repeat it back to me?" He made sure she repeated the phrase word for word then tapped the end button.

If someone were listening, they wouldn't realize Blake and Clara had prearranged a phrase years ago. It meant grab the emergency cash and rush north. Should a terrorist find out who the operators were in Echo team, they'd try to kill their family. And if the government decided not to protect them, their families wouldn't be safe.

The fallback spot was in Tacoma. Clara would check into the Candlewood Suites, a long-term hotel they could hide in for months with the money they'd set aside for emergencies.

Browning bandaged the worst of Blake's cuts and put a morphine drip into his arm. Blake fell asleep.

***

Blake woke in an empty hospital room, forearm throbbing. He lifted his arm to find a needle pricking it. *What the hell happened?* He tried to sit up, then his memories of Dex raced through his mind and he plopped down. *Dex.* If Clara and Sophia had been home, Dex would have...he blocked his imagination from moving further. A *bleep* echoed when he shifted his weight. He was ready to leave the hospital.

"Damnit."

A nurse in light-blue scrubs marched in. She strutted through the room with black, low-platform shoes like a lawyer making her opening remarks. She stopped in front of him.

"Lay down." She didn't wait for him to obey. She grabbed his shoulders and forced him down, like he was a disobedient dog.

"Now lay still. If I need you to sit up, I'll tell you. If you're thirsty, you can press this button." She pulled a button out from beneath his bedsheet. "But don't think I'll come into this room every time you call to give you a sip of water like I'm your mom. I have things to do. Patients with other needs. And I don't need you clicking away like a big baby. Got it?" She held him down with her stare.

Blake wondered if she knew his father.

"Understood," he declared back at her.

She harrumphed, heels clicking on her way out of the room. He'd faced worse. Barely.

Chapter 34

HE SLEPT AND WOKE several times over the next day with no visitors. Shadows leeched across the sterile vinyl flooring as the sun dipped away on his second day. He hated lying around. The archive called to him—he'd get his answers and be done with this mess. He switched off the alarm, hoping that wouldn't signal the autocratic nurse at the front desk. He'd rather play with a starving racoon. The tape securing the pads to his chest stripped off a layer of hair when he pulled them off. The morphine drip slid out smoothly. He stumbled out of the bed, using the wall to regain his balance. *Two deep breaths, then a small step forward.* The moment he let go of the wall and placed his weight on his numb leg, he crumpled.

"You look like a fish out of water."

Blake tried to lift himself off the ground, but his arms couldn't take his weight.

"Damnit, stop wiggling around. Kevin, I need some help in here," she shouted out the doorway.

A three-hundred-pound Black man walked into the room like a sumo wrestler stepping into the ring—not a fit fat, but a too-many-bags-of-potato-chips heavyweight. His roly-poly cheeks held back dimples that wanted to laugh. The two heaved Blake onto his bed. Nurse Sergeant Major chuckled in the most asinine way when he grunted.

"I told you not to move." She tsked softly.

It took another day of bitterness until the doctor gave Blake permission to leave after he nodded all the required nods. If Clara and Sophia knew what had happened, they didn't visit. Better if they didn't know. That meant nobody knew where to find them. He hoped Clara had gotten the message.

He had three visitors that day. Colonel Marks wished him the best, taking his report, along with an affirmation that he would find out what happened to Dex. Corporal Finnigan updated him on the night in question—dispatch had sent the officer parked at his house to another scene. The replacement never arrived. Blake was sure someone had gotten to Dex, military or not.

David came shortly before the doctor released him. He carried a fresh set of clothes. "Don't sweat the failed escape attempt. Try to remember your SERE training the next time the nurse gives you a sponge bath." David didn't stay long, which made Blake more impatient to leave.

***

Blake hailed a taxi. He couldn't lead a cab to Genesis—and he needed a uniform and ID to enter anyway—so he gave the cabby his home address.

The cab eased up behind a police car in his driveway. "You can charge this one to Colonel Marks," Blake said. Military personnel on base gave taxis most of their business, and the drivers knew the ranking officers. This driver probably assumed nobody was dumb enough to charge a cab fee to a colonel just to screw with him.

"ID card, please," the cab driver said.

Blake patted his pants, pretending to search for his wallet. "You'll have to trust me. You know where I live."

The cab driver grunted, swore he'd be back if the colonel refused the fees, and drove off.

Blake knocked on the car window of the MP watching his home. A pasty-faced juvenile stared back at him as if he hadn't heard the taxi in the driveway. *I feel well protected.*

The young officer rolled down his window.

"Who are you supposed to be?" Blake sounded gruff but wasn't. Everyone enjoyed messing with a rookie.

The officer's face flushed, his fingers pointing to his name tag as though he couldn't remember it for himself. "Private Lang, sir. I'm watching the house, sir."

"Sir? Do you know whose house you're watching?" He almost felt bad for terrifying the rookie. Almost.

Private Lang scrambled for his notebook and flipped through several pages of chicken scratch. "Sergeant Blake Powell, sir."

"And who do you think I am? I'm either a sergeant, who you shouldn't be referring to as sir, or I'm not authorized to be here, and you should be on your guard."

Private Lang's mouth hung open, narrow eyes locked on Blake. He returned to the notepad, tearing through it until he pulled out an old Christmas photograph of Blake, Clara, and Sophia. "This looks like you, right, Sergeant?"

"You're asking me if that photograph is of me and my family? Is that what they teach at the academy? Let your suspect decide?" Blake smiled inwardly, his face showing none of his amusement.

"Yes, it definitely looks like you, Sergeant, and yes, that is the extent of my security check at the moment. Please step back from the car."

Blake stepped back and crossed his arms. Private Lang opened his car door.

"Do you have ID on you, Sergeant?"

Blake feigned searching his pants pocket. "No, I don't. My dog ate it."

Private Lang's lips twitched, holding back a smirk. He looked down at the photograph and up at Blake, appearing satisfied with the resemblance.

"You can go in, Sergeant." His back straightened as if Blake might ask him to balance a book on his head. "I hope you're feeling better."

My best friend tried to kill me. I don't feel better about anything. No high-energy dog waited to greet him with a wagging tail and an eagerness to please when he walked into the house. A home could change so thoroughly, so quickly.

Blake shaved and dressed in a fresh uniform, skipped a shower because of the bandages, and drove to Genesis. The trees and farms passed in blurs. He breathed in the blinding sun as if to suck up the vitamins and store them.

It didn't take long for the stacks to come into view. He marched through security and the first-floor offices, not a soul saying a word to him. *It's like my first day here. Everyone's focused on their own thing, and nobody's paying attention to what's going on.*

Blake marched through the War Room, anticipating running into Peter or David but finding neither. He sat at his desk and stared blankly at his computer, focused so intently he discerned the individual pixels while waiting for the time to pass. Colonel Marks could be in his office as late as four thirty. Overnight security requested staff leave by six o'clock so they could perform security checks and janitorial staff could do a thorough cleaning of the machines. That left him a safety net of an hour between four forty-five and five forty-five.

Blake searched through David's desk and found the key card hidden beneath folders on his desk. Worth a shot.

The wait dragged on, and each clock tick sounded like a thunderclap. At four thirty, Blake rode the elevator to the top floor. The elevator dinged open, and the smell of bleach the cleaners had used to wash the floor nearly made him choke. He walked down the hallway where he was told the archive room was. At the end of the hallway, a white door stopped his progress. A miniscule sign, barely legible from ten feet away, read *Archives*. Only a key swipe hung on the wall beside the door.

Chapter 35

Blake swiped David's card, and a tiny dot in the top left corner blipped red. The alarm buzzed defiantly. He tried again with the same result. *Damnit, he doesn't have access.*

He tapped the walls for a hidden panel. Nothing. He retraced his steps to the nearest panel by the hallway entrance. Each key of the panel lit up.

What would happen if he punched in the code he'd memorized from Billy? Would someone get a message that he'd tried the code? He punched it in. The light flashed green, but nothing happened. He punched in the code again, and again the light flashed green. This time he thought he heard a click down the hallway and headed back to the archive.

The archive door stood ajar. Blake pulled it open and stepped inside. The door drifted shut behind him. Fluorescent lights strung in dashed lines throughout the room blinded him. Nowhere to hide.

Rows of shelves stood in rank and file. Two-foot gaps separated the rows. Just enough to squeeze through. Would he find what he needed in an hour? His hope leeched away. He pulled out a random box. It was labeled "Andres, Aidan" and contained several disks and files. They'd organized the room by last name. How could there be so many files? The Genesis Project hadn't been active long enough for all of this.

He followed the rows, glancing at the last name on each box tag as he passed. *The Genesis must be older than I thought.*

A click on the door behind him broke his concentration. He knelt and listened. Footsteps clattered down the aisles, starting and stopping several times. Blake ducked down the aisles. The clattering abated, and a door opened then closed with a swish of air.

Wilburg, Hodge, and Zackery were his primary targets, Marcus Talbert if he could manage it. It was ten past five now. Thirty-five minutes left. It had to be enough time. Fifteen minutes passed before he located Hodge. The files weren't alphabetical after all. There were names like Hank, Henry, and Herman filed after Hodge. The label on the box read *Hodge, Peter (1).* There must be two boxes. The second wasn't nearby.

Inside the box, Blake found files and a few disks. *Why the second box? Maybe there isn't one.* Blake pulled one of the files out and scanned it. There was too much to read. He snagged the disk that hopefully contained his original nightmare and moved on to the next name. Box two, if it existed, would have to wait.

Five minutes later, he found Wilburg. Five thirty now, fifteen minutes left. Dust kicked into the air when he pulled a disc from Wilburg's box. He stifled a cough. *Nobody had looked at this disk in a long time. Could there be more copies or a digital archive?*

Blake risked searching for Zackery, needing a comparison between the two men's nightmares. Five fifty-one.

Zackery's box was empty. Blake shook the box, expecting something to jiggle loose at the bottom. He found a small disc tucked into the bottom flap.

Heavy clicking barraged through the room followed by a screech like an old grocery-store cart. The screech stopped, but the echo had been so loud he couldn't tell when it had stopped.

Blake crouched, stalked down the aisle and prepared to duck into another aisle. Two aisles away from the door, he stopped and listened. *Nice and easy.*

He counted to sixty. Then again. And again. Rounding the last aisle before the door, he felt dread and relief. The door was in sight, but whoever had come in wasn't.

Blake counted to ten, forcing himself to count slowly. He darted straight for the door. Quick. Slid through. Got out.

"Hello?" a woman called out from behind him. "Who's there?"

Blake didn't look back. He strode down the hallway, forced himself to walk casually even though every muscle in his legs screamed for him to hurry. They twitched in restlessness. He'd recovered two discs and would have to risk watching them in the video room after hours or waiting until tomorrow. Security would never allow their release. Either option sucked.

He sauntered into the cubicles, most of the room empty except for a few officers—probably a last-ditch effort to finish a report. They glanced up likely to confirm he wasn't there to kick them out, then continued typing.

No security guards yet. So far, so good. The elevator chimed for BL3. When the door opened, he thought his mission was over.

Chapter 36

BLAKE FROZE. PETER'S LEGS stuck out from a panel beneath the Genesis. *What now? Peter should be gone already.* The slightest noise, muscle cramp or sixth sense might alert Peter to his presence. *I need to be in that video room alone.*

He waited in his office until Peter left twenty minutes later at six thirty. If he could keep away from security and sneak into the control room where there were no cameras, he could access the files without disruption.

Don't spot me on camera. Blake reached the video control room, a small space with a computer and a large projector. A bazaar of steel chairs had been wheeled haphazardly in front of the projector. He waited several minutes for the computer to boot, anticipating security storming into the room.

He placed the Hodge disc into the CD-ROM and closed the tray. The projector immediately flickered to life and a video flashed on.

Three men sat in single file cleaning their weapons, backs facing a cave wall. Corporal Hodge whirled to the right when a rifle switch clicked. Disassembled, his weapon rested on the blanket beneath him, so he slid out his knife and crouched. Someone yelled to his left, and he whipped around to the noise. Sergeant Malcove held his throat with both hands, blood escaping between his fingers.

Corporal Hodge wrapped Malcove's neck with the cloth he'd been wiping his rifle with. No use. Another cry. Corporal Emit sat still, a thin red line drawing itself at his throat, and then blood spurted out in pulsing arcs. He fell over, gurgling. An Afghani in uniform with lieutenant bars hovered over Captain Geraro, a knife buried in Geraro's chest.

"No!" Corporal Hodge charged.

The Afghani smiled and threw a small canister at Corporal Hodge. A brilliant flash devoured the visibility on screen. When color returned, the man was gone.

The video ended.

That couldn't be. Blake whipped to his feet and cupped his chin. The Afghani was no senator. He had probably stolen the uniform. Corporal Hodge's dream had been altered. The video proved the senator wasn't involved. How had Corporal Hodge changed his nightmare? The Genesis wasn't capable of changing one of the key people in the dream. Blake had tried with Talbert. It never stuck.

Did he want to view the second disc? *Yes.* He thumped the wall. *I have to.* He slid Senior Chief Wilburg's disc into the drive. As the video played, the images of the dead bodies hanging from walls twisted his stomach. He wasn't in a hurry to see it again. The nightmare played out identical to Blake's experience with him.

The disc labeled Zackery was last to play. Identical scenes unfolded. When Lieutenant Zackery turned at the noise, it was a small boy, maybe five years old. Not the rebel Blake had seen before. Dried blood covered the boy's face, and Lieutenant Zackery hugged his skeletal frame. He hadn't strangled anyone. *So how did those changes happen? What influenced Wilburg to kill his wife? What really happened?*

Chapter 37

BLAKE PULLED THE DISC out of the tray, frozen in disbelief. He was jolted back into reality when he noticed the air tasted like ash. He opened the door, and a wall of smoke hit him so hard he dropped to his knees in search of air. *Not my imagination.* He couldn't see anything. No idea where the source of the flame was.

He kicked the door shut and yanked on the fire alarm. The sprinklers should have been flooding the room, but nothing happened. Not even an alarm. Someone must have turned the system off.

Blake pulled off his shirt and rolled it into a ball. Without water to dampen it, he placed it over his nose and mouth and crawled toward the thickest of the smoke against every instinct, knowing it was his only chance to reach the stairs.

His next cough scorched the pit of his lungs. He crawled, scrambling against the wall toward the staircase. The heat turned up and the flames revealed themselves in the lunchroom. The flames had already reached the staircase, leaving the elevator as the only option. It wouldn't be locked down with the fire system deactivated.

The elevator pinged when he pushed the button. His eyes felt heavy. *Stay awake. You have to stay awake.*

When the elevator door opened, Blake barely mustered the energy to raise his head. *Peter.*

Peter's eyes looked like saucers. He didn't notice Blake lying on the floor until he tripped forward. Blake barely felt the impact. Peter dragged him into the elevator by his armpits, the elevator pinged, and he passed out.

***

Blake snorted awake in bed, a respirator covering his face. He choked on the tube running down his throat.

"It's helping you breathe. Quit squirming."

As intense as the fire was, Nurse Sergeant Major was just as intense. He tried to ask her what happened, but the sound came out like a gurgle.

"Don't try to talk. It's better for everyone. Maybe this time you'll listen and lay still. The doctor will be in to speak with you soon." A smile, almost friendly, maybe empathetic, creased her lips. She walked out of the room, and Blake fell back to sleep.

***

A different nurse pulled the tube out of his throat and replaced it with a nebulizer. Breathing felt easier, but his chest burned.

A doctor entered the room, his voice carrying a distinct accent that hinted at Eastern Asian origin. "You're lucky to be alive," he said, his expression obscured by a medical mask.

Blake grunted as he shifted his weight. "Thanks."

"What's that?" The doctor leaned in. "Oh, don't thank me. Thank your friend, the man that pulled you into the elevator. He's the reason you're alive. I'm Doctor Aoki. No need to shake my hand. I'm sure you've already met Nurse Eleanor. Feeling a little beat up today?"

Blake faked a smile. That resulted in an outburst of coughs from achy lungs. When the doctor didn't leave, Blake assumed he was waiting for something, so he nodded. That sparked the doctor. He waved his hands as he spoke about Blake's damaged lungs and how long it could be before they'd release him. Days? Blake stopped listening.

The discs! Had the fire been for him, or for the evidence? Nobody could have gotten into that room to retrieve the discs with the amount of smoke suffocating the floor—unless they had oxygen.

"Are you okay?" Doctor Aoki said.

Blake winced and sputtered a cough. He tried to cushion it to relieve the strain on his lungs. "Feel like trash."

The doctor's head twitched. "Have you heard anything I've said, Mr. Powell?"

"I'm sorry, doctor. How long will I be here?" *I need to get out of here.*

Doctor Aoki tapped his clipboard and shook his head disapprovingly. "Another day or two and only into someone's care. We tried contacting your wife. Do you have a way for us to reach her? We can't release you without someone caring for you. It's too dangerous. You'll need minor medical care at home. Nurse Eleanor can teach your primary caregiver."

Caregiver. As if I'm eighty years old. "My wife and daughter went on a trip for two weeks. Both of them left their phones behind—radio silence so they could bond."

"Is there anyone we can contact?"

"David Guarnere." He gave the doctor David's number.

Blake spent the rest of the day breathing into a mask, avoiding Nurse Sergeant Major, when she suddenly stomped into his room.

"Hey, war hero, I got in touch with David. If all goes well he'll pick you up tomorrow morning. He's taking you to his place until your wife is back."

Blake thanked her, but she had already darted out of the room.

The next morning, Blake woke to the sun blaring in his eyes. Nurse Sergeant Major wheeled him downstairs to the front door. "David will be here soon. I have things to do. If you need a babysitter, yell at the nurses over at the desk behind you. They're not doing anything. I'm sure they'll be happy to leap to their feet for you." She placed the nebulizer in his lap and thundered away. She'd make a great drill sergeant.

Fifteen minutes later, David strolled in from D Wing, hair spiked as if he'd had a fight with a tin of hair gel. He loomed over Blake with a smirk. "Do you have a girlfriend on the side here? You keep coming back."

"You know if you're not ten minutes early..." Blake shielded his eyes from the sun pouring through the front doors.

"I'm late to avoid waiting, and learning how to care for your dumb ass. They wouldn't let me sign you out without their lesson."

Blake shrugged. "Any update on Dex?" One hand gripped the mask to his face while the other shook David's hand. He felt wobbly even lifting his arm.

"He's doing well. Typical Dex to be back on his feet. No idea what happened yet. Or they aren't telling me," David said. "They should punch your frequent visitor's card. Free ice cream with every five visits."

"I'd take a nurse that didn't behave like a drill sergeant," Blake mumbled behind the mask.

David faked a shudder. "The stories you tell about drill sergeants. Let's jet." He picked up the nebulizer in one arm and wheeled Blake with the other. He swerved, trying to balance both.

"Are you trying to get me killed?" Blake jammed down on the wheels to shift left and right, losing a layer of skin to the rubber. The sun beat hard like an overbearing inquisition light, and sweat dripped down his T-shirt. He felt grimy, as if he hadn't showered in three days. David smelled worse with the tavern odors of flat beer and chicken wings. Blake rubbed his palms dry on his pants, then he wiped his shirt across his forehead. "It looks like you found the furthest spot in the lot. Well done. Did you save thirty cents?"

David dropped the nebulizer on Blake's lap and shoved. Blake jangled down the sidewalk, the chair rattling to a stop on the dead grass. He coughed hard enough to crack a rib.

David couldn't hide his laugh behind his hand.

"You're an asshole," Blake said.

They reached David's emerald Fiat 500. David wheeled him to the passenger's side. Blake removed the nebulizer mask. "Two soldiers get into a tampon. One—"

David moved to smack Blake in the back of the head, but Blake grabbed his arm and hauled him over the wheelchair. The weight of David's body flung Blake on top of him, elbowing him in the ribs.

David ripped off Blake's mask. "You can't win, old man. You're too beat up."

Blake coughed, the exertion more than he was ready for. David handed Blake his mask. Blake sucked in the oxygen. It tasted divine.

David stood up and stuck his hand out to Blake. "Coming to my place? I can't promise the best care with Helen, but she'll feed you and keep you alive."

Blake took the hand and allowed David to hoist him to his feet and into the chair. "I need to get my car and get to Sophia."

"Are you serious? There's no way you can drive."

Blake shrugged. "I'll manage. Remember when I got shot in the shoulder? I drove all the way from Washington to Odessa in a cast."

"Your driving is crap even when you're healthy. I can't let you hurt yourself. Or someone else. Clara would never forgive me, and Sophia wouldn't stop barking in my ear for the rest of my life."

Blake smiled. If only Sophia were that persistent with her math homework. "Drop me off at home and pretend you saw Clara."

David pinched the bridge of his nose. He knew he wouldn't win this fight. He yanked open the passenger door. "Stubborn bastard. You're going to make me drive you, aren't you?"

"If you don't, I'll get there myself." Blake clutched the wheelchair to stand and wobbled into the car.

David slammed the door shut, stuffed the wheelchair into the trunk, and circled around to the driver's side. When he slid into the car, he said, "I know you. You'll drag your own sorry ass all the way there if you have to." He gripped the steering wheel. "I must be an idiot for agreeing to this." He tightened his jaw and thumped the wheel. "Fine. Just point me in the right direction. Where are we headed?"

"They're in Tacoma." Blake ran his tongue along his teeth to clear out the taste of hospital oatmeal. "In our safe zone."

"There's no such place as a safe zone. Have to try, though, right?" David shifted into reverse and screeched out of his spot. Never a gentle driver. He jabbed the car into drive and bolted down the laneway. "We have a long drive ahead of us. Why don't you explain what you were doing at seven at night in the War Room after nearly being killed by your dog a couple of days earlier?"

Blake updated David on everything he knew. He started with Peter, raising his suspicion about the dangers of the Genesis machines and the videos of Corporal Hodge, Senior Chief Wilburg, and Lieutenant Zackery. Blake hesitated to tell David about the note left for him in the explosive box, but he needed someone to talk it through, and David was his closest friend outside of Echo team.

"This keeps getting worse," David said when Blake finished.

Chapter 38

The trip from the hospital to Tacoma lasted fifteen hours. Fifteen hours of jerking from one lane to the next and playing chicken with traffic lights. David didn't pull the car over except for gas or a piss stop, and only after dismantling all the arguments about using the empty water bottles they had. He tossed Blake a newspaper and told him to read, giving him about five minutes to look it over.

"What'd you think of the article?" David asked, pulling the newspaper out of Blake's hands.

Blake shrugged. "It makes sense."

"It's crazy is what it is!" David swerved around a Honda Accord going the speed limit. The speed limit was always a minimum for David. "There are soldiers with such damaging PTSD that these doctors probed so deep into their heads the patients became vegetables. Only, they aren't vegetables, right? They're just locked away behind the doctors' lies. That other doctor, whatever his name is. He's trying to snap them out of it; get them functioning again."

"Yeah, crazy."

David threw up his hands. "Fine. Your mission. So, Peter saved your life, but you also think he's the reason Dex attacked you?"

Blake didn't know anything yet. "Peter might be okay. Maybe he's being manipulated—they have something on him, or they threatened his family. He didn't hesitate to save me when he could have left me for dead. I really have no clue." He tightly balled his hands. "Have you heard anything about the cause of the fire?"

Colonel Marks had stopped in to see him in the hospital and mentioned the fire was under investigation. They didn't have evidence to show the fire was intentional.

"No idea, Blake. Colonel Marks told me about the fire, but that was it." David veered into the lane on the left, and the driver behind him cursed at him through the car horn. "He said they had no leads. With classified tech, they investigate internally, so the investigator will probably take his time. Or her time. Their time? I didn't see Peter, but that's not surprising. He probably had lung damage. The media isn't being looped in."

Blake pounded his thigh. *There are a lot of dead people because of the Genesis, and nobody's owning up. How far will they go to cover this up?* "Any theories on what happened to General Talbert? Why he lost it when I made a minor change that shouldn't have bothered him?"

David shook his head, driving through another yellow light. "No idea."

"Under investigation?" Blake snorted.

They passed through desert, prairies, and farm country. Farming seemed simple. Plow fields, clean up after the pigs, and hunt whenever you want. But Blake would never be happy without the heart-stopping action of combat.

They entered Tacoma on Interstate 5 and exited on Bridgeport Way, which linked up with the Pacific Highway Southwest. The Candlewood Suites was north on the left side of the road.

David swerved into the driveway and parked. The hotel looked like a blindingly white version of the Holiday Inn. It was their meeting point because it accepted last-minute long-term reservations by cash, and the staff never asked questions. In addition, a few major interstates headed to Canada, Seattle, back to California via Portland, or out to sea via a nearby highway exit.

Blake's cell phone rattled with a call from the hospital. "Hello?"

"Is this Blake Powell?" said Nurse Sergeant Major, with a quiet exhale.

"Yes."

She spoke as if someone had just told her they were withholding her paycheck. "You left without taking any extra nebulizer medication with you. Your meds will run out by the end of the day tomorrow. Stop by the ER and pick up a couple of spares. You'll need them for a week, and you'll need to replace them every couple of days."

The nebulizer had run out an hour ago when his breathing became wheezes. Blake coughed up a ball of phlegm and spat it into a tissue.

"Mr. Powell?"

Blake pointed at the phone against his ear. "Thank you. We'll be by soon. Have a good d—"

She hung up before he could finish.

Blake side-eyed David. "Don't say a word to anyone about where you dropped me off. Okay?"

David threw up his hands in mock defeat. "Hey, you know me. I'll keep it quiet."

"I have to ask you a favor. I'll need to know what's going on with the investigation. It was arson, I'm sure of that. Can you keep an ear out for information on the discs I left behind to see if they get recovered? I'll pick up a disposable and text you with it."

"If they find those discs, they'll be useless. You know that, right? Nothing electronic survived that fire."

"Maybe. Can I get you a room for the night?"

"Thanks, but I want to get back to Helen. Not my first time driving for a couple of days. Sorry I can't stay to help."

David helped Blake out of the car and into his wheelchair, then careened out of the hotel lot and twisted through the streets.

Blake wheeled into the lobby. The receptionist leaped to her feet, eyes widened, hand to mouth. *Do I look that bad?* He considered reassuring her he didn't need any help as he rolled to the counter, but she hadn't offered any. Scribbles marred the walls in an infant's graffiti.

The receptionist thawed. "Can I help you, sir?" Her nametag said Cindy. She looked like a Cindy: shoulder-length dark hair, unblemished skin, not beautiful or symmetrical. She reminded Blake of a Picasso.

"My wife and daughter are staying here. I'd like to know what room they're in."

Cindy moved to the computer monitor and entered a login key with jittery fingers. "Their names?" Her voice was shaky.

"Clara and Sophia Powell."

Cindy consulted the computer while Blake breathed into the mask, pretending it still offered him help. She furrowed her brow and bunched one cheek. "Sorry, we have no guests by that name here."

"Okay, thank you." Blake wasn't surprised, and he didn't press the issue. They shouldn't be traveling under their own names.

Blake rolled into the lobby and waited to see if they walked by. The lobby was as hospitable as the parking lot: no snacks, no coffee, not even a restaurant down the hall. There wouldn't be a lot of reason Clara or Sophia would leave their room. Probably the way Cindy wanted it.

Blake's lungs burned when he rolled outside and spat phlegm onto the sidewalk. He wheeled around to the back of the hotel, knowing Sophia wouldn't stay put. She'd want to soak up the sun with a book.

The back of the hotel had a few rusted lawn chairs lined up on a patio with a three-foot brick wall separating two large barbecues. A canopy extended from the building to cover them. A hefty man laid on one of the lawn chairs, and another barbecued something that smelled fishy.

The man at the barbecue looked up after he flipped his meal. "Hello. Are you okay?" He sounded airy despite his size and facial hair.

"Sort of. I'm looking for my wife and daughter."

"We've been here three days and have met some delightful young ladies. What are their names? Maybe I can help."

"Clara and Sophia."

A big smile spread across his lips. He tapped his fish over some flame with the tongues. "Yes, we've met them. Sophia is such a sweetheart."

"Do you know what room they're in?"

The man on the lawn chair got up, moseyed to the man at the barbecue, and pulled him in for a side-squeeze. "We aren't sure. We've only talked to them outside. They're usually around."

Blake nodded and wheeled himself through the propped-open rear entrance, too excited to wait for her to come to him. "Sophia?" he shouted. This made him double over and sputter. "Sophia?"

Chapter 39

Blake waited for a ten count. He braced his lungs. "So—" He coughed, a smoldering ache in his chest. When the scratchiness subsided, he tried again. "Sophia!" Waited a twenty count. "Clara!" They probably couldn't hear his ragged voice.

A door creaked behind him, and Clara peeked out. She'd never looked so beautiful. Chestnut hair swept her shoulders, and her smile was so wide it reminded him of the day they were married. The smile faded when her eyes found the wheelchair.

"Oh, my god. What happened?"

"I'm great. It's fine. Don't worry about me." He wheeled over and hugged her legs. Sophia shoved the door wide and leaped into the embrace. Blake stifled a cough. His lungs still seared.

He wheeled into the room and pulled himself onto the bed, lying back on the pillows. His lungs felt full, and he coughed. Clara curled up to him on his left and Sophia on his right.

He slept sporadically for two days, content with knowing Sophia and Clara were safe. They took the news about Dex hard, terrified that he might never be the same. He'd been a protector and a playmate. Sophia talked about Dex's silliness whenever he rolled in the snow after a fresh snowfall or jumped on her when she was moody. He knew what to do better than anyone, licking her face or lying in her lap as if he fit. Clara talked about how much of a mooch he was—always grinning a greedy smile. Once, she'd given him a scrap of steak from the counter. The rest of the week, he came begging at exactly the same time of day.

Blake told them battle stories. He generalized about how many times Dex had saved Echo team's life by sniffing out trip flares, anti-personnel mines, or explosives. Dex led several insertions against enemy forces, never giving up a fight as if he knew what could happen to the rest of the team if he did.

Blake felt better after another day of rest. He woke to an empty room with sounds like popcorn drumming the window. He tested his legs and decided he didn't need the wheelchair any longer. He pulled open the curtains to a drizzle pattering the ground, nearly invisible, and ashen clouds. What were Clara and Sophia doing with no sun to soak up? He scanned the vehicles and people in the parking lot and gazebo, where napkins, paper plates, and plastic cups littered the ground. He whipped the curtains shut and headed to the door.

The phone rang. Nobody had the phone number. Probably reception. He followed the phone line to the wall to ensure it wasn't attached to a bomb—*old habits die hard.*

He picked up the receiver. "Hello?"

"Hello, this is room service. We are phoning in your requested wake-up call." The voice was Cindy's. She sounded annoyed that he'd inconvenienced her.

"I didn't order a wake-up call."

She harrumphed. "Well, I'm showing a request here, so good morning. If there was a mistake, we at the Candlewood Suites apologize." She didn't sound sorry. Had Clara ordered a wake-up call?

"Thanks so much." Blake hung up and sat on the bed. The phone rang again.

He slouched and rolled his eyes. "I'm awake, thanks."

"Hello, Blake." Not Cindy. The voice sounded male and robotic, disguised with some kind of digital voice manipulator.

He held the receiver away from his ear and gawked at it. "Who is this?"

"Who I am isn't important. What's important is what I know. I remember your wife and daughter. It took some time to find the terrorist who dropped the suitcase in Cantone Mall and detonated the bomb that killed all those people, but I found your wife and daughter all the same. How do you live with it? A sworn soldier. Highly decorated, living with terrorists. I have to believe you didn't know."

Where the hell were Clara and Sophia? "I'm not sure what you think you know. Listen to me. You can't trust your memories." How could he explain the Genesis? *Someone modified your memories, and now you think my wife and daughter blew people up, but it's all a lie. They want you to hurt me so I'll end my investigation.*

The man's laughter barked through the phone, drawn out and so loud it rattled the mechanism inside the earpiece. "How are your lungs, Blake? Do they burn? I hope the smoke didn't do too much damage. It's better than being dead."

Blake wanted to smash the phone against the wall. "I feel like I smoked a cigarette or two. You must be a marine, given how badly you failed that mission."

"Failed that mission? Are you trying to make me angry? Remember to laugh when you hold your dead wife and daughter."

Blake squeezed the phone until the plastic cracked. "If you touch my family," Blake whispered, "I...will...kill...you. Hang up and walk away from this mission before you do something you'll regret."

"Do something I regret?" the man bellowed. "What about your regrets? All those dead bodies your wife and daughter left behind?

Arms and legs blown apart. Bombs are ruthless." The man had to gulp a few breaths to calm down. "I guess you're disavowing any knowledge. Do you want to decide who dies first? It's a mercy to be first. They don't have to watch the other die."

No sound in the background. "Leave them out of this. It's me you want. I'm the one investigating."

"That's noble, but I know you weren't there. So living can be your penance for keeping their actions to yourself."

Blake had never wanted to kill someone so badly. "Leave my family out of this, you fuck."

"Keep your cool under stress, soldier. Acting out is a sign of PTSD. You don't want to be labeled with that, do you?"

Blake squeezed the phone cord in a fist. "My family isn't who you think they are. Listen. A piece of technology has tampered with your memories. What you remember isn't real. Someone wants you to hurt me so I end my investigation."

"I'd like to believe that, Sergeant, I would. People in your situation lie. In fact, did you know most people in your situation lie more than they tell the truth?"

Keep him on the phone. Where the hell are Clara and Sophia? "I don't know. I haven't had a lot of time to think about it."

"But it's true, isn't it? The lies? Ah, the beautiful lies. Not as beautiful as your wife and daughter, of course."

"You know where they are." Blake bit back his desperation. He had to breathe through the fear. Two-second inhalation, four-second exhalation, repeat.

"They're sitting at a table about four hundred yards away under a small umbrella, sipping on lattes and laughing. They have no idea we're speaking." A pause. "I almost forgot. We were discussing who dies first. Or do you prefer to pick? Girl first? That's normal, right? Your call. Who first, Blake?"

Blake shot up despite his recovering legs. "Yourself."

"That's not an option. Hang on. They're leaving the restaurant."

Get out of there. Hurry!

"We're out of time, Blake. Quickly, who dies?"

Chapter 40

THE PHONE DROPPED TO the carpet. Blake sprinted to the exit. His lungs burned, and he hacked while he ran. Clara and Sophia crossed the road into the hotel parking lot, headed straight for him.

"Clara! Sophia! Run!"

They both paused and gawked across the street at him.

Crack. Sophia bounced sideways into Clara. They both tumbled to the ground.

Bystanders froze or hit the pavement despite the puddles. Traffic screeched to a standstill, and metal clashed with several abrupt fender benders.

Blood seeped down Sophia's side—*no no no no*—Clara screamed. Blake ran to them, almost skidded in the rain-slicked street, and wrapped Sophia in his arms. "We need to get inside." He hurried back to the hotel among gasps and frozen onlookers. He threw himself through the door and into the hallway. He buckled to his knees the moment the doors shut.

"What did you do? What did you do?" Clara cuffed Blake in the chest. Again. And again. He deflected her next shot.

People gathered, bystanders who didn't know how to respond. Sirens wailed closer.

This is my fault. I killed my daughter. Why didn't I stop the investigation? He shook. He felt cold. He clutched her head to his cheek, curled into a ball, and rocked. *Why didn't I stop?*

"You did this." Sobs racked Clara's words into notched syllables.

"I thought we'd be safe here. I don't know how they found us." Blake kept rocking, kept mewing between breaths. *They followed me here from the hospital. Maybe they followed David.* None of the faces at gas stations or restaurants had stood out. They'd stopped on the side of the road, made circles in neighborhoods along the way, and fueled up more than they needed to. They tried to throw off any tails. *How were they found?*

Blake ran his fingers through Sophia's hair. "My baby girl. Stay with me, Sophia."

The phone rang from down the hall, a tone that cackled at Blake.

"Don't answer it," Clara said.

"They aren't going to get away with this," he said, heading to their room. "Hello?"

"Justice for all those victims." The same mechanical voice.

"You're dead."

The man laughed. He sounded as jovial as a child at Disney. Every laugh grated along Blake's spine. He wanted to destroy everything in sight.

The phone cracked in Blake's grasp, nearly drowning out the whine of an ambulance. The plastic sliced his hand. "I'm going to rip out your heart while you're still alive so you can watch your own death."

"Your wife, Blake. She's guilty too."

"I'm coming for you."

"I'm a ghost. Take a few days with the FBI. They're on the way. Hate your life if it helps. Enjoy some time with your wife while you can."

"What the hell is wrong with you?"

"Your parents, your wife's parents—they can *all* be collateral damage."

Blake ripped the phone out of the wall and hurled it across the room. It lodged in the wall. The lamp followed. He slammed his fist through the drywall. Everything he could break, he did. The walls looked like a beehive.

By the time Blake exhausted himself, the stretcher was gone. The paramedic avoided his eyes.

***

The police took statements and notified Colonel Marks, who would meet with him later. They wouldn't let Blake or Clara leave.

FBI agents arrived a few hours afterward.

"I'm sorry to have to tell you this," the agent said, his eyes focused on the blood-stained floor. "She didn't make it."

Clara collapsed. She slapped Blake away when he tried to embrace her.

The agents took more statements and asked about the shooter. Blake couldn't stop thinking about Sophia's pause when he yelled her name, or the way her head and body kicked to the side as the bullet struck.

The FBI transferred them to a safe house, a standard one-bedroom apartment with minimal furniture. Blake paced the nineteenth-century kitchen—old cupboards and a small table he could barely play cards on. The fridge and the stove looked ready to fall apart. The paramedic had offered a sedative before departing, but Blake refused to be in a vulnerable state of mind.

"I'm leaving," he said to the FBI agent standing guard at the front door.

The agent glared. "Sit down. I'll let you know when authorization comes down the chain of command. Go be with your wife."

Blake stepped closer to the agent until they almost pecked noses. "This is your last chance to get out of my way."

Chapter 41

THE AGENT FROWNED. "I know you just lost your daughter, Sergeant. But I can't let you leave."

Had they not briefed her on who she's protecting? Blake sidestepped to get around her and she popped in front of him, arm locked in extension, hand out like a stop sign.

"Get out of my way. Last chance," Blake said.

"You're not leaving. *Sir.*"

Blake punched her in the throat. She crumbled, gargling, hands on her neck, trying to carve out a new hole to breathe through. "I warned you." Blake shoved her out of the way, took the keys from her pocket, and marched out.

An icy breeze blew across his face—a night Sophia would sit on the porch with popcorn, rocking in her favorite chair, listening to pop music, wrapped in a blanket. What he would do to see her dancing to Lady Gaga right now.

He opened the door to the FBI sedan and started the car. The engine purred like a Leopard tank and smelled like cigarettes and coffee.

Time to get offensive. He'd drive to Genesis and beat an explanation out of Peter. Failing that, he'd find Colonel Marks and do the same. The time for worrying about military discharges and assault charges was gone. The sniper hadn't understood what taking Sophia away from him would do.

The radio squawked constantly, nothing about a stolen car. Either they kept it under the radar, or the agent hadn't reported it yet. Blake felt himself nodding off while driving. He pulled over for a few minutes of sleep. *Just a few minutes.*

He lurched awake with a sharp breath that reminded him his lungs were still recovering. He checked his watch when he woke. *Damnit. Five hours?* He expected to see a helicopter and twenty armed FBI agents, but only the sun crested the top of the trees. He rolled down the window and took a breath. *Man, it's cold out.*

He drove until he reached Fort Thompson, trying to think of anything but the bullet spinning Sophia into Clara. *Focus. Find the sniper. That's the mission.* He pulled over a couple of blocks from his house. Streetlamps lit the way, so he stalked through the bush to hide his silhouette.

He tucked tightly to the siding at the back of the house and followed it around. No police cars waited in the driveway—the MPs must have been called off.

The humidity clung to his shirt and chilled it against his skin, each breath damp in his lungs. His cough echoed through the yard as sharply as porcelain shattering. Both of his cars were parked in the driveway with their keys in his locked house.

Blake grabbed a piece of plywood and glanced around the street. Nobody. He broke the glass on the front porch window as quietly as he could, hoping neighbors hadn't heard. *Ten minutes maximum, to be safe.*

He kicked out the shards of shattered glass and stepped through. The keys for Clara's Dodge Caravan lay on the stand, the big D reflecting the moonlight. He snatched them, retraced his steps, and started the van.

Getting Peter out of the building wouldn't be easy. If security cameras spotted Blake, MPs would arrest him or, at the very least, detain him. He needed a plan.

He entered the compound and turned right toward the parking structure. Private Donald waved as he pulled up. Two other soldiers stood nearby, their faces obscured in the darkness.

"It's late to be signing in, isn't it, Sergeant? Building is closed after six."

Blake glanced at the display on the radio, as if realizing for the first time how late it was. "Sorry. Didn't see the time. My wife and I had a fight. I thought I would get some paperwork done. Maybe camp out in the office."

The private nodded, his lips curled. "Security doesn't like anyone inside. But I won't stop you. I've had my share of problems with the old lady—no place to fall back to."

Blake whipped off a casual salute. "Thanks, Private. I appreciate it."

Peter complained months ago about how parking on the lowest levels felt like a sausage jamming into a hot dog bun so Blake parked at the top—level three. He didn't find Peter's car in the lot.

When he entered the building, lazy security guards came to life, hands on pistols, scowls locked and loaded. One guard hung back while the other strode up. He planted his feet in front of Blake and peered down, intimidation forced through every pepperoni-scented huff. He stood a foot taller than Blake, but the act wasn't working.

The guard grunted. "Building is closed until morning, Sergeant." No questioning why Blake was there. He expected Blake to cower away.

"I'm investigating a malfunction that caused the fire. Call Colonel Marks and disrupt him and his family to clarify why I need access at eight p.m. It's not the middle of the night." The MP insignia on the guard's uniform had two hooks. "The brass is asking for an immediate resolution—all hands on deck. *You* take the load for bothering Colonel Marks. Last time I called him at home, he wanted to jump through the phone to rip off my epaulet."

The corporal hesitated. The act was cracking. The huffs were less forced. Blake heard the thought pinging around his head like ticks on a clock. "How long you planning to be here?"

"In the War Room, two hours tops."

"The War Room wasn't damaged in the fire."

"It's an investigation, Corporal. You're not authorized to know the details. Call Colonel Marks or get out of my way."

The corporal glanced at his partner who shrugged. "Okay. I'll check on you in an hour."

"Appreciated. Thank you, Corporal."

They both returned to their booth behind the screening room. Blake went through security and rode the elevator down. When the elevator door whirred open, Blake smelled the smoke from the fire still spicing the air. The ventilation tried its best, but the sting might not dissipate for a few weeks. His jaw dropped when he entered the War Room.

It was pristine—the fire doors had kept the fire out. They must have closed independently of the alarm that hadn't activated.

Blake hustled to Genesis I. The screen responded to his touch, and he browsed through the dream sequences to find the one that matched the mall murders. If he could locate the dream and the soldier it came from, he'd have his sniper. Nothing came up on Genesis I. He scanned

II and III. Still nothing. He'd need to go inside to find it. Anyone could have renamed it. *No easy day.*

***

A familiar darkness surrounded him. The Genesis took longer than expected to respond. Blake couldn't exit until the controls loaded. "Hello?" His voice echoed around in the tomb stillness of the setting. He waved his hands around.

White streaks ran like rain in front of him. *It's malfunctioning.* His vision blurred, and for a moment, he thought he fell unconscious. Then the room buzzed to life, and the menu popped up with six options for missions—the general's mission appeared with an asterisk and a list of other missions from David and Isaac. Nothing related to Canton Mall or a bombing. Dead end.

He exited the Genesis and sat up, catching his breath as the lid whirred away. Normally brimming with noise and bustling with energy, the room remained quiet and empty. It was worth a try. He'd have to get answers from Peter.

Blake returned to the garage and parked near the lot entrance. He slept in his van, startling awake when he couldn't remember where he was. If he could make it through the night without dreaming about Sophia, he'd be happy.

Shortly after the sun came up, a car grumbled into the parking lot. Not Peter's. Another car twenty minutes later and then several more. *Where the hell is Peter?* Blake gripped the steering wheel and wrung it, rolling his skin into pinches. *There he is.* The tiny lemon box drove past him. Blake waited to make sure Peter didn't know anyone followed.

Blake drove up to the third floor, passed Peter, and parked several spaces away. He sprang out of the van, impatient to wait for a perfect moment to sneak up on him.

Peter looked up. His breath clipped. "Hello, S-S-Sergeant. I'm g-glad you're o-okay."

Blake bolted to him. He gripped Peter by the throat and slammed him against his car. Peter put up his hands, and Blake punched him in the ribs before placing him in an arm bar and slamming his head onto the hood.

"I'm going to ask you some questions, and you're going to answer them. If you don't tell me the truth...or if you refuse to answer...I'll kill you. Do you understand me?" Blake's eyes burned like smoldering embers in the darkness. "If you'd rather be dead than talking, that's up to you."

Chapter 42

Blake let Peter think about it. Peter used that time to urinate in his coveralls instead. "Are you ready?"

Peter tried to nod with his head pressed into the dent on his hood.

Blake lifted Peter's head slightly and slammed it back down. He suppressed the urge to do it again. Peter's face crunched, and blood splattered across the hood. "I want verbal answers. Not body language."

As Blake pressed Peter's head harder into the hood, Peter whimpered. "Y-yes...y-yes, I u-understand."

Blake's lip curled. "Good. What was on the chip I took with the encrypted files?" A good warm-up test; Peter probably didn't know he already had the answer. If Blake were a lie detector, this was a baseline question.

"O-o-kay, just don't hurt me p-p-please." Peter threw his hands up and winced. "P-pictures of m-me o-on vacation w-with a girl f-from the department, o-o-okay? S-she's married. I-I'm not supposed to..."

Blake speared his foot into the side of Peter's kneecap. The crack of his knee reminded Blake of being in the bush. Blake covered Peter's mouth to stifle the scream.

"The next time you lie to me, you die. What was on the chip?"

If Peter hadn't realized the danger he was in, he understood now. Blake heard cars in the lot, but none had driven to the third floor; it wasn't busy enough yet. When Peter began mewing under his hand, Blake eased it off.

"I s-saved your l-life," he cried. "I-I pulled y-you out of th-the fire."

"My little girl is dead, and you know something. What was on the goddamn chip?"

"C-coding," Peter cried. "Coding f-for Genesis. It l-looked like r-remote access. Please s-stop h-hurting me. I s-swear it's t-true. Just s-stop."

Now Blake was getting somewhere. "What were you planning to do with it?"

"A s-security p-protocol test to s-see if the i-information could m-make it out of," he sucked in a ragged breath, "out of the b-building. It's p-procedure, I s-swear. N-none of the c-coding worked."

Blake pressed on the side of his busted knee. "That's convenient. Who were you running the test for?"

"Marks!" Peter bellowed.

Blake slapped him. "Keep it to a murmur. You don't want anyone coming to investigate. Trust me."

"O-o-o-okay," Peter's eyes crept around, "o-okay." He choked on a snivel. "Colonel Marks. F-for C-Colonel Marks, okay? I a-always run t-tests for h-him. E-every month. W-we test n-new security p-protocols to m-make sure w-we're impenetrable."

Colonel Marks again. Blake would have to visit the colonel next. *Wonderful.* That meant the end of his career and cementing himself as a traitor to his country. But what price was that in contrast to Sophia's death? "What resulted from the test?"

"It n-never made it o-out of the b-building. Security c-caught me o-on the w-way out."

I hadn't been stopped by security, so why had Peter? Had Colonel Marks warned security? Were more people involved?

"What's wrong with the Genesis Project? You came to me to tell me something but changed your mind. What was it?"

Blake applied more pressure on his knee. Peter gasped. He'd pass out soon.

"Someonewas-t-tamperingwi-withthem-machines." Peter gunned the words.

Blake leaned in. "Say that again? Slower."

Peter bit his lip so hard from the pain that he drew blood. He shuddered, caught his breath, and then tried to even his words out. "Someone was t-tampering with the m-machines. I th-thought it might h-have something to do w-with the s-soldiers that were k-killing people." He swallowed. "I f-found a m-microchip that shouldn't h-have been in the m-machine. Th-the chip went to C-Colonel Marks. I n-never heard about w-what happened, s-so I was going to w-warn you about u-using the machine. I s-swear I don't kn-know what the chip did. B-but with th-the murders...No p-protocols were b-being put in p-place to prevent f-further tampering. I was t-too afraid to t-talk to C-Colonel Marks, and w-when I t-tried, he was b-busy."

Blake let Peter go, and he dropped to the concrete with a yelp. His knee bent unnaturally. "You'll need a hospital. I'm sorry to hear your knee gave out and you fell on the hood of your car, smashing your face into it."

"I'm c-clumsy." Peter pulled up his pant leg to check his knee. Swollen and bruising.

So what next? Colonel Marks was the best target, but he wouldn't go down easily. If they had to fight, it needed to be away from Genesis. He drove down to the first floor and waited, leaving Peter to sort out his knee problems.

An hour later, Colonel Marks drove into the parking garage in a clean black Mercedes Benz. Sunglasses hid his eyes.

Blake waited until Colonel Marks headed out for the day at four thirty. Blake followed a minute later.

Private Donald waited at the security exit. "Have a good day, Sergeant. I hope things get better on the home front."

Blake nodded. "Thanks."

It didn't take long to find Colonel Marks cruising down the road. Blake slowed, maintaining a cautious distance. Blake hoped he didn't notice the vehicle behind him, especially on the interstate.

They drove down Willowcrest Road until reaching Fort Thompson. Blake lost sight of the colonel but found him a minute later, headed to Ortona Crescent, a wealthy officer's lane. Colonel Marks pulled into the driveway of a two-story brick house with a large front yard and lush grass. A balcony and large tinted glass windows watched sentinel over the front yard.

The colonel disappeared inside. Blake waited until the sun dissipated, then rang the doorbell. He rubbed his hand along his pant pocket, feeling for his knife. The cold steel pressed against his thigh.

A tall, slender woman in pink jogging pants and a Berkeley sweater answered the door. "Hello." She smiled brightly and ran her fingers through short, curly blonde hair. She didn't look like the type of woman that belonged with Colonel Marks. Blake imagined a serious, rigid woman, unwilling to relax.

"Hello," Blake said. "I'm Sergeant Powell. I'd like to speak to Colonel Marks."

Her smile grew. *She's too beautiful for him.* He nearly felt bad for what he was going to do to her husband.

"Sure, I'll get him. I'm Joyce."

Blake shook her hand. She had a firm grip. "Thanks."

She stepped back and signaled for him to come inside. He wavered, not wanting to deal with the colonel inside their home with his family watching.

"I'll wait out here. I need the cool air to clean out my lungs."

A few minutes later, Colonel Marks stepped outside wearing jogging pants similar to his wife, but black. He wore a T-shirt with *Army* written on it.

"Sergeant? What the hell is going on? Who gave you my address?"

"We need to talk." Blake turned and walked to the front lawn.

"You don't come to my home and tell me we need to talk, Sergeant. You book with my office and we talk during office hours. This is a serious breach of security protocols. I won't discuss anything with you here."

Blake spun, his leg coming up high and striking the colonel hard in the face. The colonel collapsed.

Chapter 43

"WHAT THE HELL ARE you doing?" the colonel bellowed. He rubbed a smear of dirt on his chin.

Blake kicked him in the face again, hearing a pleasant crunch. *Second broken nose of the day.*

Colonel Marks leapt up and ran toward home. Blake caught up in four steps and kicked the colonel's legs out from under him.

"I told you we need to talk, Colonel."

Blake lifted the colonel by his T-shirt, now bloodstained, and scanned the windows to make sure nobody was watching. Satisfied that military police weren't on the way, Blake pulled the colonel down the driveway and shoved him into his van.

"You'll be court-martialed for this." The colonel sounded nasal, as if someone pinched his nose.

Blake nodded. "We're beyond a court-martial, sir. My daughter is dead."

"I'm sorry, Sergeant. But that won't get you out of assaulting a superior."

"A sniper killed her." Blake shook. "I have some questions for you, and I'm going to need answers."

The colonel stared at him—his face shifted from furious to disconcerted. His jaw loosened.

Blake drove down a dirt road soldiers used to hunt small game birds. Hunting was technically illegal on a military base, but the police didn't enforce it. Since it wasn't hunting season, nobody was on the road. The road wound on for miles until they reached a sandpit used for target shooting—unofficially.

He stopped the van and put the key in the pocket opposite his knife. The colonel stepped out of the van, hands in his own pocket. Blake watched him closely. *Pull a knife and I'll kill you.*

Blake climbed out of the van. "There are a lot of questions I need answers to. And I need the truth. You know how this works."

The colonel shook his head, careful of what the motion would inflict on his nose. He yanked a tissue from his pocket, flapped it out, and wiped the blood trickling down to his chin. "No, I *don't* know how this works. You already think I'm guilty, don't you? That's why I'm here. There's something messed up in your brain." He winced. "I don't think they'll be able to set this back right, you ass."

Blake gritted his teeth. "I used to carry out assassinations for the government. People like you have been using me to kill for years." He pounded the hood of the van. "But that was fine—it got personal when someone killed my daughter."

"I'd like to help, even after you broke my goddamn nose. But I don't have the information you need. I don't know who killed Sophia. Jesus, I'm sorry, Sergeant. Why would you think I know who killed her?"

"Let's start with what you know. There are security tests being conducted, forcing internal staff to steal classified information and sneak it outside the Genesis. Is there a security leak? Is that why you're running tests?"

The colonel shrugged. "We don't know. That's why we run tests. If we successfully extract classified documents, something in the system is broken." He held the bloody tissue at his side. It was soaked, and he needed another.

Blake breathed in the colonel's face. "This is you being cooperative?"

The colonel didn't back away. "What do you want me to tell you? The successes and failures of every attempt? Who is involved? What do you want to know? The security checks have been going on for years."

"Recent activity. Who made the last attempt and what happened?"

The colonel stepped out of Blake's reach. "Peter was the last person to attempt it. Security caught him on his way. The information didn't leak."

"What information?"

"Coding software that looked like a back door into the Genesis." The colonel stuffed the rag in his jogging pants pocket. "In case it got out and we wanted to track it, we could detect the coding parameters, and it would walk us right to the user's front door." He screened his eyes to look in the van window. "Do you have any more tissues in there? My nose is gushing."

Blake breathed deeply. The fresh air suddenly felt suffocating, as if he had a gas mask on. "The information got out. I got it out."

The colonel's face reddened. "Not anything of value, you didn't."

"How did Peter get caught?"

The colonel paced. Sand kicked up, nearly making Blake cough. "I don't know. When I received the chip from security, the report showed they searched Peter. They'd questioned him about the content on the drive, but he didn't have satisfactory answers."

"They didn't search or question me."

The colonel's eyes found the ground, his hands out to his sides, his fists clenched. "Then there are security issues." The blood had leeched all the way down his shirt, blotching out the word *Army*.

"Major security issues, Colonel. My daughter is dead!" He cracked his fist against the passenger window. *Anyone involved in Sophia's death...* He needed to focus up, but he couldn't, the rage pulsating in his body like lava coursing through the veins of an erupting volcano.

"I have a son. I'd act just like you if someone hurt him, but I can't help you." Colonel Marks covered his nose. His breaths whistled, and the bridge was purpling. "Who did you give the information to?"

"A contact. I kept a copy of the data. It had access codes on it."

"The information on the disc isn't compromised. It's fake." The colonel sputtered a quick laugh. "Did you look closely? If you tried to access the building using the codes, you would fail."

"The archive code is accurate," Blake spat. "I used it to access the archive."

Colonel Marks' brows frowned. "That's not possible. I entered the fake codes into the files myself."

"You did a shit job, sir. Or someone else accessed your file and entered the proper codes. Why would they do that?"

"What were you doing in the archive?" The colonel scoffed. "You know you're going to prison for a long time, Sergeant."

"Live long enough to tell someone, Colonel. I'm going to kill everyone involved with my daughter's death, including you."

"I had nothing to do with your daughter's death."

Colonel Marks was the only man that had access to the Genesis and could authorize the modification of the sniper's nightmare. *What was his motivation to hurt Sophia?* Blake hoped he would find out momentarily. "All the information I have points at you. I need a reason not to kill you." Blake rolled his shoulders back. "Sir."

Colonel Marks squared his stance with Blake as if to challenge him. "What can I tell you? Might as well kill me. You can torture me into telling you what you want. It won't be the truth."

Blake needed to tread carefully. He didn't want to give too much away. He weighed his next question. "Why did you deny David access to the archive?"

"The archive? He has access. Has for months."

Blake noticed bright stars in the sky. There were as many stars as he had problems. His gaze returned to Colonel Marks. "David didn't have access. He went to you to request access two days ago. You denied him. Why do you think I stole the access code? His card didn't work."

"David was working on two projects that required access, and he had it. His cases are ongoing, so his card works...assuming he gave you the right one."

Blake pulled his knife from his pocket and flicked it open. The four-inch blade glinted in the moonlight. He raised the blade to the colonel's throat. The colonel deflected the attack, knocking the blade away. With his free hand, he reached into his pocket and pulled out a similar knife.

"Is this who you want to be?" the colonel said. "Just another screwed up operator? I should have left you with Echo team to remain a trigger-happy Boy Scout."

Blake caught his knife in the air before Colonel Marks flicked his open. If he let the colonel go, he'd never get to interrogate him. Why would David lie to him? David knew where Blake and his family were staying. Did someone torture the information out of him? "How are the killings linked?" Blake asked. "Do you know about the problems with the Genesis?"

Colonel Marks looked away when a wolf howl in the distance drove through the field. "We are looking into the possibility of nightmares returning over time with Corporal Hodge, but that doesn't make the Genesis a failure. Sometimes soldiers revert. That's the way it is."

"And what about Peter's report on the microchip hidden in one of the Genesis computers? What was the microchip for?"

The colonel shook his head. "What microchip?"

"Peter found a microchip that shouldn't have been in the Genesis. He didn't know what it was for, but he gave it to you to check out. What was it for?"

"Peter didn't give me anything."

"I'm going to get the truth, sir. Get in the van." Blake returned his knife to his pocket. He wasn't an expert at reading people, but the colonel's steady gaze and relaxed shoulders made Blake fairly confident Colonel Marks was telling the truth. The colonel complied but didn't put his own knife away, choosing to use it as a barrier between them.

Blake stopped in front of the colonel's house. "I'm going to continue this investigation, sir. I need some time to figure it out. There's something wrong with the Genesis, and the soldiers are killing because of it. I'm asking for time."

"Go to hell." Colonel Marks revved up and spat blood on Blake's dashboard. He raised his hand and put pressure on his nose and cheek. He disappeared inside his home.

Nothing Blake could do now. He'd head to David's home to find out what he knew. Hopefully, a parade of military police wasn't waiting.

Chapter 44

Blake arrived at David's home after midnight. He imagined David cuddling with his wife while his kids slept comfortably and safe in their beds. The house looked modest for someone with David's salary—a single-story bungalow huddled with other bungalows on both sides as if for warmth against a frosty night. If Blake broke in and someone screamed, the sound would wake the neighbors. The best approach would be the same as the colonel: knock on the door and get David outside.

Blake walked up the driveway to the front door. A small lamp revealed the living room. He rapped on the door, then harder when nobody responded.

"One minute please," a nervous female voice said...Where was David? Blake stepped back from the door and scanned the street for movement.

The door crept open, and Helen's head peeked out. Seeing him, she opened the door, tears building in her sunken eyes. Strands of hair reached out in all directions. Her cheeks were puffy with the saturation of tears. "Is he dead? He better be dead if he's not home." She sniffled.

Blake's head jerked back. The one scenario he wasn't prepared for. "Are you kidding? He's not home?"

Helen wiped the back of her wrist against an eye. "He didn't come home yesterday. I thought the worst. Haven't been able to sleep or eat. Can't concentrate. He always calls to tell me he'll be at the office late. He didn't call, Blake. But he's okay, right? Right?" A hushed sob racked her body.

She must have panicked all night. Whenever the families got together, she smiled and looked happy, but Blake never bought it. She seemed miserable, maybe a bit unsure of herself. Though pudgy from a lack of exercise and two children, she had a plain beauty about her.

"I'm sure he's fine. I haven't seen him today. A lot has been going on at work."

Her brows furrowed. "What's going on? I know, I know. You can't say. He's been working late at the office for weeks, and I feel like I never see him. Is he with someone else? Would you tell me if he was? No, you wouldn't, would you? Goddamn brotherhood."

Her words struck a chord. "He was at the office the last few nights?"

"Longer. The last week? Maybe two."

David hadn't told his wife he had driven Blake to Tacoma. "Did you try calling him at the office?"

Helen waved her hand dismissively, which was the first time Blake noticed she held a wadded-up Kleenex. "The operator gave me the runaround. They kept connecting me to his office, but he didn't answer. If he was even there."

She ran her fingers through her hair several times, using them like a brush. She stepped to one side and swept her arms into the foyer. "I'm sorry, where are my manners? Do you want to come in? I have tea or coffee or...a Coke. I'd like to say he'll be home soon but..."

Blake smiled. "Thank you, but I should be going. I'll swing by the office and see if he's there. I'll tell him to call home if I see him."

"Thank you, Blake."

Blake had no other play than his office. He'd find out if David was there, or he'd wait for him to show up.

***

Blake waved to Private Donald, who waved him into the parking garage without stopping him. Blake thought about asking if he'd seen David, but he didn't want to get questioned. The lot was nearly abandoned. He parked on the first floor. No sign of David's car.

He entered the building and flew through security without being questioned. They must have assumed he was there for the same reason as last night. Someone should have asked anyway.

He reached the War Room, scanning for movement. Empty, but all the lights were on. Blake headed to his office...and stopped short. Had he heard something? A crinkling noise. He followed along the wall and peeked around the corner. David studied a paper in his hands. Not even looking up, he walked to what used to be an empty desk beside his. Papers now littered the desk.

Blake knocked on the doorframe. "Working late?" He stepped into the office, blocking the door.

David startled and almost toppled backward into a chair. He put a hand to his chest. "Frig, Blake. You scared the hell out of me. What are you doing here? Why aren't you in Tacoma? You look like death."

"I'd ask you the same thing."

"Working late. I have a few projects on the go."

"Did one of those projects include killing my daughter?" Blake swallowed down his emotions.

David had recovered from his shock, but a new shock paled him. "Wait, what? What the hell are you talking about? Jesus Christ, Blake, Sophia's dead?"

Blake fiddled with his knife, flicking at it in his pocket. "I spoke with the colonel. You never went to him to get access to the archive. You already had access. All of your support was bullshit. My daughter is dead. Did you do it?"

David straightened and opened his hands in surrender. "Blake, look. I'm sorry about the archive. I made a judgment call that you were going to get yourself into a lot of trouble, so I wanted to slow you down until things blew over. But you were like a stray bullet, and nothing was going to stop you until you hit something—no matter how far off the mark you might be."

A footfall dragged across the floor behind Blake. He turned to Peter breathing down his neck, his face swollen and his leg locked in a cast to his thigh.

"So, you're in on it too?" Blake stared at him.

Peter growled. "I'm j-j-just ending your r-rampage. You're h-hurting people. You h-hurt me."

Blake snarled. "I should have broken both kneecaps. The colonel never received the chip. Is it still in there, corrupting operators?"

"Peter came to me because you broke his leg, Blake. You're out of control. I didn't know someone got to Sophia. No!" David reached out, his palm blocking something.

Blake whirled around, aware of how much time he'd given Peter with his back turned. Peter pointed a Taser at Blake. Two coils shot out and hit Blake, then—darkness.

Chapter 45

SEVEN MONTHS IN THE Genesis, and Blake never got used to the dark.

"Comfortable?"

A lamp illuminated the space. General Talbert sat at a wooden desk. He lowered his hand from the lamp switch. Blake found himself in a chair as comfortable as sitting on barbed wire. His wrists were cuffed to the arms.

Blake thrashed around to break free of the cuffs, but they held. "What's going on?"

General Talbert smiled. "Well, that depends on you. This environment can go a few ways at the push of a button." He waved, and a small box with a button appeared.

The Genesis should only load dreams and dream sequences from a client's dreams. This must be what the chip did. It removed those limitations so Genesis could do more—like programming a soldier to think someone else committed a crime. "You can shove your button up your ass. Tell me what's going on. Where's Peter and David?" He shifted to get his hand in his pocket. His knife was gone.

"Missing something? There's no need for violence." General Talbert tented his hands in front of him. "I do plan to answer your questions. You're in the Genesis. I control what's happening here. You're here because you need to understand what we're doing."

"We?"

"There are a lot of people involved in the Genesis, some at official capacities and some with investments. That's not important. You know Corporal Hodge killed the senator because of implanted dreams. You know the same of Senior Chief Wilburg, also known as Lieutenant Zackery, who killed his wife."

"Implanted dreams?" Blake wished he'd figured it out sooner.

"You aren't stupid. You must have connected the dots by now." General Talbert's thumb circled the button as if he considered pressing it.

"You weaponized the Genesis against soldiers with post-traumatic stress. Manipulated them to get what you wanted." Blake's breathing labored.

General Talbert studied him, gauging if Blake was full of it. His lips opened, then shut.

Blake leaned forward in the chair. "Isn't it easier to find a highly trained operator to hit targets? Why all the trouble with Genesis?"

"Spare me that look on your face, Sergeant. The Genesis is still being used as intended. But we shouldn't ignore the opportunity for advancement. We can sell the Genesis to combat PTSD to other countries, not only the US. The mental health of everyone should be a priority."

"Why was I assigned to your nightmares?" Blake attempted another tug at the cuffs. They only clattered against the chair's arms. Still no give.

General Talbert smiled. "Your help sustained the rest of the project. I'd lost focus with those nightmares, drinking too much and...wanting to die. I couldn't close big deals or do demos. With your help, the screams of the nightmares have faded to whispers. I've proven the capabilities of the Genesis and closed a major deal. You've done well by me, Sergeant, so when you started poking around, I didn't have you killed. The project needs you to continue your work. We're here to discuss the terms of you keeping quiet and doing your job."

"Sir, are you asking me to look the other way while you implant memories into soldiers so they can unwittingly murder people for you? Why did you have Corporal Hodge kill the senator? Why did Senior Chief Wilburg kill his wife?"

"We're turning lesser-trained soldiers into heroes. We're giving them a purpose they believe in and will fight for. They won't question, they won't hesitate. Hodge and Wilburg were required demonstrations of the Genesis's potential. The senator was near the end of his tenure and not very popular in his state. Senior Chief Wilburg was a mistake; he was supposed to kill a judge's son. You probably didn't recognize the boy."

Blake shot forward in the chair. "The rebel wasn't the target? It was the little boy?"

"Made a mess of things. I admit, we rushed that one. I should have held back another month. He would have killed the judge's kid instead. Who knows, maybe not." General Talbert's gaze flickered to the left as if he were thinking back on something. "It's different in the psyche...killing a kid. Not enough research on that."

"And my daughter. Who did you send to kill my daughter?" Blake almost stood up, cuffed to the chair or not.

General Talbert raised his hands. "Relax, Sergeant. I don't know."

"You're lying. The killer thought my wife and daughter set off a bomb in a mall. The Genesis is the only way that could have happened." Blake heaved on the cuffs until the chair's arms broke. He bounded over the desk and landed atop General Talbert with his hands wrapped around his throat. General Talbert's eyes popped as he grappled Blake's clawed hands, trying to pull him away. Blake bashed him across the face, and again, each strike doing more damage than the last. Blake's fists chewed up his chin, his lips, his nose. Blood covered Blake's knuckles and spattered on his face. He punched until General Talbert's skull caved in and tears brimmed in Blake's eyes. Blake collapsed backward on the desk, and when he opened his eyes, General Talbert's body was gone.

"I had hoped you'd be more reasonable, Sergeant." General Talbert snarled from across the room. He stood beside a desk. Another lamp clicked on. "How many times will you have to kill me to get it out of your system? Should I mirror myself so you can kill two or three of me at once?" His words echoed as if playing on a speaker. "Your daughter was innocent, I know."

"How does this end?"

"You return to your duties and use the Genesis to help soldiers. If you don't, I'm afraid you aren't going to make it out of here alive. We will eventually sell the Genesis hardware along with the microchip that allows for its manipulation to foreign countries, and they'll never know they've allowed us a back door into their soldiers' minds."

"You killed innocent people for the purpose of killing more innocent people so you can control the bad guys?"

"Collateral damage. Buyers wanted proof of effect, and it had to be big enough to draw attention. Corporal Hodge is being held for murder, and his trial will never become public. He'll live the rest of his life in prison. If I'm lucky, they will release Senior Chief Wilburg. They can't hold him accountable for what he did in a dream. Thanks to your report, he might spend some time in a psych ward, but that should be it." He grinned like the Grinch stealing Christmas. "I might even use him again."

"You're just like the terrorists we've been trained to fight."

General Talbert laughed. "I was afraid you might not see it my way. This is disappointing, but we're here because I had my doubts."

"Why my daughter? That's why I'm here."

General Talbert emerged in front of him. Blake clenched his hands and almost felt General Talbert's neck in his grip again.

"I told you I don't know. We want you to stick with the program, helping us turn soldiers into heroes, driven with purpose and passion. What sense would it make to kill your daughter?"

"And yet, my daughter is dead. All of this," Blake raised his arms to indicate the Genesis, "is the cause."

"I can bring your daughter back. The Genesis will allow you to spend time with her. As much as you want. You can help soldiers by day and spend time with your daughter at night. She can live again." Talbert's eyes twinkled.

"She won't be real. Won't grow up. Won't get a job and have a family."

"I'm afraid there isn't much time, and your loyalty is in question. You're a man of your word. I'll need at least that."

Blake saw Sophia's body hitting the ground again. He heard the crack of the shot splitting the air. They'd do this to other girls—to anyone they wanted.

"Did you start the fire? Was Peter supposed to let me die?" If Blake had died, Sophia would be alive.

A table appeared between them. Chairs surrounded it. General Talbert sat in one chair and beckoned Blake to do the same in the other.

"Peter was a pawn." General Talbert crossed his legs. "A working-class grunt that's smart in his own way but dumb in most. He had his uses, but he was never meant to pull you from the fire. I set it when

I saw you inside the video room. It's like operators have nine lives when they sign the paperwork."

"You should have done a better job with that fire."

General Talbert slammed his fist on the table, and it crumbled under his virtual strength. "I'm sorry we couldn't come to an agreement. Let's not waste any more of my time. There's one test I haven't conducted yet. That's seeing how far I can push someone's mind before they lose it." He lifted the box, which had a small button on it. He raised an eyebrow to prompt Blake to change his mind, and when he didn't, General Talbert pressed the button.

The darkness faded, and Blake stood in the upstairs hallway at home. A growl revved behind him. He turned to find Dex with his teeth barred, foaming at the mouth.

***

"Dex, sit." Blake gave a commanding and unwavering order. Dex stalked forward, the same unrecognizable rage he'd seen last time. What had they done to turn Dex against him? Could Blake undo it?

He felt for his pocketknife, keeping his eyes locked on Dex.

"Daddy? What's going on? Why is Dex growling at you?" Sophia peeked into the hallway from her bedroom.

"Sophia! Get back in your room." Blake's knees buckled, and he fought to keep steady against the wall.

Dex tore past him like he wasn't there. Blake lunged for him, but his muscles jelled, and his jump fell short. Sophia heard Blake but hadn't moved. Her face contorted, her hands shot up to block Dex. She didn't have time to run—Dex leaped and locked his jaws onto her throat. Blake tried to pull Dex off, but Dex wouldn't relinquish his vice grip.

Sophia screamed, but it was hopeless. *She's already dead. She's already dead.*

With a snarl and one monstrous tug that defied Dex's strength, Dex ripped out her trachea and disappeared. She gurgled. Blake cradled her body. It felt so real, even though he knew she'd already died. Blood pooled around him. He smelled rotting flesh and tried to swallow, but his throat was dry.

Darkness. Then light again.

Blake stood in the hallway with Dex growling once more. "Enough!" Blake leaped at Dex with clumsy reflexes. Dex jumped out of the way, standing between Sophia's room and Blake.

She poked her head out her door. "What's going on, Dad?"

"Sophia, stay in your room!"

Dex raced to her. Blake wanted to cover his eyes and pretend it wasn't happening, but he couldn't. He ran to her and watched Dex kill her all over again. Splashes of blood decorated the walls. It smothered him...until he stood in an empty hallway again with Dex in front of him.

The nightmare looped a dozen times. Watching her die didn't get easier. He couldn't save her, no matter what he tried. The dream always allowed Dex to charge past him and maul her.

The general must have changed things up. When the darkness lifted, he lay prone on a building roof with a sniper rifle on his shoulder. The rocks beneath him jabbed his stomach and legs. Several large buildings stood like giants in front of him. He looked through the scope as if a puppet on strings and saw Sophia and Clara walking away from the coffee shop.

No. No. Not this.

Sophia approached the hotel, pausing on the street—he yelled for her. He tried to take his finger off the trigger, but the machine overrode him. Blake turned the dial on the scope two notches right to adjust for the wind, and he felt himself slowly squeeze the trigger.

"No!" he cried.

He relived the scene several times, swallowing vomit. Each time he felt himself breaking inside a little more. He needed to plunge deeper within himself if he had any hope of surviving this assault. As if General Talbert could sense his thoughts, the room darkened.

Blake stood at the entrance of a hospital—the same dream as Senior Chief Wilburg. In this sequence, he didn't see bodies strung against the wall, but rather people walking the hallways, talking and laughing. General Talbert planned to make him the killer in Wilburg's nightmare.

He fought to keep his body from stepping forward, but the Genesis dragged him in anyway. Blake focused on withdrawing to another place in his head. He knew the soul could barricade itself behind a wall, so he built a barrier in his mind and felt himself drift away from the Genesis and into oblivion.

Chapter 46

Clara sat opposite Colonel Marks. They weren't in his office—no personal effects for a man so highly ranked, a cheap desk, and uncomfortable chairs. Nearly an interrogation room.

"Why am I here? I don't like driving to Fort Thompson." Clara had almost refused to show up at the meeting. Blake had abandoned her to the FBI, forcing her to cope with her daughter's death by herself. *He's out there looking for Sophia's killer like a pissed-off vigilante, when he should be home with me. She's dead. No amount of killing will bring her back.*

Colonel Marks ignored Clara's statement. "How are you, Clara? I'm very sorry for your loss."

Formality. It's not why I'm here. The colonel had strict fraternization rules, so he'd only seen her twice and never stuck around at a barbecue. Not that Blake had ever been there mentally either. She peered out the window, then back at the colonel. She wondered why his nose looked broken. "I'm here, Colonel. What do you want?" Her shoulders lifted and sagged as she breathed.

The colonel pulled a small wooden box from a drawer in the desk and placed it on the table. "Do you mind?"

She shrugged. "It's your office. It won't kill me." She almost laughed at that.

Colonel Marks lit a cigar and puffed a few times. The smell wafted to the ceiling fan. She coughed. The bitterness in the air was stifling, and she almost put her hand over her nose. She licked her lips, tasting ash.

Colonel Marks noticed her sour face and opened the window to let the smoke escape. "Sorry." He wafted out the smoke and then returned to his seat. "We found Sergeant...Blake. We found your husband."

She wanted to feel relieved, but she felt only anxiety and rage. She wanted to slap Blake in the face as badly as she wanted to bury herself in his arms. "He's okay?"

Colonel Marks looked at the door.

"He's dead, isn't he?" she asked.

"He's alive; not really cognitively."

"Get to the point." She leaned forward with a glower. "What aren't you telling me?"

His lip curled. He set the cigar in the ashtray. "A police officer recognized him in the streets and picked him up. The officer tried to talk to him, but he was catatonic. I haven't spoken to him."

Clara stared at the cigar box on the table. "Where is he?"

"He's being held at the Fort Thompson Psychiatric care facility."

Clara slapped the table, almost pouncing to her feet. "Being held? What did he do?"

"He has his own room." Colonel Marks put his hands up to disarm her. "He doesn't interact. Medication hasn't helped. He's *catatonic*." The colonel stood. "They want you to visit him to see if you can help. Brain waves show there isn't much going on. I'm sorry to tell you this: they don't have hope that he'll ever be the same. Clara. I wanted to tell you in person. He accomplished a lot of good in his career. I'm very sorry, Clara."

This is the colonel's fault. My husband. My daughter. Colonel Marks had invited her to an office that wasn't his, puffed smoke into her eyes, told her that her husband was brain-dead, and offered no support. Goddamn military. When she'd met Blake, he'd been all she needed—caring and compassionate, bold and driven. He'd helped her save children under her care in Bangladesh. He was supposed to head straight to India to eliminate some security threat, but when the storm hit, he stayed with her. Back then, he did what he felt was right. The military should have fired him. She wished they had. His men covered for him, making it seem like he couldn't get past the storm even if he wanted to; the timing was wrong. All the Delta guys looked after each other, and it seemed Blake felt forever indebted to them. Over time she'd gotten used to him in faraway places, and she'd sucked it up and adapted until he disconnected and she shriveled up inside. *I've sacrificed so much, and this is what's left for me. It's not fair.*

"I should see him." She shot to her feet and turned to leave.

"You've lost a lot," he said as she reached the doorway. "It's not easy. I know. I've lost people close to me too. If you ever need to talk..."

She left before he saw her tears. The heels of her shoes clicked like a soldier on parade as she headed into the elevator and pressed G. She turned from the elevator mirrors. *Ugh,* weathered—old and scraggly. *Alone.*

***

The psych ward was a fifteen-minute drive away. Just as she pictured, the ward was a single-story brick rectangle bereft of character. Inside, the clean ivory walls and spotless laminate flooring gleamed more fiercely than those elevator mirrors. The thick odor of bleach made it difficult for her to breathe. The front desk would have passed any white-glove inspection. "I'm Clara Powell. I'd like to speak with my husband, Sergeant Blake Powell."

"Certainly, dear. Let me pull up his file." The front desk nurse tapped away at her computer keyboard. She wore a v-tent cap atop hair pulled back so tightly it almost stretched her temples. The woman's smile gleaned with the walls until she read something and cocked her head. "You'll have to speak with Doctor Stillman before you see your husband."

Chapter 47

Clara followed the nurse down a corridor in sharp contrast to the celebration of lights before: drab and underlit. They entered an office with sun shouting through full-wall windows. She shielded her eyes as the light glared off the corner of the room so loudly it obscured it.

"Have a seat on the sofa. He'll be with you in a few minutes."

She stopped at an aquarium to admire the reptiles and goldfish. They swam helixes around each other like choreographed dancers. She sank on the gunmetal sofa. The doctor would likely take the love seat and prop a notepad on his lap, just like the movies.

"I'm sorry to keep you waiting," Doctor Stillman said before even opening the door the whole way. He floated to the couch like a wraith and offered his hand. She took it reluctantly, barely getting her hand into his before his grip bit down like a shark.

Clara hefted up to a half-stand and then sat back down as Doctor Stillman did. "Where is my husband?"

Doctor Stillman flipped his notepad open and clicked his pen. "Before you see your husband, I want you to be aware of a few things. First, his condition isn't rare. The lack of means to explain his condition is. We can't find swelling in his brain or signs of trauma. Typically, with sudden onset, there is damage in the brain. We sent him for a CT scan and found nothing. Then we transferred him to neuroimaging, and the results were inconclusive."

"Exactly what is your specialty, doctor?"

He smiled. "I'm a psychiatrist that specializes in psychoanalysis. I've been helping patients recover from brain trauma for many years. My success rate is about forty-two percent, which is the best amongst my peers."

She didn't return his smile. *Forty-two percent? Is he justifying his failures?* Her heart might have turned to stone when Sophia died. She straightened her pants as if his words had wrinkled them. Something about him felt...off. Fabricated. Clandestine. His smile didn't fade as he stared, as if trying to penetrate her soul and ensnare her without her consent.

"When can I see him?"

He folded his hands on his lap, pen diagonally over the notebook. "That's what we need to discuss. We should proceed slowly. He stares at pictures—doesn't interact at all. It's possible that talking to you will be more effective since your voice might trigger him. But I want to limit your time." He paused. "We don't know what he's capable of. With his training, he could seriously harm you before he understands who you are. Like a dream you wake up from that's so vivid you react to it for a few seconds before your mind wakes up. Except in this case, we're not sure his mind will wake up at all. So, you understand the danger." The doctor stood and motioned for her to follow.

He doesn't care if I have questions. He thinks I'm an obedient soldier's wife, following orders.

In the hallways, they passed male nurses so jacked they probably couldn't wipe their own asses. The doctor said hello, and they grunted their nods.

The doctor tapped his card at a door with a plastic barrier, which beeped open to a flurry of aimless wanderers dressed in white gowns. A twig-like man, maybe mid-twenties, spoke in fits and starts—definitely not English. An old lady with dark hair hunched over a table, drool running down her face. *She doesn't look like a soldier.*

Doctor Stillman noticed who Clara was looking at. "She's a widow. When the chaplain delivered the news that her husband died in combat, she had a seizure. Her brain hasn't recovered. Thirteen years." He sighed. *So she's one of his fifty-eight percent.* "Haven't been able to help her." He turned and pointed. "Your husband is over here, through the door in the back." The doctor led her to the far end of the room and down another hallway. Barred doors with small windows flanked both sides like soldiers standing at attention at a funeral.

They stopped in front of room seven. The doctor glanced inside, then at her.

She squinted through the window. A small bed sat in one corner, a bookshelf in the other. The shelf was empty and as white as the walls. Blake sat on the bed, hands on his legs, feet on the floor, staring at the wall but not seeing it. It wasn't until the doctor spoke that she realized she hadn't taken a breath.

"You can go in."

She backed up a step. She still couldn't breathe. She stared at the door, swallowed, and stiffened one lip against the other. The doctor's hand grazed the small of her back. She flinched away.

Okay. She threw open the door and marched in. "Hello, Blake." She had expected anything...anything except him sitting and drooling in his lap.

"We shouldn't expect too much today."

Clara glanced at Doctor Stillman, breathing in to ask a question but not asking. A nurse stood beside Doctor Stillman, his eyes locked on

Blake like an eagle circling its prey. He folded his cannon arms. *Is this what's left of Blake? Being monitored by a steroid junky?*

She finally spat the question out. "What kind of medication is he on?"

The doctor considered his answer, probably what to divulge, what to hide, and how to alter the truth. "Mood stabilizers mostly. There isn't a lot we can give him without a diagnosis. The mood stabilizer controls his emotions if he wakes up, but otherwise it's not doing much in small doses."

Is that right? Blake would accept and override, not caring to get a second opinion on the dosage. Clara should want to wrap her arms around him and tell him how much she loved him. In a happy marriage she would have. If only she had meant enough to him, he wouldn't be in this mess. Instead, the bastard abandoned her for his own needs. He forced her to bottle up her emotions like he always did.

Clara couldn't take it. She elbowed between Doctor Stillman and the nurse to escape the room, not trying hard to hide her tears.

***

Clara returned daily. Days turned into weeks. Blake's state didn't change. She hadn't given him any affection and, as time marched on, she felt less inclined to. Doctor Stillman asked her to extend her visits until she was in the room for over an hour. The nurse had monitored them for the first couple of weeks but stopped bothering. *They've given up on him. I'm here, but I've given up on him too.* Was she visiting daily to hold back her loneliness?

On day thirty, she sat on a wooden bench outside, back against a mottled wall, arms hugging against autumn wind, facing skeleton trees instead of the hospital behind her. Blake drooled two feet away. She squinted from the sun's dominant glow, feeling as crusty as the grass and as dry as hay. Doctor Stillman had wanted her to test the outdoors. She'd watched Blake be carried out like a helpless child and hated him for it. Where was the man she had married? He was supposed to be stronger than her. When the nurses had left, she felt her hand shaking, lip quivering—

She slapped him. "Where are you?" She bit back another scream, but it spewed out anyway. "How dare you leave me like this? Why won't you answer me?" She slapped him again, her eyes burning. "I'm alone. Did you know that? I used to go home every night to a house that was maybe not booming with joy, but was better than this. I hate it. I hate you for doing this to us. Where the fuck are you?" She slapped him again, much harder. It sounded like a breadstick snapping and left a pink welt.

Drool ran down the scruff of his overgrown beard. She cried until there were no more tears. Her hands cupped her face, and she bent forward, staring at the dead grass, losing herself in the individual yellow needles—

"Clara?"

She gasped. *Blake?* She jumped and slapped out at him in reflex.

The slap didn't connect.

Blake caught her hand midflight.

She stared down. This couldn't be real. Not a chance. Her breath sounded ragged. She blinked. She didn't want to remove her hand from his. *No, this can't be real.* "Blake?"

"What's going on?" His jaw hung open. His eyes shifted around the field, but his head remained facing her until his eyes found their home in hers.

Clara swallowed. Not real. This wasn't real. She was dreaming, right? *Right?*

She collapsed onto him and draped her arms over his shoulders. "We're in a hospital for people with brain injuries, Blake. You've been catatonic for weeks." She pulled back when she realized he hadn't embraced her. "What the hell happened to you?"

His eyes were on hers, but he didn't acknowledge her. They were hollow and soulless. She waved her hand in his face.

"Blake?" He still didn't care about her. His mind was off on another mission.

"I don't know what happened. I heard you yelling for me, but I couldn't get to you." Blake's eyes still didn't move.

"I don't understand."

"Can't remember. I'm trying to. The last thing..." Finally, his gaze shifted to the ground. "Is she really dead, Clara? Is she gone?"

"Yes." Clara found fresh tears to cry.

Blake nodded. "I think I'd rather not be here."

Clara stood, blood rushing to her head. "What about me? Did you think about what that would do to me? Do you know what it's been like alone? Coming here every day to a zombie? Sophia's memory for company? I'll never see her smile again. I'll never hear her laugh. She was the best of both of us, and now she's gone! And you left me alone to deal with it." Ignore and override. That would be his advice.

"Sergeant Powell?" Doctor Stillman crunched on the dry grass toward them. A clownish smile stretched his face.

"Your plan worked. Only he doesn't want to be here. Do us all a favor and beat him over the head until he's dead or a zombie again!" Clara stormed to her car, hearing the doctor yell for her to come back. Nothing from Blake.

She yanked open her door—probably damaged the hinges—and threw herself in. She shrieked and slammed the door. Opened it just to slam it again. When that didn't satisfy her, she pounded the horn, screaming. No matter how much she hoped, the man she'd met in Bangladesh wasn't coming back.

Chapter 48

BLAKE WATCHED CLARA MARCH away. He tried to follow, but his muscles didn't respond. When was the last time he'd used them? A security guard tried to stop her at the gate, but she launched her car past the parking booth. He wondered if it was the last time he'd see her and it made him sick. *Go after her.* He couldn't will himself to move. She would be safer on her own.

A man in a white gown reached his hand out. "Sergeant Powell, I'm Doctor Stillman. You're in a psychiatric hospital. How are you feeling?"

That name sounded familiar. "Did you drug me?"

The doctor chuckled. "A wee bit." His finger and thumb nearly pinched together. "It's to help you relax, I assure you. What's the last thing you remember?"

Blake should be asking the questions here. "Do I have to stay here?"

"No, you're not in custody, but I *would* like to run some tests for safety."

Blake needed to get away—find a place to hide and think. "No, thanks." He stood, his head spinning like the time a mortar had gone off near him, and he'd struck his head against a stone wall. His leg buckled, and he fell back.

"You haven't moved a lot. Take it slow."

Blake denied the weakness in his legs. He stood...and nearly fell again.

Doctor Stillman grabbed his forearm to keep him from eating dirt. "Blake, let me help you back inside so we can run a few tests."

Traffic blared across the lawn, scaring seagulls from the lot. *Did Clara say I'd been out for weeks?*

Doctor Stillman struggled to keep Blake upright. "Grady, give me a hand."

An orderly with mountain ranges for arms hovered nearby. "Let me help you, Sergeant."

Blake took an uncontrolled step. He wobbled forward into the orderly's arms. His head spun, and a needle pricked his arm. "What the..."

Darkness.

***

Blake woke lying in bed in a room small enough to be a closet. The end of his bed nearly pressed against the closed door. His head felt clearer, but he couldn't remember anything after Sophia's death. Were the last few weeks sealed away in his mind?

He wobbled to the door and jerked the handle. Locked. When he peeked through the window, he saw only gleaming white walls staring back at him.

"Hello? What's going on?" He used the handle to jiggle the door.

Grady appeared at the window. His eyes glazed over. "You'll have to wait to see Doctor Stillman. You're here for observation."

Blake punched the window hard enough to crack the glass. A slot in the door opened, and a dart shot through and hit him in the abdomen.

He stumbled back, lightheaded, thoughts wavy, and fell onto the bed. All he heard was the squeak of springs and...

Knock, knock.

...he woke on the floor.

Doctor Stillman stood at the door, face filling the window view. Grady stood behind him. "Hello, Sergeant Powell."

Blake propped himself up. "Well? Are you going to let me out or not? You told me I'm free to go." He scowled.

"I'll open the door once you assure me we can talk and you won't hurt me or anyone else here."

Blake raised his hands in surrender, teeth gritted beneath his lips. "You're fine. I'm not going to hurt anyone."

A lock clicked, and Doctor Stillman swung the door open. "How are you feeling?"

Blake frowned. He lifted himself onto the bed and clutched his reeling head. The tiles under his bare feet might as well have been dungeon stones. "Like I've laid in bed way too long. Why am I locked in here?"

"A precaution. We have a responsibility to keep our patients safe."

"It's safe. I'm ready to leave." He plucked at his hospital gown in disgust.

Doctor Stillman opened his notepad and scanned a few lines with his eyes and pen. Did he ever put that thing down? "Before you go, I want to talk about your test results. They're inconclusive; I've seen nothing like it before." He looked up at Blake. "Do you remember anything that would explain what happened to you? At all? You have no swelling or damage in the brain. You are perfectly healthy. There's no explanation for your state."

Blake rested his elbows on his legs. Why did he feel so tired? "Sorry, I can't help you, doctor. I don't remember anything."

"I've looked into your file. There are inconsistencies with your employment. I've seen it before. I want to help you, Blake, and I think I know why you don't remember. It's because you were in the Genesis, isn't it?"

Chapter 49

"LET'S TALK IN PRIVATE," Blake said.

Doctor Stillman shooed Grady away with a dismissive flick of his wrist before easing the door shut with a quiet click. "These rooms are soundproof. Anyone standing outside the room can't hear what we're saying."

Blake stood so fast his bare feet slapped against the tiles. He wanted to grab Doctor Stillman's collar and shake the answers out of him like change from a piggy bank, but he promised he wouldn't hurt anyone. "How do you know about the Genesis?"

"I designed it."

Right. Colonel Marks had mentioned a Doctor Michael Stillman. *He worked on the Genesis Project until...until...What had happened to him?*

"We have a lot in common," Doctor Stillman said. "The Genesis nearly wiped my memory clean. I woke up years later, and I spent months piecing together my life. I still feel like I fabricated some memories. Is my wife my wife?" He grimaced and shrugged. "Hard to say. I don't remember meeting her and falling in love. I don't even remember our wedding day. She has been true and loving since, but I wish I could remember." He flipped his notepad closed, slid his pen into a pocket, and sat on the bed next to Blake. "I studied brain trauma here, hoping the research would lead me to recover lost memories. I medicated, tried inhibitors and memantine, electroshock therapy. A combination of all three helped release a few earlier memories—my work on the Genesis, in flashes, too scrambled to figure out." Doctor Stillman pulled at his hair. "It's all in there somewhere, but I can't get it out."

Is he keeping me here to study me? "Do you remember any problems with the project?"

"Problems?"

Blake scanned Doctor Stillman's reactions for deceit: eye contact, contradictory body language, sweating or fidgeting. All Doctor Stillman's reactions seemed genuine. Being vulnerable grated under Blake's skin, but there was no other way to get answers and if Doctor Stillman already knew about Genesis, what were a few more details? "Someone murdered my daughter. They accused her of setting off a bomb in a mall. Someone used Genesis to place the memory in the killer."

Doctor Stillman swallowed. "I'm sorry for your loss. In theory, with upgrades, it's possible to alter memories. However, not with my design. Do you remember anything after your daughter died?"

"No," Blake said.

Doctor Stillman shuffled closer and grabbed his pen and pad again. He scribbled a note. "Do you remember a mental marker?"

"What?"

"A mental marker. The trauma to your brain marked a moment, like a bookmark in a novel. You woke up and your brain has blocked anything after that bookmark. What do you remember before your daughter died?"

"Everything. What normal people would remember."

"Fascinating. I lost all my memories, but you lost only recent memories."

"You think the same thing happened to both of us?"

"Yes. The Genesis is central to all of this."

Doctor Stillman sat still as Blake relayed what he knew about the murders, only nodding with the occasional "uh huh" and "I see." He mentioned the note on the explosive, his dog dying, and the fire. He needed to trust someone. *Anyone.*

"Wow, that's incredible." Doctor Stillman chewed the tip of his pen. *The creative side of his brain or the scheming side?* "We should try treatment. Your memories are important."

There were dangers in letting Doctor Stillman mess with his mind, but what choice did he have? No way he'd let Sophia's killer live. It didn't matter what happened to him. His life didn't mean anything anymore. "Okay, run your tests. But I want to know what tests. If I don't like them, I walk away."

"Agreed. We start now."

Doctor Stillman led Blake to a cozy room with a computer on an oak desk so big Blake wondered how they'd gotten it through the door. A chair that looked like a cross between a lounge chair and the Genesis huddled against the desk, straps dangling from the head, abdomen, arms, and legs.

"Have a seat."

"What is this?" Blake lifted the head strap and flipped it in his hand. He knew Doctor Stillman could feed him a story, and once they strapped him into the chair, they could do whatever they wanted. But he still had to ask.

"Of course. My apologies. Full disclosure. This is a little unorthodox, but it has the best chance of success. No doctor would recommend this step. Jump-starting the brain is dangerous. But, we are as certain as we can be that the Genesis caused your amnesia. This machine is going to deliver several shocks to your brain. The shocks will be very mild at first, but they'll get stronger until it's either no longer safe to proceed or you get flashes of memories."

"No drugs?" Blake raised a skeptical eyebrow at Doctor Stillman. He intended to keep a clear head.

"No drugs."

Blake swept the straps aside and sat. The chair smelled like bleach. *What happened to the last guy who sat here?*

An orderly stepped into the room, white gloves snapping into place. He pulled the straps so tightly they chafed. "Say aah," he said and jammed a mouth guard in before Blake could respond. Blake gagged and bit down.

"I hope this is clean," he said around the polymer. His eyes wandered to the ceiling, where he saw swirls and a patch of mold in the far corner. He was about to comment when a jolt forced him ramrod straight. He bit into the mouth guard.

Jolts crackled through him a minute apart. Each jolt felt as painful as the last and knocked his head against the back of the chair. He almost spat up the mouth guard.

Doctor Stillman stood at the console, finger poised to deliver the next outburst of electricity. "Are you okay? Anything happening?"

Blake shook his head and mumbled a no. Not a single memory after Sophia dying. The pain kicked up a notch.

When the procedure ended, Doctor Stillman signaled for the orderly to unstrap Blake.

"How are you?"

Blake tongued out the mouth guard. "You tell me. You fried me for, what, twenty minutes? And there's nothing to show for it. I think I smell smoke."

"We don't know if it worked yet. It's too early. We have to give it time. Your memories may not come back quickly or easily. It took me years, and I still don't know everything."

Blake didn't have the energy to argue. He slinked off the chair and stumbled down the hallway. *I'm not staying here to get fried every day. He's got one more chance. That's it. Then, I'm getting answers my way.*

***

The treatments went on for two weeks, with Blake clinging to the hope that one of the sessions would restore his memory. Occasionally two or three days passed between them, but they spoke daily, mostly about the days leading up to Blake's memory loss. Doctor Stillman continued to prod for information on the Genesis Project. Blake kept his answers as vague as possible, relying on the excuse of a lack of memory to explain his unwillingness to talk. Blake had become weary of the treatments; each one seemed more painful than the last and never produced the results he needed.

After another tough round of treatment, Blake collapsed onto his bed and slept. He dreamed, brief glimpses of memories acting as commercial breaks, mostly ones he'd forgotten: David laughing at him, shattering Peter's kneecap, threatening Colonel Marks. *Is any of this real?* Why would he shatter Peter's kneecap?

When he woke, he wandered down the halls, too frustrated to sit still. He passed a wide range of patients of different cultures, as if the facility needed to fill a quota for the spring calendar.

Blake reached an exit where an orderly nodded him through. "Go ahead. You're permitted outside."

Haphazardly arranged trees rose at least ten feet high. He sat against a tree on the outskirts of the field. The wind, the clean air, the smell of the forest—all familiar friends.

He fell asleep and dreamed once more. He broke Peter's kneecap again, this time accusing Peter of lying. Then he sat in the hospital surrounded by the dead—they begged for his help, but he couldn't move. Last, he dreamed of threatening Colonel Marks and reaching for his pocketknife, intending to kill him.

He thrashed awake. Doctor Stillman jiggled his shoulder, silhouetted between bright sunlight and gentle shade.

Doctor Stillman hunched next to him. "Are you okay? You were talking in your dreams. It didn't sound English."

"I...I think so. I think I remember."

Doctor Stillman smiled. "Brilliant. I didn't expect this to work so quickly."

Chapter 50

Throughout the evening and into the creaking hours of night, the memories hit him like rounds from a machine gun—quick, hard, merciless. General Talbert might not admit to killing Sophia, but he must have ordered the hit.

Blake ran to the front desk. "I need you to call Doctor Stillman." He almost lunged at Tracy, who he'd come to know over the last few days as a bubbly mother of two. While everyone else treated him like a nuisance, she'd offered him homemade muffins a couple of times. She was the only one in the joint that he was on a first-name basis with.

"Please quiet down, Blake. It's the middle of the night." Tracy's face reddened in frustration. She examined the hall for anyone wandering out to see the commotion. She padded the air to shush him. "You'll have to wait until morning." Under the desk, her hand slithered toward—

Blake snatched up her hand. "Don't."

"Let me go." Tracy tried to jerk free. Her defiance turned to panic. "Blake, what's gotten into you?"

"I said do not." His grip on her tightened. "Call Doctor Stillman. He'll want to hear what I have to say."

"Let me go," she blurted, on the verge of tears. She lunged for the panic button with her other hand, but Blake caught it.

"Call Doctor Stillman. Now, Tracy. Now."

"Okay. Okay, I'll call him. Just let me go. You're hurting me." Tracy tried to pull away.

"I'll release one hand slowly. I want you to call Doctor Stillman when I do. Clear?" Blake bit back his own regret at threatening her. "Tracy, you know me. Trust me. Please."

They locked eyes. Blake pleaded with apologetic eyebrows for several breaths.

"Tracy. Trust me." Blake eased one hand. She snapped her arm away and slammed her hand under the counter. Blake let go of her second hand and smashed his fist on the counter. "Please."

"You're an asshole," she said.

"He needs to know I have my memories back. They're going to come for both of us. His family needs to know."

Tracy's shock dissipated. "There is nobody coming after you or Doctor Stillman. Please calm down."

"Time to go back, Sergeant Powell." Grady stood behind Blake with crossed arms. Blake could sense his robotic energy even without hearing him. "You're having an episode."

"I'm not having an episode. You know that. I'm still here because Doctor Stillman is trying to help me access my memories. They are back now. I need to leave."

Grady put his baseball-mitt hand on Blake's arm. "I can't let you leave without the doctor's permission."

Grady outweighed Blake by fifty or sixty pounds. Three more orderlies marched down the hall. One slapped a fist into a palm. *Was that really necessary?* Four against one. Blake was trained for odds like this, but he didn't want to be responsible for any broken bones.

Blake shook off Grady's grip and fanned his hands in mock surrender. "I just want to talk to Doctor Stillman. My memories are back. I'm not catatonic anymore. Grady, you know that."

"I don't know nothin'. Get back to your room until the doctor comes in on Monday."

Monday? What day is it? Blake glanced at Tracy's cat-a-day desk calendar. It was Saturday. "You're not listening. Doctor Stillman is in danger. So is his family. He needs to know what's going on."

"He will once he's in," Grady leaned forward, "*on Monday.*"

"I'm leaving this hospital." Blake sidestepped toward the front door. The orderlies converged on him.

"Like hell you are." Grady cracked his knuckles—too many *Fight Club* reruns.

Blake planted his stance. Everyone moved at once. A quick throat punch sent Grady to the ground, gasping. Blake ducked, assuming they'd try to grab him, then donkey-kicked the next orderly, who yelped as he buckled over. Two on one. Squeaking footsteps gave away the third orderly. He seized Blake's arm and yanked him down, the other doing the same with his other arm, trying to pin Blake to the ground.

He pulled his knees tightly to his chest and kicked the third orderly in the face. The orderly's head snapped back—blood arced out his nose.

One on one. Better odds. Before Blake could stand, what felt like a mosquito bit his neck. He punched the orderly in the face. The orderly fell away.

Blake lumbered to his feet, plodding lethargically toward the door. His thumps became thuds became dragging feet became a drop to his knees.

He teetered to the tiles, and his eyes clamped shut.

***

"He'll wake up soon. We'll get some payback on him then." Grady snorted. Blake recognized Grady's raspy snarl anywhere.

Blake kept his eyes closed. At least two people breathed near him. From the echoes of footsteps, he guessed he was in a small room—confinement, probably.

"Did his eyes move?"

"No, he's been twitching since you put him out."

"His leg moved. See that?"

"It ain't nothin'. Will you stop being so damn paranoid? He's strapped in. Who cares if he wakes up? I even want him to."

"You report already?"

"I sent the details up the chain. I dunno what they'll do with it."

A phone rang like a duck call. "Hello? Yeah. Okay. He's still out, yeah. What? No man, I ain't doing that. Our agreement was I let you know if he regained his memory. I ain't killing nobody."

"Damnit."

"They want us to kill him."

"Us? They don't know me. They want *you* to kill him. I ain't part of that."

"I've never been asked to kill anyone before outside a *Halo* tournament."

"He kicked all our asses."

"Who is he?"

"I don't know, man, but that don't matter. He kicked all our asses."

Blake fought the urge to lift his legs or arms to test the straps' range of motion. If they saw him jerking around, they might kill him before he worked the problem.

"How'm I s'posed to kill him, Grady? I don't kill people."

"Give him an overdose?"

"That's suspicious. If the coroner checks, they'll blame us for giving it to him for sure. He'll be dead, but we'll be in prison."

"Well, how much are they paying you?"

"Too much. And not enough. I can't get out of this. Fuck. Grady, think, man. I ain't good at this stuff."

"Put a pillow over his head."

"This ain't one of your stupid movies."

"Pillows were assassins' tools for centuries."

"I ain't an assassin. Jesus."

"No evidence. It's quick. Nothing we could do to bring him back."

"This don't feel right. Grady, this don't feel right." What sounded like a hand slapping a wall. "It don't feel right!"

"I heard you the first time!"

The idiots might be brave enough to kill him while shackled. *Work the goddamn problem.*

"So what we do? Just press it over his face and...what...push down?"

"Are you an idiot? It's not rocket science."

The pillow pressed against Blake's face. He choked. He thrashed his arms, kicked out his legs, twisted his head, hoping to snatch up a sip of air. The shackles were tight.

"Oh, he's awake. Just push down. Grady, c'mon, man. Quick!"

Struggling sapped his strength. *Calm down. Work the problem. Play dead.* He quieted his muscles, hoping they'd release the tension on the pillow before he needed another breath. Keeping control was the hardest thing he'd ever done. This wasn't training. It wasn't a dream. He'd be dead in less than two minutes.

He heard a creak, a door opening.

"Doctor Stillman!"

A scuffle ensued. Crashes, smacks. It seemed as if it would never end.

The pillow lifted away to reveal Doctor Stillman looking down at him. "Sorry it took so long."

The two orderlies lay on the floor face down while six others secured their arms with zip ties.

"Thank you." Blake watched Doctor Stillman unstrap his arms. He sat up and rubbed a wrist. "You saved my life."

Doctor Stillman tilted his head in concession. "I put your life in danger. I shouldn't have left." He went to work on the ankle straps.

"Who called you?"

Doctor Stillman cleared his throat. "I knew someone from Genesis would watch you." One ankle strap was off. "They had to. If they let you live, it's because they didn't think you'd come back. So they kept tabs on you, thinking you wouldn't get your memory back." The other was off.

"How do you know all of this?" Blake rotated his arm to check the redness of his wrist.

"I don't. Not for sure. I suspected."

"Then you know you're in as much danger as I am. Your family too."

"They're safe. As safe as I can make them. What did you remember?"

Blake scanned the room. "Not here. We need to leave. Let's take a drive."

Doctor Stillman rushed to the exit. "I have a spare set of clothes in my office. You should change, then we'll go."

Chapter 51

Ten minutes later, they sat in Doctor Stillman's car, the radio playing Damian Marley. "Where to?"

"Drive. I'll fill you in."

They snaked down country roads. Blake told Doctor Stillman everything he remembered about Genesis and General Talbert's attack on him.

"They must have done that to me too. Used Genesis to wipe out my memories." Doctor Stillman turned off the radio and smacked the wheel with his palm. "What did those animals do?"

"Watching my daughter die so many times—I ran away in my mind. I don't think the Genesis did it. I did it to myself. When Clara pleaded and slapped me, her emotion must have brought me out. I don't know if there's a way back for you, or if you would want to remember." Blake's palms were sweaty, so he rubbed them on his pants. "We have to destroy the Genesis," Blake said.

Doctor Stillman ruffled his hair, as if shaking the cobwebs off.

"I know it's your machine, and you had good intentions when you built it, but that's gone now. They used your tech to brainwash soldiers into mercenaries, not help them."

Doctor Stillman stopped at a yield sign to let a driver through, then proceeded. "You think they're going to let you just walk in there and blow it up?"

"It's a high-tech military operation. They'll have a weapons vault somewhere in the building. A bit of well-placed explosives will work."

They drove within a few miles of the base. Doctor Stillman parked on a side road.

"This is as far as I can take you. They removed my access years ago." The steering wheel groaned beneath Doctor Stillman's grip. "Now that you remember, would you rather forget?"

Blake placed a hand on Doctor Stillman's shoulder. "Ignore and override. The people running this farce need to be stopped. That's why I became an operator. I believe in the mission."

"You're just going to walk in wearing jeans and a golf shirt?"

"I'll wait until daylight when the office opens. They know me. They'll let me in." Blake leaned back in the seat and slept.

***

"Blake? Blake, hey." Doctor Stillman shook him awake. "It's eight o'clock. Time to move."

"I'm up, I'm up." Blake yawned and checked the window. "Give me five minutes, and we're a go."

Doctor Stillman pursed his lips. It was obvious he was hesitating on a thought.

"What's on your mind?"

Doctor Stillman didn't look at him, perhaps nervous about how Blake would react. "Look, I don't remember what happened to me, but I know the machine helped a lot of soldiers. Blake, if there's a way to take out the bad tech and make it usable again, it's worth it to figure out how."

"I appreciate what you're trying to do. But the Genesis needs to end. There has to be another way to help those soldiers."

"Okay." Doctor Stillman nodded. "Just keep it in mind, okay?"

Blake walked down a dirt road. The car started, swerved around, and squealed away.

Three miles to the base. Before he could get half a mile, a car rumbled up behind him. Blake thought Doctor Stillman had reconsidered. When he glanced over his shoulder it wasn't Doctor Stillman's car.

David rolled down the window. "Need a lift?"

Blake got into the car. A coat of Armor All made the dash sparkle in the sunlight. "What's going on?"

"Why are you walking to base?" David shifted into drive. The tires took half a second and then found traction in the dust.

"Morning PT. Why are you driving this early in the morning?"

David scoffed and looked Blake up, then down. "Morning PT with that outfit? You look like you just finished drinking at The Saloon, not running a few miles."

Blake studied a glint of sunlight cutting across the dash. "What do you think happened? After Peter shot me with the taser? That's the last thing I remember before the Genesis."

David raised one hand up. "After Peter tased you, he told me what you did to him. Colonel Marks ordered you to the infirmary under watch. That's the last I saw you. Everyone knows something went wrong in your brain. If you go to Genesis dressed like that, it's going to raise a lot of suspicion."

Blake side-eyed David. "How does everyone know what happened?"

"In a briefing. You had a psychotic break while working the Talbert case. Something you saw sent your brain AWOL. Colonel Marks shut Genesis down. He's running some tests to make sure the machine wasn't at fault."

Yeah. Sure he is. "Recommendations?"

"Abort. What are you going to Genesis for?"

David snapped that out quickly, almost rehearsed. He already knew what he was going to say. He just needed Blake to prompt it. "You know what I'm going to do, don't you?"

"With what you've been through, I don't blame you for wanting to destroy the place."

"Colonel Marks sent you, didn't he? Come on, David. Don't buy into his lies."

David sighed. "He wants to talk about it. Before you do anything stupid. Blake, we've been friends long enough. Hopefully long enough for you to trust me. Let's at least hear him out."

"How does he know I have my memory back? It hasn't even been a day."

The front gate of the Genesis facility loomed in the distance. Two soldiers stood silhouetted at the front. *They should have prepared an army if they wanted to stop me.*

"This whole thing is FUBAR. You need to hear Colonel Marks out."

Blake grabbed David's shirt. "Stop the car. What's going on?"

If David had slowed the car, Blake might have strangled him. Instead, they raced toward the gate even well after they should have slowed their approach. David didn't reduce speed until they reached the front booth, too late for Blake to do anything without losing his opportunity to get inside.

"Just heading in to work, Corporal. Here with Sergeant Powell." David plastered on a smile and even threw in a casual wink at one of the guards. He flashed his ID. Blake threw on a smile and nodded. The corporal stared, shook his head, and waved them through.

David closed the window and glanced back at the guards as if they could overhear him. "I'm taking you to talk to Colonel Marks. He's in his office."

"How did you know I was on the road?"

"Colonel Marks told me you'd be here."

But how did Colonel Marks find out? Doctor Stillman wouldn't trust him. So who told him I'd be walking to base?

They drove into the garage and found a space on the second level. David had a set of dress clothes in the trunk that he pulled out. "Put these on."

They raced down the staircase. Blake paused and cleared his throat. "Hey, David, next beer's on me."

"What? Why?" David turned.

"For this." Blake punched him in the jaw, knocking him out. Blake caught him and lowered him to the ground.

"Glad that only took one punch." Blake checked the stairwell up and down. Nobody. He tapped David's shoulder. "Sorry, buddy. I know you're just following orders, so I can't hold it against you. But no more lies. They killed my little girl."

Chapter 52

Blake passed through security. The guards either didn't remember he was supposed to be in a nuthouse or didn't care. Small victories. He headed to Colonel Marks' office. If the colonel had set a trap, Blake had no intention of making it easy. David wouldn't be his backup.

He kicked the door open, pulverizing the latch and sending the door crashing against the wall. A picture fell, and glass shattered on the floor.

Colonel Marks sat at his desk, leaning back, arms crossed. He moved only to examine his cuff. "Well, that was unnecessary, Sergeant." He pointed at the goddamn uncomfortable chair. "We need to talk."

"I have questions. You better have answers."

"Where's David?"

"He needed a nap." Blake sat. "Let's get this going."

"I'm sorry about your daughter. It never should have happened."

"No kidding, sir. What do you know about it? Did you kill her?" Blake launched forward, swiping at Colonel Marks, who pushed off his desk and wheeled out of reach.

"No. This isn't over yet, Sergeant."

"It will be soon, sir. Answer the question."

"The senator's death wasn't the first time someone linked to the Genesis murdered a civilian."

"Something I don't know, sir."

Colonel Marks straightened his tie. "I've been trying to figure out what's been happening with the Genesis, but I haven't been able to break in. That's why we recruited you."

"What?" *He's stalling.*

"I knew something was wrong, but it wasn't the machine. The Genesis was doing what we built it for."

"So how the hell, sir, does General Talbert fit into this mess? And Peter?"

"General Talbert? What are you talking about?"

Blake quickly explained what had happened to him, how Peter hit him with a taser, and the general made him relive Sophia's death.

"How is he doing it? How did he get access? He's not an operator. He's supposed to be my patient."

"He's with DARPA. DSO."

"He's leadership for this shit-show?"

"I didn't know he was involved in the assassinations or the issue with the Genesis. I was trying to figure that out."

"That's why you brought me in, let me visit Corporal Hodge, assigned me to Senior Chief Wilburg. You knew what was happening, and you didn't stop it. You threw me into a gopher hole to see what would pop out the other side." Blake swept a framed picture off the desk.

"Sergeant, no!" Colonel Marks retrieved the frame. It had split at the corner, and he tried vainly to fit the pieces together and then gave up and tossed it next to his keyboard. "I couldn't stop it. I had suspicions but no proof. Someone needed to expose it. What they did, who did it...why they did it. Thanks to you, we have those answers.

The tech we haven't figured out. We will. We have to keep going. If we shut it down now, the general will run."

Blake ground his teeth. "Sophia is dead because of this."

David walked in, holding his jaw. "What the hell was that for?"

Blake fumed at Colonel Marks. "Who went after Sophia?"

"I'm sorry, Blake. We don't know. Probably General Talbert or someone in his chain of command."

"Where is he?"

"He's due to be in the Genesis this morning."

"So it's operational." Blake shot David a glance. "With who?"

"Isaac," David said. "His case went to Isaac."

"Is General Talbert's PTSD real?"

"You helped him get through it," Colonel Marks said. "I imagine when he realized the machine's potential, he took steps to make changes."

"I want in the Genesis with him." Blake leaned into the colonel. "A modified Genesis."

"We don't know how the tech works," David said.

"Peter knows. He's been swapping chips and playing with security protocols for weeks. He knocked me out with a taser before the general got to me. He needs to be interrogated."

"Not by breaking his other kneecap, I hope," Colonel Marks said. "Let's give him a chance to defend himself."

"Call him in," Blake said. "Let's find out."

Colonel Marks drummed his fingers on the desk. "Fine." He seized his phone. "Can you send someone to bring Peter to my office? Yes. Yes. Good, thank you," Colonel Marks hung up. "He's on the way."

***

Peter poked his head through the doorway. "You w-w-wanted to see me, s-sir?" When he saw Blake and David, his face paled.

"Come on in," Colonel Marks said. "Close the door."

Peter wobbled in on one leg, the other in a brace. He stepped only far enough into the room to close the door. "Yes, s-sir?"

No salute, feet apart, a general lack of respect. A civilian through and through.

"I need to ask you a few questions, Peter. You're not on trial. Answer them honestly, please. Okay?"

Peter inched toward the corner. If he could burrow into the wall just to be farther from Blake, he would. "Sure. O-o-of course, sir. Y-yes."

"Go ahead, Sergeant," Colonel Marks said.

Blake stood, sick of the uncomfortable chair. He motioned for Peter to sit. "Genesis hardware. I've seen you messing around with it. Changing or adjusting the software."

Peter turned for the door, but Blake grabbed his shoulders and threw him into the chair. Peter winced.

Blake slapped Colonel Marks' desktop. "What are you doing to the Genesis hardware?"

"N-n-nothing. I..." Peter gawked up at Blake's scowl. "Y-y-yes. Okay, I g-go in the machines—you've s-s-seen me—and adjust some things. Y-yeah. Th-that's my job."

"You're messing with the machines, adding a microchip for General Talbert, and I want to know what it does."

"W-who?" Peter's face reddened.

"General Talbert. What did you change in the Genesis? How does the tech work for you to change memories and weaponize soldiers? General Talbert tried to kill me. He thought he succeeded. Right after you tased me."

"Wh-What? N-No. The microchip d-doesn't do that. It's a m-modification. C-clearing bugs from the system. I tased you b-be-cause you b-broke my kn-kneecap and w-were hurting people. We took you to the infirmary. David and I. N-not the Genesis."

"Who told you that the microchip is a modification?" If Peter wasn't lying, General Talbert must have gotten to him at the infirmary.

"J-Jacob told me to p-put it in." A bead of sweat forged a path down Peter's cheek.

"Who is Jacob?" David twisted a confused gawk at Peter.

"H-he's in IT. He w-works with the e-engineers, I th-think. They d-design the ch-chips. The chips u-update the G-genesis. I-I've been in-installing them for months."

Colonel Marks leaned back in his chair. "You installed a microchip without confirming with Major Graham?"

Peter had kids at home. He probably couldn't afford to lose his job and certainly didn't want to go to prison. "M-major Graham yells at m-m-me when he d-doesn't like what he hears. I try n-not to tell him a-anything if I don't have to." Peter's words sounded moist. He snorted back some tears. "J-Jacob said Major Graham a-allowed it. W-why wouldn't I b-believe him?"

"It almost killed me, Peter. Doctor Stillman, too."

"Wait." Colonel Marks leaned forward. "What do you know about Stillman?"

Blake brought Colonel Marks up to speed on Doctor Stillman, how they'd connected at the hospital, and how nurses tried to kill him. It was time to get everything out. "They were watching me. They knew the moment I got my memories back, and then they tried to kill me. How did you know I was coming, sir? You sent David to get me. How did you know?"

"I also had someone watching you. Not the people that tried to kill you—a nurse. Tracy. She reports in on soldiers in the ward in case there are things we need to know about. Many of the soldiers there...they came here for help. But Tracy didn't tell me about Dr. Stillman."

Blake felt his stomach churn like he'd eaten too much for breakfast. He'd helped them, even if he hadn't known how corrupt it was. Soldiers murdered innocents, believing they were doing the right thing. This was worse than being ordered to kill people on the battlefield.

"How the hell is this program still operational?"

"It's needed." Colonel Marks leapt to his feet. "To save lives. To help others with PTSD. Research has casualties just like war does."

Blake grabbed Peter by the front of his shirt. "How many Genesis terminals have the chip installed?" Nobody in the room moved to interfere.

"A-all of them."

"And they are all connected by the same network right? Any operator can mess with another Genesis? How does it work?"

"I d-don't know anything. It's j-just a ch-chip. I-it's supposed to update the m-machine, like a s-security update."

"Your update got Sophia killed, and it wants to kill a lot more people. We're all targets now." Blake tightened his grip on Peter's shirt, wanting to choke the life out of him. The only thing saving him was that it wasn't his fault.

"Nobody could have known what the general had planned," Colonel Marks said.

"Without the microchip, the machines are safe." David stood and checked the others for agreement. "Aren't they?"

Blake let go of Peter. "There's no chance I leave this place without those machines destroyed. I don't think it's that hard to duplicate. Someone will get the plans out if they haven't already."

"You're going to destroy them? How?"

"Explosives, from the armory."

"Jesus Christ." Colonel Marks massaged his forehead. "There aren't explosives in the armory. I'm not going to allow you to hurt more people on your crusade. We all need to slow down a second."

Blake pointed at Colonel Marks. "General Talbert first. Then the machines."

***

"Almost ready?" Blake lay on the Genesis bed. Sergeant Martin struggled a few feet away, hands and arms tied, murmuring mouth gagged.

"R-r-ready," Peter said, extracting himself from inside the Genesis panel.

"It will work? I'll have control?"

"I d-double-checked the chip. It's r-r-ready to go." Peter hobbled to the bed. "You don't h-have to do this."

"I need answers, Peter."

"Good luck," David said, his eyes on the console.

The lid hummed down over Blake. He waited in the familiar darkness as the Genesis loaded. A slew of options dropped from a menu. A swipe would activate the sequences. *Waiting for Others to Connect* pulsed under the menu in vehement blue. Blake wondered where General Talbert was. Usually, he was already waiting. They'd scheduled him ten minutes ago.

Waiting for Others to Connect flashed on Blake's screen.

He reached for the button marked *Exit*. If General Talbert knew he was free and coming after him, the Genesis could be a trap.

Blake pressed the button. In the background, the screen continued to blink *Waiting for Others to Connect.* In front of him, the Genesis displayed, *Exit now? Yes / No.* Blake reached for Yes, but the blinking screen disappeared.

"Sergeant Martin? Ready to proceed." General Talbert's voice came over the speaker, calm and nonchalant.

Blake pressed *No,* then pressed *Sequence One.* The Genesis loaded.

Chapter 53

THE CROWD SHOUTED FROM the bottom of the embassy wall. General Talbert stood beside Blake. Controls popped up in front of him, offering options to take over crowd-member actions and add, remove, or swap characters and scenes. A major upgrade from the few options he'd seen before.

General Talbert paced along the wall when gunfire erupted in the crowd. Blake made an adjustment, and one of the American soldiers fired.

"Cease fire. Cease fire!" General Talbert shouted.

His soldiers weren't shooting at the terrorists. They shot at the women and children.

"It looks like you've lost control of your men," Blake said.

General Talbert's eyes looked like saucers. "Blake? What the hell is going on?"

He pressed another button, and a round hit General Talbert on the back of the knee, dropping him to the ground.

"Sergeant, what the hell is going on?"

General Talbert swiped for options he wouldn't have without an active chip. The harder he swiped, the bigger Blake's smile.

"No way out of this one, General."

"What do you want?"

Blake ended the sequence. "Who killed my daughter?"

"I told you I don't know. I had nothing to do with it. How did you—Peter. He activated the microchip."

"Someone on your team was brainwashed with memories of my wife and daughter setting off a bomb. They killed Sophia. Who killed her?"

When General Talbert didn't respond, Blake pulled up the menu and made another selection. They sat in a Humvee. General Talbert lay sprawled on the ground with another soldier.

"You abandoned us," the soldier said. General Talbert tried to shove him away, but the sergeant leaned back, pointed a gun at his own head, and pulled the trigger. Gore splattered out like a water hose, disintegrating chunks of his face. "You deserve to die," the sergeant said with half his head missing. "You're the reason we're all dead."

"This isn't real," General Talbert said.

They stood with the general's men outside the Humvees. As bullets rained down, General Talbert watched his men die. He took many bullets before Blake reset the machine. General Talbert's wide eyes scanned the area, presumably looking for a way out. Blake wished the same when he'd watched Sophia.

"Who killed my daughter?"

The general dropped to his knees, eyes closed and hands reaching for one of the dead soldiers at his feet. "I don't know."

"Who?"

"I don't know," General Talbert whispered.

For the first time, Blake considered that General Talbert might be telling the truth. "What happened when you lost it during our sequence that day?"

"Colonel Marks couldn't keep his nose out of my business. He confronted me the night before our session. Told me the truth about my nightmares. It's not like I didn't know you were altering my dreams, but he fed me the details. He reminded me of what had happened. It screwed up my dreams that night and our work that day."

"Why would he do that?"

"You'll have to ask him."

"If you didn't kill my daughter, who could have? Who else is there?"

"Doctor Stillman."

Blake sent them back to an empty room with a small lamp reflecting a silver beard and white hair on General Talbert's face. "That's not possible. He helped me get out of the hospital."

General Talbert still quivered from the nightmares on the battlefields, his legs crossed. "If you're here, then he's hoping to get rid of me and toss you in a cell after I'm dead. He's covering his tracks now that there's a spotlight on soldiers being turned to assassins. When this is over, and we're all dead or discharged, he'll get back to killing people."

"He's not the reason I'm here. He let me leave the hospital. Colonel Marks let me in here. Peter helped with the tech."

"Pawns," he said. "Colonel Marks knew something was going on but couldn't prove it. He needed someone inside. A soldier that could operate the machine and had the willpower and politics that aligned with his objectives." He paused to let that sink in. "I oversaw the updates to Corporal Hodge's memory as we programmed him to become the perfect weapon. Doctor Stillman designed and implemented the tech from his own Genesis. He used men on the inside to get to Peter so he could retrofit the others. I agreed to go along with it."

"Why did you come after me?" Blake said.

"You were getting too close to the truth. Too much was on the line. We'd come too far for you to destroy what we'd created. Think about it. Corporal Hodge's memories may be flawed, but he believes he just saved the country and took out a terrorist."

"Someone knows who ordered my daughter's death, and I'm going to find out." Blake took two deep breaths. "You tried to turn me into a drooling vessel. I'll give you the same courtesy."

"No, don't," General Talbert shouted.

Blake sent General Talbert back to his nightmare, playing it on a loop. Someone would need to log in to save him. Maybe he had someone who cared that much for him. Maybe not.

Chapter 54

Blake exited the Genesis to find Peter hovering over him as the lid buzzed away.

"W-what happened?" Peter said, slack-jawed.

"He's taking some time to think about what he did."

"W-what did he tell y-you?"

"I have to go." Blake shoved past Peter, stripped off the gown, and pulled on his own clothes. His fingers brushed the pocketknife in his jeans as he returned to Colonel Marks's office.

"So?" Colonel Marks said.

If General Talbert had told him the truth, the only people that could have been involved in his daughter's death were Doctor Stillman and Colonel Marks. *Do I tell him what I know or confront Doctor Stillman first?*

"Sergeant Powell?"

"He admitted to his part in the microchip, the tech, and connecting soldiers to the Genesis with the modifications for reprogramming."

"Who did the reprogramming?" David asked.

"Tell him why you brought me in, Colonel," Blake said.

Colonel Marks sighed and sat back in his chair, his hand reaching for a cigar.

David leaned forward, eyes shifting between them. "Did I miss something?"

"Colonel Marks knew about more than the problems with Genesis. He knew about the assassinations. A bunch of small ones, prior to the senator."

"Prior to the senator?" David coughed into his fist. "What other murders?"

"The colonel couldn't figure out how it was being done, so he brought me in and practically fed me the case while acting like he didn't want me to eat a thing. That's why I got so far. He made it seem like the investigation was my idea, but he'd been guiding it. The threat at my home? Was that you, Colonel?"

Colonel Marks hesitated, eyes wandering, so David pressed him. "Colonel?" His voice had an edge. "Did you put his family at risk to get answers you couldn't get on your own?"

Colonel Marks sighed. "Sergeant Powell was the only one that could do things none of us could without raising eyebrows. His connection to Corporal Hodge. The questioning of orders. Accessing the archive without authorization. The explosive at his home forced him to pick up his pace."

"You couldn't figure it out on your own? It's your operation!" David said.

"I knew several soldiers and civilians were involved. I needed to go after the source, not pick at it like a scab. Blake was new, motivated, and did the job. Now I need to know who the source is."

"I'm going after the source. You can pick up the pieces." Blake headed to the door. He turned back to Colonel Marks. "One more thing. Did you inject Dex?"

"No, whoever went after Dex wanted you dead. General Talbert. Maybe your source."

"Why did you remind General Talbert of his nightmare? You erased all our work and set him back."

Colonel Marks clenched his fists. "To keep you focused on the mission."

"The one you told me to stand down on?"

"There are a lot of politics on this one, Sergeant. A lot of eyes are watching. I had to look like I had you under control."

Blake shook his head. *I'll deal with him later.* He walked out.

David marched alongside him. "Let me go with you. You don't have to do this alone."

Blake rubbed the sweat from his palm, feeling the steel of the knife in his pocket. "I can't drag you into this with me. I appreciate it, brother. But this isn't going to be a simulated battle operation we can wipe from memory. Good chance the target doesn't live through it. I might be on the run after this. Or in prison."

David followed Blake into the parking lot. Blake stopped when the door banged shut behind them.

"Forgot you didn't have a car here? I'll take you."

"Accessory to commit," Blake said. "I can't let you do that. I'll take your car. My go-bag still in the trunk?"

David grabbed Blake's shoulders. "Sophia might not have been my daughter, but I loved her like one. She was an incredible kid. Too young to go out like that. Whoever did it...they need to end. Let's do it together, brother. If anyone in Echo team were here, they'd be with you on this one."

Blake nodded. "Okay. But the moment you hear the police, you get out. You don't need to go down with me. You have a family."

David chuckled. "A wife who'd prefer I was dead and a son she brainwashed to believe I'm doing the Devil's work. They'll be fine living off the insurance money."

"She cares, David. She really does." Blake couldn't hold back a chuckle to reduce the tension. "She thinks you're having an affair."

"Figures." David shook his head. "She's worried I'm having an affair because of how it will tarnish her reputation with her family. Our marriage ended years ago. Besides, I have to keep tabs on you if I want that beer you owe me. Come on, let's jet."

They parked at the back of the psychiatric hospital. Blake tucked a holstered Glock 19 into the waistband of his jeans. "We'll have cover of darkness until we get close to the building."

"Mission is to kill Doctor Stillman?"

"Make him squeal first. Until then, he's a DNK."

"Are you thinking of walking through the front door?"

Blake smiled.

***

Blake limped through the hospital main entrance, an arm over David's shoulder.

"This isn't an emergency hospital." The nurse pointed the way they'd come. "Back to your vehicle and hit the highway. Three more exits." She ran a finger through her knotted hair, spinning it further into a web.

"He needs medication," David whispered.

"Excuse me? I just said this isn't an emergency hospital. It's a psychiatric hospital. We aren't trained for emergencies."

David lifted Blake's head by his hair. The nurse's finger paused. "He was wandering down a dirt road, wobbling. Something happened to him. He isn't saying a word and can barely walk. He needs help."

The nurse pulled her finger from her hair, picked up the phone, and murmured into it. A large orderly burst through a pair of sealed doors down the corridor. He pushed a wheelchair along. *They certainly have their ideal employee visualized.* "We'll take it from here," the orderly said, nearly hip-checking David out of the way. "This man is a patient of ours. He signed out this morning. I knew he needed more help."

"I'm coming with him."

"Authorized employees only." The nurse stopped in front of them and poked her finger back into her hair-web. "He's going to see the doctor right away."

"Good. He should. Since this isn't an emergency hospital, there's no reason I can't stay with him."

The nurse's finger caught in her hair. She exchanged a nervous glance with the orderly. The orderly shrugged. He didn't seem to know how to get rid of David, either.

"Come on, come on!" David said. "We're wasting time."

All four rushed through the double doors, down a hallway, and into a small room with a bed and straps. The same bed they'd strapped Blake in when they tried to kill him. No way would Blake get on the bed. He didn't want to blow his cover, but he had his limits.

"Where's the doctor? He doesn't need straps; he needs a doctor," David shouted.

"I'll get him." The nurse ran down the hall, the nest on her head bobbing as if it might break loose.

The orderly crossed his arms, waiting at the door. David carefully lifted the gun from behind his back, waited for the orderly to look the other way, and cracked him hard behind the head. The orderly crumpled.

Blake leaped out of the wheelchair. "That wasn't part of the plan." He darted to the door and ducked his head out into the hallway. Two patients had seen the orderly fall. Both looked pleased. "I think we're clear. Two eyes on. Not alarmed."

"We need to get to him before she does." He checked the orderly's consciousness with a light kick. "Help me pull him into the room, and let's get after her."

They dragged the orderly into the room and used his keycard to lock the door. Blake dropped the card in his pocket beside his knife. "We have less than a minute before someone comes by on their rounds, if the timings haven't changed."

An orderly rounded the corner, saw them, and marched toward them. David reached behind his back. Blake waved him off with a lowered hand. The orderly looked half as big as the other. "What are you doing in here? How did you get in?"

"I was looking for the bathroom. We were in Doctor Stillman's office, discussing my recovery," Blake said. "We took a break to use the pisser and got turned around."

"His office is that way." The orderly pointed down the hall. He looked Blake over, then smiled. "I remember you. Congratulations on your recovery." He placed a hand at his side, wrapping his fingers over the top of a Taser.

David slapped his hand on Blake's shoulder and chuckled. "He's better, but we have a lot of work to do."

Thunk. The noise came from the locked room. The orderly? *He couldn't have woken already.*

"What was that?" The orderly in the hall tried to peer over Blake's shoulder but Blake shuffled to the side to block his view.

David pointed his pistol at the orderly's head.

"Relax," David ordered. "Slow movements only. Anything quick, and you don't screw your girlfriend tonight."

The orderly jutted back and threw his hands up. "Look man, just let me go, okay? I won't say anything. The pay here ain't worth it."

David chuckled. "Look no further for a hero."

"My life for those people?" The orderly threw his thumb over his shoulder to indicate the patients. "They don't care about anyone."

"We don't have time for this," Blake said. "Doctor Stillman's office. David, take point. You're in the middle. Don't fuck with me."

"I won't. I swear I won't," the orderly said.

"What's your name?" Blake gripped the orderly's shoulders with one hand, applying pressure to his clavicle and guided him down the hallway to Doctor Stillman's office.

"Kyle. Is Dominic going to be okay?"

"Dominic?" Blake said.

"The guy I think you stuffed in the observation room," Kyle said.

"I need you to focus and shut up, okay Kyle? Can you do that for me?" Blake said.

"Yep, yep."

"Good. Doctor Stillman's office. Now."

Kyle pointed. "That door down there. Third on the left."

Chapter 55

THEY REACHED THE DOOR as Doctor Stillman and the receptionist exited. David grabbed the receptionist, spun her, then wrapped an arm around her throat and pointed his gun at Doctor Stillman. "Back," David said.

Doctor Stillman stutter-stepped back into his office until his heel banged on his desk. "Blake? What's going on?"

"Just shut the hell up for a minute," Blake said. "General Talbert sold you out. Told me everything about the Genesis and your involvement." Blake pulled his pistol and pressed it against Doctor Stillman's forehead. "Did you have my daughter killed?"

Doctor Stillman sighed and spoke slowly. "Blake, if you want to talk, I want you to take the gun out of my face."

Blake wrapped his finger around the trigger. "Not a negotiation. Did you kill my daughter?"

"Blake, General Talbert accused me out of desperation. But now he's out of the way—you saw to that. It's over, Blake. I had nothing to do with your daughter. I'm so sorry for your loss. There are a few doctors in the city who can help you. Keep it away from official channels if you need to. But you can't go around hurting people."

"Where's the Genesis?" Blake said.

"I imagine it's where you left it, Blake." Doctor Stillman's eyes jumped to the orderly and back to Blake.

"Stop repeating my name! There's one here. Where is it?" Blake asked.

"You're welcome to look for it. Kyle can take you where you want to go. Could you point the gun somewhere else?" Doctor Stillman raised his arm as if he were blocking out the sun.

Blake holstered the gun. David did the same. *If he doesn't have a Genesis here, where would he have it? His home would attract too much attention. The hospital would be the perfect cover. It* had *to be here.* "We'll go together," Blake said.

David whispered in his ear. "You're sure it's here?"

Blake leaned in. "Unless he owns another property, yeah."

"What are the odds he actually takes us where we want to go?"

"Lead the way, doctor," Blake said. "David, take the rear. The orderly and receptionist behind me." *He'll take us as far from the machine as he can, so when his tour is over, we'll go the other way.*

The five walked through the hospital. Doctor Stillman used a master keycard attached to a belt chain to unlock the doors. Blake paid little attention to what Doctor Stillman showed him. What was important was what he *wasn't* showing. The giant orderly banged helplessly on the window in the observation room when they walked by. David waved.

"Satisfied?" he asked when they returned to his office.

"I don't remember seeing confinement," Blake said.

"I can't take you there. It's restricted. For the patients' safety. We've come as far as I can take you, Blake. You need to let this go. Start healing from what happened to you. The general is gone. Nobody is coming after you."

Someone killed my daughter. "Confinement, doctor. Now."

The receptionist whimpered, "No."

"Just you and I," Doctor Stillman said. "The others can wait here. The more faces in that wing, the more likely a patient will become aggressive."

"Wait here with them," Blake said to David.

David stood by the door, one foot planted on the wall, one hand planted on his holster. "Copy. We'll be here when you get back."

"Let's go." Blake shoved Doctor Stillman out the door and to another door marked *Confinement* in bold, red letters. Doctor Stillman swiped his card and entered a code. Inside the zone, several patients walked the halls, muttering.

Doctor Stillman noticed Blake glancing around at the patients. "They're on a timed rotation. Every three hours, they return to their rooms, and other rooms open. Only three patients are allowed in the hallway at any one time. It's more manageable for the danger they pose to each other." An orderly Blake had never seen before—lanky, deep sockets revealing large dark eyes—guarded the far corner of a large, quiet common room, his arms crossed. Doctor Stillman nodded at him. "Good morning, Stewart. We'll be gone soon."

A patient's eyes bulged at Blake. "Your soul is so dark." The patient pointed at Blake, white hair dancing on his head like a toupee sliding off as he bobbed closer. "You've buried it deep." A smile spread across his lips and revealed beige teeth.

Doctor Stillman stepped between them. "We'll be gone in a moment. Thank you for sharing your thoughts. I will discuss it with him."

"He knows. It's overflowing." The man gestured like a volcano erupting and danced away.

"We should go," Doctor Stillman said.

"Keep moving."

Doctor Stillman led them down a short hallway, opening doors or letting Blake see through glass windows.

"All clear?" David said when they returned to the office.

Blake pulled David to a corner of the office. "I thought it would be here. It's the most logical place. A Genesis has to be here."

"Have you considered that Doctor Stillman might have been honest about what General Talbert was doing? Peter could have swapped the chips in the machines under the direction of General Talbert, and they did all the brainwashing in-house."

"No. There's something I'm missing. When I asked General Talbert about Sophia, he had every reason to tell me the truth. I don't think he lied. He didn't know who killed Sophia. That means there's someone out there that's involved in this that hasn't paid for it. And who developed the chip in the first place? Unless..."

"Unless Colonel Marks is lying," David said. "If Doctor Stillman isn't involved, then Colonel Marks would have to be. That doesn't fit either. He's not a programmer."

Blake grabbed a lamp from a book table and hurled it across the room. It shattered against a wall.

Kyle stepped toward them but stopped when David pulled his pistol.

"It's fine," Doctor Stillman said. "It's just a lamp."

David returned his attention to Blake. "What do you want to do? We should jet. Either way, I'm with you, brother."

"All these people. Twisting the truth. Sending me on missions half blind."

"What did they gain by killing Sophia?" Doctor Stillman said.

Blake's and David's eyes snapped to the doctor. "They killed her because I was getting too close to the truth. They wanted me to back off," Blake said.

"Oh man," David muttered. "Anyone who knows you would know killing Sophia wouldn't take you out of the fight. It would send you into the fight like a hammer against a board of loose nails. Think about it, Blake."

Blake squeezed his pounding head. The throbbing pulsed down to his chest. *Calm down. Calm down.* "I'm going in circles. Colonel Marks? General Talbert? Doctor Stillman? They all have agendas. They're all hiding things from me."

"We should go," David said. "There's nothing more we can do here."

Blake massaged his forehead. "We need to find the fourth Genesis."

They left the hospital, Doctor Stillman swearing he and his staff wouldn't call the police, hoping Blake would trust he had nothing to hide.

They took Highway 15, heading south to San Diego.

"Turn around." Blake slapped the dashboard.

"What?"

"Turn around."

"To the hospital? It's not there. He let us go, Blake. We're lucky we aren't in prison." David yanked the car two lanes over to the side of the road, causing one car to swerve and blare its horn. "I know you want answers. I can't imagine what—"

"David, how did Doctor Stillman know I took care of General Talbert?"

"What?"

"In the office, he said I took care of General Talbert, so this was all over. How could he know that?"

"He has someone on the inside?"

"He knows more than he let on and we walked right out of there."

"What if it doesn't exist? What if General Talbert lied to you?"

Blake tapped his finger on the dashboard, running the tour through his mind, trying to spot something he'd missed.

He knew where he'd find it.

"The only place we didn't check. When the orderly tied me down in the observation room, there was a second door in the room's corner. Too big to be a closet or a bathroom unless it was wheelchair accessible, but none of the other rooms had a door. What if observation is for after Genesis experiments? I left the room with Doctor Stillman after he unstrapped me. We never checked it."

David got out of the car and paced the gravel shoulder. "It was probably a bathroom. Are we going back to search again? How are we going to get in *this* time?"

Blake pulled the card from his pocket. "I didn't give this back. You still have that can of spray paint we used to paint my fence in the trunk?"

David threw the car keys in the air and caught them. "We'll be in jail before the night is out." David chuckled wryly and shook his head.

They returned to the hospital. Five seventeen. They would have changed shifts at five. David led the way to the back door and blacked out the camera with spray paint. If security was paying close attention, they'd have seen him do it. *We'll keep going until we can't.* Blake pulled the card and swiped. The door opened. They went inside, recognizing the hallway from their tour. They weren't far from the observation room.

They stalked down the hallway. When they reached the observation room, Blake opened the door and stepped inside.

"Wait here and cover the exit. Don't let anyone in." Blake opened the door he'd written off as a bathroom.

Chapter 56

A Genesis machine stood in the middle of the room with the lid closed. Someone lay inside. Blake checked the monitor and saw Doctor Stillman in a conversation with Peter.

"I'll watch for him," Peter said. "When Blake stumbles onto the note at the office, he'll kill Colonel Marks." *No Stuttering.*

"That should wrap up this mess. Any idea who killed his daughter?" Doctor Stillman said.

"No idea. I don't think General Talbert did. It wasn't our team."

Doctor Stillman chuffed. "It's a loose end I don't like. If someone else put that sniper in play..."

"If they killed his kid, they aren't on his side."

"What's happening with Senior Chief Wilburg?"

"MPs picked him up for processing at Miramar. He won't make it to the prison alive. We have operators on the ground to intercede."

"Corporal Hodge?"

"He's going to take his own life."

"Any other problems?"

Peter smiled, pleased with himself. "Only Sergeant Powell and Captain Guarnere. Without them, Colonel Marks has nothing. The board should move forward with the project, having no solid link between the killings and the machine."

"They both need to die. Make it look like an unrelated accident. Away from Genesis. Colonel Marks' home, if we're lucky. A tragedy for the Genesis team—nothing that comes back on me." Doctor Stillman pointed at himself. "The board wants the project to move forward, and with the team dead, they'll turn to me again."

"I'll arrange it."

"Thank you, Peter." A glass of wine appeared in both their hands. They clanged glasses. "To years of successful missions."

Blake pulled the cord on the Genesis, killing the power to the simulation. The lid opened and Doctor Stillman sputtered, as if in the middle of gulping wine. When he saw Blake, he froze.

"Blake, it's not what you think," Doctor Stillman said.

Blake pulled his gun. *Calm. Breathe. Don't kill this asshole. It's the easy way out.*

Doctor Stillman raised his arms. "Stay calm."

"You may not have killed Sophia, but you led her to the sniper's scope. I should kill you." *He deserves to die. People are dead because of him.* Blake could walk out of the hospital, and there would be no proof he'd been in the room. The investigation would reveal what Doctor Stillman had done. No detective would be eager to find the killer. *The asshole deserves to die.*

"Everyone has a price," Doctor Stillman said.

Blake's eyes narrowed in concentration. "The truth. That's my price."

"You know the truth. I wasn't lying when I said I don't know who killed your daughter. I had nothing to do with it."

"Nothing to do with it? *Nothing?*" He squeezed the trigger, and the hammer pulled back. Before it slammed forward, enormous arms clutched Blake's arms and shook him so violently the gun flew across the room.

"You should have named a price." Doctor Stillman chuckled. "Bargaining is no longer available."

Blake squatted then exploded up, his head cracking against the face behind him. Hopefully the snap he heard was the man's nose breaking. The grip relaxed, and Blake dropped, arms pressed overhead, falling out of the man's grasp. He felt the knife in his pocket and pulled it out. Dominic punched him in the face before he could use it.

"Watch out!" Doctor Stillman said. "Knife."

Dominic grabbed Blake's arm at the wrist and snapped the arm against his knee twice until the knife joined the pistol on the floor.

"Get the gun." Doctor Stillman pointed to where it had fallen.

Blake stomped on Dominic's foot, whirling him off balance, then pulled him close, dropped onto his back, and threw him over and into the Genesis. Dominic's head cracked awkwardly between the floor and the Genesis. Bones fractured, echoing in the room like snapped celery stalks. Dominic didn't move.

Gun. Blake rolled over and spotted his pocketknife on the floor. He flicked it open, stood up, and threw it just as Doctor Stillman's hand came up with the pistol. The knife hit Doctor Stillman in the shoulder, and he dropped the gun. *Ten steps.* Blake sprinted across the room and slid to the gun. He caught it by the handle and squeezed the trigger. A bang echoed in the room as the bullet struck Doctor Stillman in the head. Blood spattered the wall behind him.

David burst into the room.

"It's time to go," Blake said.

"No kidding!" David shook his head and followed Blake to the car. "What happened? You look like hell."

"Thanks for the backup."

David shrugged. "I knew you could handle it."

Blake told David what he'd heard from Peter and Doctor Stillman in the Genesis.

David punched the steering wheel. "Peter's been working us for years. I thought he had a disability. Acting lessons paid off. Prick. He's next?"

"Yeah, he's next. Vehicle interdiction." Blake spat blood. He must have been punched in the lip so hard his tooth cut into it. "I don't want to take him at Genesis, and I don't want anyone in his family getting hurt. Once he knows Doctor Stillman is dead, he'll run. He was talking to Doctor Stillman in the machine. That means he's on site but will leave soon since I cut Doctor Stillman out. We wait for him to leave and snatch him en route. Have you ever seen him in the Genesis before? He seemed comfortable with it."

"Peter never used it to my knowledge," David grumbled.

"He must be using it after hours. Any bets he's able to work later than us? Especially if he claims a programming glitch that needs overtime to fix?"

"Let's jet and catch him on the way out. I hope you're right."

Chapter 57

They parked on a side road near the Genesis compound and watched vehicles drive by until they saw Peter's bug. Peter never looked their way.

"Intersection of Stanwood and Oakview. It has an all-way stop."

"Copy."

The intersection was ten minutes ahead. Blake checked the remaining rounds in his pistol. Peter might be on his guard. He'd know Blake was close.

David barely threw on his clicker to change lanes. "Ready? It's just up ahead."

"Let's finish this."

The brake lights on Peter's car lit up, and his vehicle eased to a stop. David screamed past on Peter's left, swerved into his lane, then slammed the brakes. Peter slammed his brakes so hard his tires shrieked in protest. Blake leapt out of the car before it stopped, charging toward the front door. He yanked the handle. Locked. He smashed the window with the butt of his pistol.

"Let's go." Blake reached through the window, unlocked the door, and yanked it open. "Get out."

Peter kicked back into the passenger seat as much as the seatbelt would allow and threw his hands up. "What are you doing?"

Blake cracked the end of the pistol across Peter's face. Blood dribbled from a gash in his forehead down his cheek. "Get out."

"Take that gun out of my face. I kept my mouth shut about my knee. I-I shouldn't have. Th-this is insane." His hands trembled as he used the steering wheel to pull himself out of the car.

Blake grabbed his shirt and yanked him into the back seat of David's car. Peter bonked his head on the door's rim but tumbled in. Blake sat beside him. The car tore away from the intersection.

"I've had a hard time getting the truth out of people." Blake turned his pistol over in the light of streetlamps streaking past. "Everyone who lied to me is dead."

"Blake, l-look, I—"

Blake backhanded him across the face, further opening the gash. "Think about the consequences of lying to me before you talk. And we all know you don't stutter, so knock it off."

The car swerved between lanes. Peter used the momentum to try to grapple the pistol out of Blake's grip. Although larger than Blake, Peter's grip was weaker, and Blake had leverage. Blake twisted and elbowed Peter's throat. Peter gagged. The blood from his cheek smeared Blake's sleeve.

"Oh man, hang on," David said.

"Keep driving." Blake shoved Peter against the door with his boot. "I'm good." Peter raked at Blake's face, and Blake raised his knees to put distance between them, then kicked him back. With a click, he pulled back the hammer and aimed his pistol between Peter's eyes. "Give me a reason not to kill you."

Peter got the hint and stopped struggling. "I didn't kill Sophia."

"I know you didn't. Who did?"

Peter shook his head. "It had nothing to do with us."

"Who is us?"

"You know. General Talbert. Doctor Stillman." Peter wiped his gash on the back of his wrist and checked the blood. "The only reason Doctor Stillman left Genesis was because General Talbert was on the panel that fired him. The general knew what Doctor Stillman was doing with the tech. They wanted a place for him to experiment outside of military eyes. During the changeover from Doctor Stillman to military leadership, Doctor Stillman told me exactly what to do to get hired as a civilian tech. I work both sides."

"How the hell does nobody know who killed Sophia?"

Peter clamped his eyes shut as if to brace against a bullet. "I don't know, I don't know, I don't know. We've been trying to figure it out. Please, don't kill me. I was doing my job." His lower lip trembled.

"Sophia would be alive if it wasn't for this project and the work you did for them," Blake said.

Blake felt David's eyes on him from the rearview mirror. "Your call," David said.

"Please." Peter buried his head in his hands, and tears fell from his eyes. "I'm sorry. I wanted to tell you the night I came to your office. I was going to tell you everything I knew. But they'd come after my family like they did to yours."

Blake's jaws tightened. Peter was only sorry that he had got caught. He knew people were going to die when he put those chips in the machines. The conversation in the Genesis with Doctor Stillman confirmed that. Senior Chief Wilburg's wife was dead because of Peter, accident or not.

Sophia. Blake saw her in her last moments, looking at him, confused that he'd yelled her name, and he'd never forget the moment the bullet snapped into her. He raised the pistol to Peter and pulled the trigger three times.

"Jesus Christ, Blake, in my car?" David slammed on the brakes and threw the car to the shoulder. No honks or flashing lights. Range Road was quiet at night. He spun in the front seat. "You couldn't wait until we reached the pits, at least?"

Blake shrugged. "Help me get him out of the car, and you won't have to clean up all the blood that pools."

"We can't leave him here. They'll find him."

"Not before I finish what I have to do."

"You shouldn't have to go to prison for this."

"I've killed a lot of people, David. This time, the government didn't order me to."

"Jesus. If that's how you want it. It didn't happen in this car."

Blake stared at Peter's pulverized head. "I borrowed your car and brought it back cleaned up. That's the story if anyone asks. Get it cleaned up before you go home."

"We should bury him somewhere. Burn the body. You don't have to go down for this. You deserve better."

"Sophia deserved better."

They got out of the car and threw the body into a ditch, concealed for the night. It would be visible in the early trickles of daylight.

"Now what?" David sat in the car, wiping the sweat from his face onto his sleeve. "We don't know anything more than we did before you killed him."

"Sure we do. We know for certain he didn't kill Sophia."

"Who's left?"

"Colonel Marks."

David squinted at the blinding lights from an oncoming car. "Damn high beams." David flashed his lights on and off. "Let's hope he doesn't notice the body."

"Doesn't matter. They'd never connect it in time."

"We've gone down the Colonel Marks rabbit hole already. Is there something you haven't told me? Because I can't think of any reason he knows more than he told us. We have to trust *someone*."

Blake caught a whiff of copper from the gore splattered on the rear window. "Do you remember when you said the point of killing Sophia, for anyone that knows me, wouldn't be to take me off the hunt, but to send me straight into it with guns blazing? Colonel Marks admitted to setting me up for this when he hired me. He got me in so I would push buttons and discover what he couldn't. When I was with Clara and Sophia, I would have sat back and relaxed for a while, rethink what I was doing, maybe leave the project. Doctor Stillman would have wanted that. Do you know who didn't want that? Killing Sophia sent me back on the path like a rabid dog. Who would benefit from that more than Colonel Marks? Everyone involved in the scandal that we know of is dead."

"So, you're going to kill him, too?"

"I'm going alone. Nobody knows you're involved. Last anyone saw, you drove me home. I didn't say a word to you about what happened."

"I can go with you. I loved her too."

"The mission doesn't need two operators. Drop me off on Laforest Road. I'll hump it in from there."

Chapter 58

THE AIR WAS MOIST with a chilly wind. It would rain soon. Blake checked the weather app on his cell phone: heavy rain was expected to begin later this morning, probably sooner. His stomach growled. He pushed the hunger out of his mind.

David had driven off five minutes ago, leaving him on an abandoned dirt road, the forest creaking with insect life on both sides. Blake's little girl was gone, Clara was torn apart and would never speak to him again. Maybe his purpose on Earth was this very moment, and then he'd return to the dirt from which he came. A bullet. That's what he deserved, too.

Mission update: kill everyone involved in Sophia's death before morning. If more people were involved, he'd have to hurry, but he didn't think there were. The puppets in this show had to stop at some point.

Blake ejected the magazine from his pistol, counted twelve rounds, then returned the pistol to its holster. He veered off the road and walked through the forest. The colonel's neighborhood was on the other side. Covering five miles took an hour at a jog. He found a dog-walking trail and followed it onto a concrete sidewalk. To anyone watching, he'd have taken a midnight walk and just come out, his hood hiding his face. When the police found Colonel Marks' body, the neighbors would remember the man in the hood and wish they'd called the police.

He walked like he had nowhere to go, suspecting not a soul stirred at this desolate hour, although soldiers lived here, and many could wake from nightmares. How ironic would it be if a soldier with PTSD called Blake in and the police arrested him?

When he reached the colonel's house, he ghosted across the lawn to the door and pressed his ear against it. No sounds, no activity. It would be easier if the colonel was awake. Blake tried the doorknob—locked. He walked around to the back, stepping carefully to ensure he didn't alert a neighbor's dog. Blake wasn't the only soldier with a retired police pooch.

The gate to the backyard opened easily, and Blake minimized the creak. He walked to the patio door and listened. The wind blew the squeaky swing set, and a vent flap on the side of the house clunked.

Two lock-picks later, he slid the door open, anticipating squeaking but hearing none. He stepped through and edged the door shut behind him.

Colonel Marks had a wife and son. He'd need to get the colonel downstairs while the others slept. His watch read four forty-five. Waiting for the colonel to wake might be best. He'd be up first, probably in the next forty-five minutes. If someone else woke before him, he'd have to play out the consequences. No collateral damage. Colonel Marks was a coffee guy, so he took a seat in the gloom of the kitchen.

Twenty-seven minutes later, the floor squeaked overhead. Blake's body electrified, and he perked up in the chair. A toilet flushed. The footsteps sounded heavy. Could be Colonel Marks. The creak descended the stairs and thumped around the corner. Blake slipped his pistol out and lay it on his thigh.

The footsteps changed direction. *Coffee isn't the most important thing in his day.*

The television came on. A song introduced Paw Patrol. Not the colonel. Must be his son. What was the boy's name? Darrell? Derek? He would come to eat soon, if he was like most growing boys sitting in front of a television. Early riser like his dad. Sophia was an early riser, too. Tears soaked his eyes, but he pushed out the memory. He needed anger.

Ten minutes later, he heard footsteps upstairs, and a toilet flushed again. The footsteps tapped down the stairs. Blake heard a grunt, definitely masculine, near the bottom.

"Daniel, it's five in the morning. What are you doing up? You should go back to bed," Colonel Marks said from the other room.

"It's five thirty-three," Daniel said. "I'm awake and hungry. Can you make pancakes?"

"No. I have a lot to get done today, Daniel."

"Can you ask Mom?"

"I'm not going to wake her up. She needs to rest."

Something hit the floor, a dull thwack. "I'm starving," Daniel groaned. "Too starving to move."

"I'm not your mother. That's not going to work with me. I'm getting coffee. If you want help making breakfast, get off your butt. Soldier on."

"I'm not a soldier, Dad. I want to be a gamer. Like PewDiePie."

"Who? Turn off the TV and come help."

"Can you make me cereal?"

"If you have time to know who PooDeePipe is, you have time to get your own cereal. And you don't *make* cereal, you add milk to it."

"Pew...Die...Pie," Daniel said.

"Kaw...fee." Footsteps headed for the kitchen. Colonel Marks turned the corner and flipped on the light. Blake still held his pistol inconspicuously at his thigh but pointed at the colonel. He put a finger on his lips. The colonel paled.

"What are you doing?" Colonel Marks whispered. He glanced at the other room, then back at Blake. "Let's go outside."

Blake needed to control the environment, the players, and the threat level. He shook his head. "Here and now." The colonel glanced to his side. Blake followed him to the blades sitting in the knife block ten steps away. The math equated to nine bullet holes and the colonel never reaching the knives. "You were the sniper, weren't you?"

"I need you to trust me, Blake," Colonel Marks said.

"Daddy?"

Blake hid the pistol behind his back.

Daniel appeared around the corner. "Who is that, Daddy? You look sick." He pointed at Blake, his French fry fingers shaky. "Did you make my daddy sick?"

"Daniel, go watch some TV, okay?" Colonel Marks scooted Daniel out of the room.

"I'm hungry, and you told me to make my breakfast. I want to make breakfast," he whimpered, on the verge of tears. "Who is that man? I don't like him. He looks mean."

Colonel Marks put his hands on Daniel's shoulders to usher him away. "We work together. He lost someone close to him. He's having a tough time. You remember when Gammy died? How sad and upset we all were? It's kind of like that. Now, I need you to go back to watching your show for a bit, okay?" Sweat dripped down Colonel Marks' face. *At least he can save his son.*

With Daniel gone, the colonel returned his attention to Blake. "I need to show you something. I need you to trust me."

Blake slipped the gun out from behind his back. "Did you kill Sophia?"

"No. I didn't kill Sophia."

Liar. "What do you know about the shooter? About her death?"

"You've trusted me this far. Can you trust me a little further?"

Blake lowered the pistol. "If you try anything, I'm going to shoot you and leave you in a pool of blood while I come back here and kill your son, so you know what it's like to lose someone you love more than anything in your life."

"You can trust me," he said. "I'll drive."

They got in the car. Daniel begged his dad to stay, never taking his eyes off Blake. Colonel Marks assured Daniel that his mom could help make breakfast and that he'd be back later.

"Where are we going?" Blake asked.

"Your home," Colonel Marks said, both hands tight on the steering wheel, eyes locked on the road ahead.

"What for?"

"You won't believe me if I don't show you."

Blake kept his pistol pointed at Colonel Marks. They pulled into the driveway. Clara's van shined like new in the sunrise. "Clara won't be happy to see us," Blake said. "Last time I saw her, she hit me and stormed out of the hospital."

"Come on." Colonel Marks led the way to the front door and knocked. Blake shifted his weight from leg to leg and holstered the pistol. He felt strange, waiting outside his own home for someone to answer. *Sophia is gone. Clara will want to be alone.*

The door flung open, and Sophia beamed when she saw him.

Chapter 59

Blake felt breathless. Sophia ran into his arms. He barely had the sense to hug her back, feeling tingles all over. *This can't be real. I saw her die. I held her in my arms.* He touched her with a few fingers, terrified she'd blow away in the wind. *She's real.*

Sophia looked up at him. "Can you stop poking my face? You're a little too much, Dad."

He refused to let her go. Her dark hair, her thin frame—so real. Was he in the Genesis? No, he couldn't be. "How is this possible?"

"We need to talk." Colonel Marks raised a hand and indicated inside.

Blake squeezed her again. She moaned, guarding her shoulder. "My arm hurts, Dad. I got shot, remember?"

Clara stood grinning in the doorway. She joined the hug as if all the frustration in their marriage disappeared with the revelation that Sophia was alive.

"I don't understand. I thought you hated me," Blake said.

Clara's brows furrowed. "I was angry you had put the military first again, but I know it's who you are. And Sophia is okay. She's alive. Look. She's okay."

Tears brimmed in Blake's eyes. He heard his dad in his head calling him a Girl Scout for crying. Blake didn't care. He tightened his grip on both of them. "I'm sorry I wasn't there," he said.

Colonel Marks placed an arm on Blake's shoulder. "We really should talk."

"Colonel," Clara said. "Thank you for bringing him home."

A soft click of nails tapped against the hardwood floor in slow, careful steps. Blake stiffened. He knew that sound.

Dex appeared at the end of the hallway, his eyes locked on Blake.

"He's okay?" Blake asked, but he already knew he was.

Blake's breath left him in a broken exhale. He took one step forward, slowly raising a hand.

Dex tilted his head, then padded forward and rubbed his head in Blake's hand.

Blake wouldn't be home for long. He'd killed Doctor Stillman and Peter. They'd lock him up. Sophia was alive. If he'd known she hadn't died...*I held her body—she was dead, and Clara hated me for it.*

Blake and Colonel Marks headed into the den and sat.

"This is going to be challenging to understand," Colonel Marks said. "I was the sniper."

Blake took several calming breaths. He knew this already, but he had to give the colonel a chance to explain, even if he wanted to put his head through the coffee table.

"You were hesitating. I needed you to go all-in on figuring it out. And you did. I'm sorry so much went down to complete the mission. I couldn't let the Genesis fail." Colonel Marks sighed. "I had two sons. The picture in my office? My wife and two sons before my son Geoff died." Colonel Marks' words dampened. He wiped an eye. "A private under my command came back from Afghanistan with serious PTSD. He blamed me for nightmares I couldn't erase. We had no help for him because of his rank and waiting lists. If the Genesis had existed, my son might be alive."

Clara stepped in and offered to feed them. Both declined. Blake had no appetite. He'd killed Doctor Stillman. Peter had a family, and he'd killed him for his involvement in Sophia's death. "Do you know how many people are dead because of me?"

"Mostly."

"You shot her. How is she alive?"

"I shot her. I didn't kill her. The FBI wanted to protect her, so they told you both she had died, in accordance with my request. You were angry. General Talbert put you through the loss so many times you lost the thread that she might be alive. I think he wanted you to focus on the shooter because he didn't know who the sniper was. I wish we could have done this another way."

"You're no better than the private that killed your son. How do you think Senator Fredrick's family feels? Senior Chief Wilburg? What his kids are going through? You knew the Genesis was creating assassins. You might as well have pulled the trigger yourself."

Colonel Marks nodded.

Blake punched him hard in the face, knocking him back against the chair. "You could have killed her."

Colonel Marks rubbed his jaw. "I had to take the risk."

"She would have been what? Collateral damage?" Blake felt the weight of the pistol tucked into the back of his pants and his knife poking him in his pocket.

"I needed you at your best. I didn't program the soldier that killed the senator. If it came back on us, they would have shut down Genesis. We need Genesis. It's my atonement for not helping that private—for not saving my son."

"Did you drug Dex? Place those explosives at my home with the threatening note? You knew what I'd do."

"I'm sorry about Dex. We gave him a drug that should have temporarily made him dangerous enough for you to focus up. It wasn't supposed to go as far as it did. The dosage was wrong."

Blake gripped his pistol. "You stopped helping soldiers with PTSD. You force-fed the project to me—used me like a weapon to protect the machine."

"You trust in the Genesis mission. I know you do. Protecting the project is the best way to help."

Blake felt sweat run down his spine despite the chill in the air. "What's stopping you from killing me and using the machine to assassinate whoever you want? I know you're capable. The best thing for the project is for it to die."

Colonel Marks didn't seem fazed. "Someone else will figure out the technology. The only way to keep the machines from being used that way again is if I oversee it."

Blake thought he'd lost everything. Sophia wasn't dead. Doctor Stillman and Peter didn't have to die. He felt the room spin, his memories bursting in agonizing flashes.

"We can rebuild it the way we meant it to be," Colonel Marks said. "We destroy the chips and carry on with our research. Let's change lives."

"Trust you? You fucked with my mind. You made me believe my daughter was dead, and I killed people for it."

Colonel Marks sighed. "Your brothers need you."

Blake slammed his fist on the coffee table. One of the legs cracked. "My family needs me. How did you know I'd come out of that coma?"

"I didn't know you'd end up in a coma. I didn't know the Genesis could do what Talbert made it do. Clara tried to help, but she couldn't reach you."

"Clara? She hated me at the hospital. I woke up because she slapped the shit out of me. And she packs a punch."

"When the ambulance arrived to take Sophia away, the FBI insisted she'd be able to identify the body later. It wasn't until after you woke up from the coma that we told Clara the truth and reunited her with Sophia. They were with the FBI in witness protection until we knew it was safe to bring her home."

Blake felt his neck tense. "Your mission. Son of a bitch."

"Spend some time with your family, Blake. Take a couple of weeks to recover. We can talk later."

Blake wondered what would stop Colonel Marks from killing him if he thought he was a threat. How could he go back to Genesis? "Doctor Stillman and Peter? I killed them both."

"I'll take care of it. We'll clean the scenes and make sure there's no link. Police won't be able to implicate you."

"Cover it up. I guess that's what you do."

"Nobody is perfect, Blake. Get off your high horse. You've killed people for a lot less critical reasons than national security."

"Corporal Hodge? Is he alive? Senior Chief Wilburg?"

Colonel Marks' shoulders slouched. "Unfortunately, someone got to them first. We found Corporal Hodge poisoned in his cell. Senior Chief Wilburg took a shiv twelve times in his back. An unaffiliated inmate." He shrugged. "Doubt we'll ever know who paid for it. Safe to say Doctor Stillman or General Talbert."

Or someone else involved in this mess. Blake felt as though a heavy weight lifted from his shoulders and another one slammed down on him at the same time. He escorted Colonel Marks out and watched him drive away. He should have shot him. He wrapped Sophia in one arm and Clara in the other. Dex wagged his tail, his nose nudging at Blake's leg to go for that run he owed him.

"What are you going to do?" Clara said.

"I don't know."

Chapter 60

THREE WEEKS FLEW BY. Blake devoted all his time to Clara and Sophia. Still, the tension in their relationship reemerged, as the novelty of what they'd been through wore off. Blake found himself desperate for action. Relaxing wasn't in his nature and he felt increasingly jittery with each passing day. He kept his phone turned off for the first time since he'd joined Delta. Every car that zoomed past his yard, every dog that barked, every visitor reminded him that his family might never be safe again. A few days ago, someone from Genesis called Clara, asking him when he'd go back to work. He kept asking himself if back to work meant Delta or Genesis.

He went to Genesis first. Getting into the building and down to the machines went smoothly as if the last few months hadn't happened. His office looked the same as he'd left it.

The War Room continued its work with soldiers—just with one fewer operator. *I'm thirty-nine. If I go back to Delta, I might get to operate for a few more years. In the Genesis, as long as my mind stays sharp, I'll always have a mission.* Clara and Sophia wanted him to make his own decision. They'd support him either way. As brief as the family discussion had been, the wedge between him and Clara eased slightly when he pulled them into the room and asked them what they wanted him to do. That small thing mended a tiny piece of their relationship, giving him hope that maybe it could be fixed.

"Nice vacation?" David leaned against the Genesis, hands in pockets. He'd come by the house several times during Blake's time off, but they'd never talked about what happened. "I heard you were back today. Had to see it for myself."

They shook hands and hugged. "Good to see you, brother."

"I missed you."

Blake chuckled. "Yeah, sure you did."

"He's waiting for you."

"I know," Blake said. "How have things been?"

"Quiet. Smooth. Things changed when your mission ended. All the tension went out of the place."

"When all the right people ended up dead, you mean."

"Know what you're going to say?"

"You mean, do you think I'm out of a job?"

"If you wanted to go to prison, you would have come out with the truth already."

It hadn't taken a lot of time to talk himself out of going to the media. If he did, the military would just cover up what they needed to and blame him for the rest—rogue soldier suffering from PTSD. They might cut the project, but chances are they'd rename it and rebuild. The organization or the culture would never face blame for Senator Fredrick's death.

Blake had killed people overseas while defending his country. Why go to prison to defend it at home? He knew how it worked. Kill one leader, and another would rise in his place—sometimes worse. To keep the project focused, he'd be better off supervising it from the inside.

Blake headed to Colonel Marks's office. The colonel's secretary waited outside, her hands clasped together, her blouse straightened. She reminded him of Doctor Kendra.

"I'm here to—"

"He's waiting for you." She turned and opened the door, never looking him in the eye.

Three men stood in the office. Colonel Marks behind his desk, Major Graham in the uncomfortable chair, and Major Lokey standing in the corner. Blake hadn't expected company.

"Sir." Blake cracked to attention and saluted. Colonel Marks gave a snappy salute and pointed to a third chair—steel and probably the most uncomfortable. Major Graham and Major Lokey glanced at him, then returned their attention to Colonel Marks.

"I've brought the majors up to speed on the Genesis. They were both instrumental in resolving the links between the traitors and the project. They're the reason you aren't in prison right now."

Blake felt the frame of the knife against the cotton of his pocket. *He's acting like he did me a favor.*

Major Lokey cleared his throat. "Sergeant, thank you for your service in taking down those responsible and maintaining the integrity of the project."

Major Graham nodded.

"We'd like to discuss your next mission," Colonel Marks said.

"If I want to stick with this project or move back to Delta?"

Major Lokey turned his chair to face Blake. "No. That's not an option for you. There's a lot of heat regarding the project. A lot of people affiliated with it are dead. We can't allow you to operate outside the wire. General Bradford is stepping into General Talbert's role and has canceled all leave and transfers until further notice."

"Look, Sergeant, we want to present you with an opportunity." Major Lokey folded his hands on his lap.

Now what?

"We all feel the technology Doctor Stillman designed is superior and gets results for PTSD more efficiently than its predecessor," Colonel Marks said.

Jesus Christ. They want to use the tech.

"We want you to be the senior officer in command of the tech and the project. The promotion needs to happen today." Major Lokey stabbed Colonel Marks' desk with a downward finger. "Before the parade places General Bradford in command."

"I'm not an officer. I'm an operator."

"And we'd want you to continue operating. Under the rank of Sergeant Major, you'd have operational control on decisions involving the Genesis." Colonel Marks said.

"What happened to the fourth Genesis?"

"It's here in a separate War Room. The only machine with the chip installed. We don't plan to jump into this. You can decide, Sergeant Major, when we move the tech to other machines."

The deal is buttered up nicely. Is there something I'm not seeing here?

"What do you think?" Colonel Marks said.

Blake had walked into the office expecting a completely different conversation. Putting him in charge didn't change the politics that would force his hand or the orders they'd give when they needed it.

"Sergeant? Sergeant Major? What do you think?" Major Lokey said.

"I decide when and if the tech makes it into the other machines? I'm the only one that operates the Genesis that has the tech installed?" Blake stared at Colonel Marks.

"You know I can't promise that. As of right now, the tech won't move. But if anything happens to you, or if you procrastinate, we may move without you. We're still in the military, Sergeant. You'll be the only one using the V2 Genesis, and if that changes, we'll let you know."

"The goal of this project was to help soldiers recover from PTSD," Blake said as much to them as himself. "That's still the mission?"

"Yes, that's the mission," Colonel Marks said.

He didn't trust any of them. Probably never would. That didn't mean he couldn't do a lot of good for his brothers. The kind of good that Peter, Doctor Stillman, and Talbert should have been doing. They paid the price for their role in corrupting soldiers and destroying lives. The project would outlive his career as a Delta operator. "I have one request."

"A request?" Colonel Marks looked red enough to smoke from his ears.

"Let's hear it," Major Lokey said.

"Remove Colonel Marks from his position and give him the opportunity to retire honorably. Assign someone else to lead the project. One that we all agree on."

Author Note

The idea for this book came while I was reading *Unflinching* by Jody Mitic, a memoir about a Canadian sniper, his injuries, and the impact military service had on his life. I started thinking about PTSD and what it costs soldiers and their families long after the war ends.

Then the question shifted.

What if we could treat trauma by stepping inside a soldier's nightmares? What if we could help them confront the memories that haunt them instead of letting those memories control them?

And then the darker thought followed.

If you build a machine that can guide someone through their worst moments, what else can it be used for?

Genesis was born from that tension.

This story went through multiple drafts before it became what you just read. Some versions were darker. Some characters didn't survive. In the end, I chose the version that best served Blake's journey and the ethical battle at the center of the project.

At its core, this book isn't just about technology. It's about responsibility. About how far leaders are willing to go in the name of mission success. About the cost of loyalty when the chain of command is compromised.

Thank you for stepping into Blake's world.

Acknowledgements

Thank you to all the wonderful people who made this book possible. Every person made a difference in this project, so I've listed them in order of the novel's development, rather than in any special order.

Ione Jayawardena and Jennifer O'Neill for being my beta readers and sharing your thoughts and insights. We need to do more Zoom beta reading calls. Sorry O'Neill, I didn't get much deeper with Clara and Blake's relationship. Liam Gibbs for your developmental / line / copy edit rolled into one. I appreciate all the moments you suggested using five senses in the scene and the work you put into the edits to make the book better. Ayden Rails for your copy / line edits and thoughtful insights into character development. Ione Jayawardena (again!) and Duby for your proofreading and helping bring together the final product.

Finally, thank you to all my Kickstarter backers (listed in backing order). Your support means the world to me: Lejeune, Robert Wein, A. Graham, Marcus Johnson, Patricia, Daniel Z, R.G. Roberts, Cathy Anderson, Brooke & Steven Coté, Jennifer O'Neill, Stephany, Z.S. Diamanti, Joe Barros, Ione Jayawardena, Liam Gibbs, Nadon-Nadeau Family, Cozzie & Grover, Amanda, RMJ Nadon, Duby, Gomez & Diaz, Roger Freedman, Dorothy N, Kamilia Rostom, Jeannie, Sebastian Zanker, Erin Messaros, Morris & Szaryk

Read Next

Cognitive Breach: A Genesis Project Novella

The Genesis machine was built to treat PTSD.

Now Captain David Guarnere is using it to stop a terrorist attack.

To uncover the truth, he must enter the dreams of a brilliant scientist before thousands are killed.

Scan the QR code to download your free copy

What's Next?

The Treatment Room

A Psychological-Tech Thriller

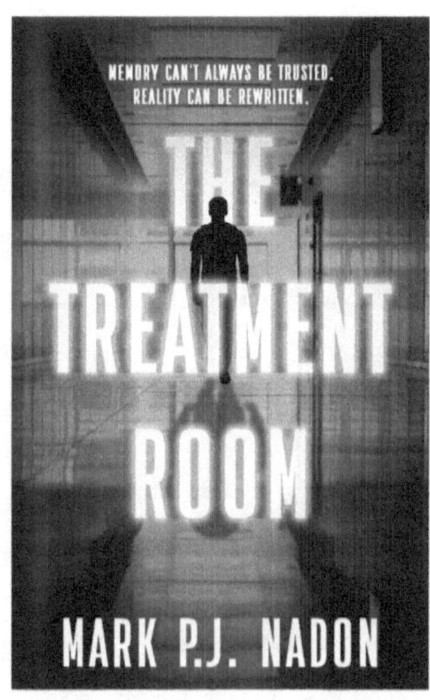

When his client is arrested for murder and blames therapy, Lucas O'Rourke's career implodes overnight. To clear his name, he infiltrates a VR clinic—but some truths destroy the people who find them.

Scan the QR code to order. Available April 14, 2026

Book Review

If you enjoyed this book, I'd be grateful if you left a review.

Reviews help other readers discover stories like this, and they make a bigger difference than you might think.

Thank you for reading.

About the Author

Mark P.J. Nadon writes pulse-pounding thrillers that blend relentless action with psychological depth, exploring the darker corners of the human experience. A former Canadian Forces Reservist and ultramarathon runner, he brings real-world grit and resilience to every story. When he's not writing, Mark runs a fitness company, hosts the Thriller Pitch Podcast, and lives in Ottawa, Canada, where he enjoys gaming with his son.

Content Warning

The Genesis Project is a psychological tech thriller set within a fictional military environment. It delves into themes of war, battle, PTSD, and hand-to-hand combat, alongside depicting perilous situations, blood, intense violence, brutal injuries, death, substance abuse, and the use of graphic language.

* 9 7 8 1 7 3 8 3 0 7 7 0 8 *